"Let's walk, Zamyatin said and again they moved down the narrow, deserted Moscow street, the rain seemingly colder and more intense now.

Mahoney kept his right hand in his coat pocket, his fingers curled around the butt of the .45. During the war Zamyatin had been a ruthless man. Perhaps he *was* telling the truth, and he indeed had changed, softened. But he had also been a very careful man and Mahoney doubted if that had changed. Certainly, this was a time for caution. Two pawns, arm in arm on a rain-swept Moscow street while around them the KGB and CIA move their men in a desperate search for a missing weapon and the scientist who could start World War III.

SEAN FLANNERY

A DIVISION OF CHARTER COMMUNICATIONS INC.
A GROSSET & DUNLAP COMPANY

THE KREMLIN CONSPIRACY

Charter Books
A Division of Charter Communications Inc.
A Grosset & Dunlap Company
360 Park Avenue South
New York, New York 10010

2 4 6 8 0 9 7 5 3 1
Manufactured in the United States of America

This book is for B. & J.,
we had hoped for so much for them.

Saturday Night

It began late on Saturday night, the fifteenth of April as two men, one of them driving, headed toward Moscow State University in a black; Soviet-built Zil limousine.

The weather for the previous five days all across east central Russia had been filthy. Miserable even for an April. It had rained—never pouring, only misting—and the temperature had gone up and down like a roller coaster between a damp fifty degrees Fahrenheit and a damned cold two above.

That evening it was even colder. The temperature hovered around the zero mark, and patches of slick ice had formed here and there in the streets so that the big automobile coming around a corner slewed to the left and then came back on track. The passenger, a solidly built but nondescript-looking man, swore sharply in Russian.

The driver glanced his way, grim-faced, but said nothing as they continued along Kaluzhskaya Street, Lenin Park between them and the Moscow River.

Moscow, the home of the Bolshoi Ballet, proclaimed the brochures put out by the Ministry for Tourism.

Moscow, city of 125 square miles, population approaching seven million, the atlases recorded.

A town plagued with the pollution and filth of any large Western city, with few or none of their redeeming graces.

Moscow, the largest industrial center in the Soviet Union: manufacturing and trade center for steel, machinery, precision instruments, automobiles, aircraft, rolling stock, chemicals, and textiles, the trade atlases listed.

The home of the *Komitet Gosudarstvennoi Bezopasnost'i*—the KGB—with its offices at 2 Dzerzhinsky Square in town and its new modern building of glass and steel just outside of Moscow on the Circumferential Highway. The new building was copied after the American Central Intelligence Agency's new headquarters outside of Washington, D.C.

Moscow, home of dozens of universities and schools, including the Lomonosov University founded in 1775, the much newer Moscow State University, the Soviet Academy of Sciences, and numerous technical institutes, the world educational almanacs recorded.

Pockets of happiness here and there in apartments and clubs despite the lack of adequate housing, the lack of consumer goods, the lack of hope in the Western sense of the word, and over all of it the low-keyed fear: the constant turning over the shoulder to see who was behind.

Past the Donskoy Museum the limousine turned east on Vorobyevskoye Road, then speeded up. There was no traffic here at that time of the night, and both men would have been surprised if they had encountered any.

Moscow was a city of darkness. Despite its size, the Soviet capital was unlike New York or Paris or Amsterdam where lights shined twenty-four hours a day, where traffic never really ceased, where the ever constant press of humanity was highly evident.

That evening the city seemed particularly dark and brooding.

Moscow first became a gathering place in 1147. By 1271 the city has been made headquarters for Daniel, the son of the Grand Duke Alexander Nevsky of Vladimir-Suzdal.

When the Dukes of Vladimir took the title of Grand Duke of Muscovy in the fourteenth century, Moscow had become a very important trade center. A short time later the city's place in world events was assured when Ivan III made the town the capital of a new, centralized Russia.

The limousine slowed down as it approached the broad avenue that turned left into the Moscow State University complex. The passenger instinctively stiffened and sat forward in his seat as they came around the corner and halted at the gate. Across the wide avenue from them was the embassy of the People's Republic of China, dark like the rest of the city.

A uniformed guard came out of the gatehouse, and the driver cranked the window down. Instantly the car was filled with a damp wind that drove before it the filthy, penetrating mist.

"Your papers, please," the guard said, his AK-7 automatic slung casually over his shoulder, the barrel pointing down out of the rain.

The driver handed over his identification card, which

the guard instantly recognized and handed back.

"Yes sir," the guard snapped. He saluted, then marched smartly back to the gatehouse. A moment later the heavy iron gates, closed at night, swung open. The limousine driver cranked the window back up, and the car proceeded along the avenue toward the huge, gray, central building.

Moscow was burned twice by invading Tartars: once in 1381 and again in 1572. The Poles conquered the city and held it briefly until a volunteer army under Prince Pozharsky freed it in 1612. Two hundred years later, in September of 1812, Napoleon entered the city, but he had even less luck than the Poles. The city burned to the ground a few days after Napoleon had conquered it, forcing the French into a retreat that meant disaster for them because the Russian winter was fast approaching.

The capital city of Russia was moved to St. Petersburg in 1713 where it remained until 1922, five years after the Communist Revolution. Since that time Moscow had grown steadily not only in size but in importance. Worldwide.

The limousine pulled around to the east side of the main building, and the driver parked it in front of the glass doors of the physical sciences wing.

He and the passenger got out, pulled up their coat collars against the wind and hurried into the building.

Just inside the front entrance two uniformed guards were seated at a table, an open magazine spread out in front of them. They looked up as the two men came in, and one of them started to get up, but then sat back down saying nothing.

The two men strode purposefully down the long,

deserted corridor, their heels clattering hollowly on the parquet floor.

Light shone from under only one door off the corridor; the two men paused briefly by it, then went in.

An old man was seated behind a desk in the small, book-lined office. He was already dressed in a shabby topcoat and dark hat pulled low, and in front of him on the desk was a fat briefcase. When the two from the limousine came in, the old man rose.

"I am ready," he said timorously, but he stumbled as he tried to come around the desk, so that the passenger had to take his arm and help him out into the corridor.

Then the two men, one on either side of the older man, the driver carrying the briefcase, retraced their steps down the corridor.

Again the two guards at the door said nothing, in fact did not even look up from the magazine they were reading, and the three men left the building, got into the limousine and departed.

The weather seemed to close in after that as a heavy fog began forming from the birch forests to the west. The city seemed to be a sleeping giant; fitful and restless with its nightmares past, present, and future.

I

Sunday Morning

WASHINGTON, D.C. (AP) . . . President Forsythe met today with Egyptian President Anwar Sadat and Israeli Prime Minister Menachem Begin, capping off a three-day series of meetings concerning the tense Middle East situation.

Begin and Sadat are both scheduled to return to their respective homelands this evening.

In a brief announcement following the meeting, which was held in the Oval Office, President Forsythe confirmed that his conference on Thursday in Moscow with Soviet leaders had not been canceled.

He was aware of the downstairs door slamming and a moment later of someone climbing the rickety wooden stairs. He rolled over and looked at the clock on the small table next to the bed. It was barely 10:00 A.M.

At sixty-one, Wallace Mahoney had plenty of vices. He smoked too many cigars, drank too heavily at times, and he could not abide stupid people.

There he was, he had told himself once in a rare fit of self-analysis. At least the cigars were good ones—Cuban Gondoliers—that he bought from a tobacconist downtown.

His bourbon was, as far as he was concerned, among the best available anywhere, a nine-year-old Kentucky that came in on Fridays with the diplomatic pouch. He drank it neat. No water. No ice. None of the frills.

And stupid people. Well, stupid people were to be pitied perhaps, avoided if possible, but certainly never abided.

The only vice that he would ever admit to was his love of sleeping late on Sunday mornings. And he damned well hoped that this Sunday would not prove to be an exception.

He listened as the person on the steps passed the second floor landing, paused a moment, and then resumed his climb upward to the top floor where Mahoney's apartment was located.

It was a man, probably young, a bit overweight, Mahoney guessed. He could hear the springiness and quickness of step that denoted youth, and the harsh slap of male shoe leather on the stairs.

The second man, if there was one, would be standing by the car parked out front, the building's Soviet policeman watching him.

Mahoney pushed the covers back and got out of bed. For the first couple of moments, as always every morning, the varicose vein in his right leg throbbed, the pain shooting up to his hip.

Mahoney's wife Marge, a loving, devoted, and dutiful woman, rolled over in her sleep, her right arm searching for her husband. She was awake instantly.

Mahoney put his finger to his lips, and shook his head. He could hear the steps on the third floor landing now, pausing a moment, and then they came toward their back apartment.

Marge had heard the noises, too, and she looked up at her husband with a questioning expression.

Mahoney made a mental note to speak to her about the rollers in her hair. He hated it when she went to bed with the things on, which was about twice a week. But she called them their little joke.

"Without them you might think you were in bed with a strange woman," Marge had said once in a rare joking mood.

"It's been so long, I wouldn't know what to do with another woman," Mahoney had said, and they had both laughed about it.

The steps stopped at their door as Mahoney picked up the telephone on the night table. A moment later the dial tone began its low, steady, reassuring hum.

"Have the embassy standing by," Mahoney said softly to Marge, handing her the phone.

Six months ago a junior diplomat from the American embassy whom the Russians had apparently taken a dislike to had answered his apartment door one Saturday night. A man handed him a sheaf of papers that the bewildered diplomat took. A moment later two KGB agents grabbed the man and took him to jail, as a spy. The evidence was the papers they had found on him. State secrets.

It had taken the American embassy two months to find out where the man had disappeared to, and by that time it was too late; he had been shot as a spy.

As he heard the knocking on the door, Mahoney pulled on his robe that was laying across the foot of the bed, took his military .45 automatic that was holstered and slung over a chair and went to the door.

The pounding on the door was repeated this time more heavily. In the background Mahoney could hear his wife speaking on the phone.

"Who is it?" Mahoney asked.

"Mr. Mahoney? It's the embassy, sir." It was a man's voice.

Mahoney cautiously opened the door and peered out. A young, heavyset man, in a suit and impossibly colored tie, his raincoat open, stood in the dimly lit, narrow corridor. The ever present stench of cooked cabbage was particularly strong this morning.

"Who the hell are you?" Mahoney growled.

"Siverson . . . sir. Day clerk," the young man said, and then he looked over his shoulder and lowered his voice. "The O.D. sent me, sir. Said for you to come immediately."

Mahoney nodded. He had seen the young man around the embassy at one time or another. "Tell Finch I'll be there in a couple of hours."

Siverson started to protest, but Mahoney cut him off. "How's the weather out there, son?"

The young man looked confused. "Weather, sir?"

"Yes, goddammit, the weather. What's it doing out there?"

"Ah . . . raining . . . sir."

"A couple of hours," Mahoney said, and he started to close the door, but Siverson moved closer so that his nose was almost sticking through the opening.

"May I come in, sir? Just for a moment?"

Mahoney hesitated. Goddammit, he thought. Not Sunday. But then he sighed and backed away from the door, admitting the young man who quickly entered the apartment and shut the door behind him.

Marge was at the bedroom door clutching her robe tightly around her neck. "It's all right," she said, and she looked beyond her husband to Siverson. "Shall I make some coffee?"

"Ah . . . not for me, ma'am," Siverson said, and then his eyes went wide as he saw the .45 in Mahoney's hand.

Mahoney chuckled inwardly, but he kept his face and voice stern. "What the hell has Finch got up his ass this early on a Sunday morning?"

"It wasn't . . . ah . . . Finch, sir," the young man said, stumbling over his words.

"Carlisle?"

Siverson nodded. "Yessir. Everyone is coming in."

Mahoney looked sharply at the messenger. Farley Carlisle was his boss. He was a hard man, almost Oriental in his inscrutability. Carlisle's eyes proved, so the office scuttlebutt went, that the man was really Haitian. Or at least had spent time in Haiti where some mad Voodoo doctor had turned him into a zombie, the living dead.

Mahoney had a great respect for the man, but the kind of respect one has for a cobra or a cornered lion. You never turned your back on the man.

"Fifteen minutes," Mahoney finally said, and the

young man interrupted him again, an almost apologetic look on his face.

"Mr. Carlisle said I was not to let you walk to the embassy this morning. That I was supposed to take you in the car, and if necessary—"

Mahoney started to laugh, and Siverson looked hurt. "You win," Mahoney said, and he turned and went into his bedroom to get dressed. "Give me a couple of minutes," he said over his shoulder, closing the door.

Marge had already begun to lay out Mahoney's clothes, and he crossed the room to where she was bent over the bottom drawer of the dresser and patted her on the rear.

"If you're not back by three, I'll put your dinner in the oven," she said without looking up.

Mahoney smiled, and a wave of love for his wife of thirty-nine years passed over him like a soft summer's wind rippling a wheatfield. He decided not to say anything about her rollers.

Whatever Carlisle wanted this morning must be damned important, Mahoney thought as he took off his robe, threw it on the bed and began dressing. Probably had something to do with the shit the Jews and the Arabs were getting themselves into again.

The Kremlin had been totally silent about the situation, which was in itself not surprising except for the fact that the president of the Unites States would be in Moscow within five days. The last time an American president had come to Moscow, both *Izvestia* and *Tass* had made a circus out of it for the month preceeding and the month following. This time, nothing.

He went into the bathroom, ran the hot water in the sink, lathered up his face and began shaving.

Sixty-one years old, he thought. And he damned well looked it and felt it. Twenty years ago he had still been in pretty good shape. But in that time his six-foot frame had shrunk to five-ten-and-a-half. His 190 pounds had inflated to 220, and that was cheating the bathroom scale by a couple of pounds. His face and paunch had suffered the ravages of gravity yet somehow his legs had turned spindly. And his eyes at times seemed to him to be a century old.

When he finished shaving he turned around and took his shirt and tie off the door where Marge had hung them for him, and put them on. Then he brushed his thick, silvery hair.

He had not gotten a single gray hair until his fiftieth birthday, and then for the next few years it had seemed as if a veritable blizzard had enveloped his head, turning him totally silver within five years.

"Gray is beautiful," the stateside gray liberation groups were spouting.

"When there's snow on the roof, there's a fire in the furnace," his mother used to tell his father in Minnesota.

But that was all bullshit as far as Mahoney was concerned. "When the hair turns gray, the paunch begins to drop, and you'd rather sleep with a Len Deighton novel than *Playboy,* you're over the goddamned hill," he had told a friend of his in Berlin last year before he had been handed the Moscow assignment.

"We're just as bad as the women," his friend, who was only a couple of years younger, had replied. "When we hit forty-five we stop wearing bathing suits in public, and when he hit fifty-five we stop looking at ourselves in the mirror."

They had laughed about it at the time, but this morning Mahoney felt a little used up around the edges. Eight and ten hours of sleep a night were becoming a necessity, not a luxury. And getting up in the morning had almost become a living hell.

He shook his head, went into the bedroom, strapped on his shoulder holster and stuffed the heavy .45 automatic in the thick, black leather pouch.

Marge had turned away, as she did every morning when he strapped on his gun, and did not turn around until he had put on his coat and buttoned it.

"All set," Mahoney said, and she came across the room to him and pecked him on the cheek.

"Don't work too hard, Wallace," she said, a smile on her lips.

Mahoney reached out and gently caressed her cheek with the back of his hand. "Love," he said, and then he turned and went back into the living room where Siverson was waiting for him.

"I have a car waiting for us, Mr. Mahoney," the young man said, obviously relieved that Mahoney was apparently not going to give him any further trouble.

Mahoney nodded, then the two of them left the apartment together, passing the Soviet policeman in his guardbox by the front door, and climbed in the back seat of the black Ford Cortina embassy car. The driver took them the four blocks to the United States Embassy on Tchaikovsky Street around the corner from the Moscow Zoo.

The American embassy was always a surprise to anyone who saw it for the first time. Housed in a run-down yellow stucco structure that had once been used as an apartment building, it looked more like a slum tenement than anything else. When Mahoney had arrived in Moscow a year ago he had been told that a new, modern embassy building was being constructed a few blocks away on Kalinin Prospekt, near the western bend of the Moscow River.

During that year, however, the only thing that had happened on the site was that a few buildings had been leveled. And it looked as if the present embassy building would have to do for a while longer.

Siverson dropped Mahoney off at the front door, then rode with the driver around back to the garage. The older man mounted the three stairs and entered the embassy through the thick glass front door.

The marine guard on duty at his desk in the foyer looked up and nodded pleasantly. "Good morning sir," he said.

Mahoney signed in, quickly scanning the previous signatures and time-ins. Siverson had been correct. Since eight this morning the embassy had been busy, and the register looked like a who's who of the staff.

"Where is everyone?" Mahoney asked, straightening up.

"Third floor conference room, sir," the marine said, and Mahoney nodded and went down one of the narrow corridors toward the back of the building. The young guard picked up the phone and spoke softly into it.

Farley Carlisle, Chief of Station for Central Intelligence Agency activities in Moscow, was waiting for Mahoney when the ancient, creaky elevator stopped on the third floor and the iron gates slid open.

"Sorry to get you out on a Sunday, Wallace," the man said, and Mahoney was certain he could detect a note of genuine concern in the man's expression. Odd.

"I'll bet," he said dryly as he followed the man down the narrow corridor and into the conference room.

Not many people in the embassy knew much about Carlisle, but from what Mahoney had been able to piece together, the man had first proved himself in Chile, and then had been sent to Portugal where he had converted three men at high levels of government.

That operation had gone on for almost three years until the entire network began to crumble. Whether Carlisle's assignment to the Moscow embassy two years ago was a promotion for work well done, or a slap on the wrist for not maintaining his network longer than he had, was a subject of speculation among the junior staffers.

Mahoney did not care one way or the other. Carlisle was good at his job, was obviously angling his way upward, and until or unless the Russians openly tumbled to him, he would remain.

Carlisle's conference room was electronically clean and was often used for discussions of sensitive subjects even by the ambassador himself.

Six men were seated around the long, low, mahogany table, and they all looked up as Carlisle took his place at the head chair, indicating a spot at the opposite end for Mahoney.

"You should know everyone here," Carlisle began, and Mahoney quickly catalogued the faces, his interest rising.

To Carlisle's left was Colonel Howard McCann, chief U.S. military attaché to the embassy. The man was fresh from a Pentagon assignment, and had seen no action since Korea. It was his bitter plight, he told everyone, to sit out the Vietnam war as a logistics officer. He had come to Moscow eleven months earlier, a bitter man, and his attitude had gotten steadily worse.

"Patton was right, goddammit," he would tell anyone who would listen. "When we were in Berlin with the men and materiel, we should have kept going all the hell the way to Moscow. Wiped the sonsabitches off the face of the earth. Now look at us, kissing ass and sucking hind tit to the bunch of squarenecks."

Next to McCann was Stewart Anderson, a man whose quick, brilliant mind was successfully hidden beneath a mousy exterior. He worked as the chargé d'affaires during the ambassador's frequent absences from the Soviet Union. But unlike most embassy staffers, he was not isolated from the Soviet population in general. Anderson had several Soviet friends, he attended many Soviet dinner parties, ate in Soviet restaurants, and generally was a highly visible American.

Next to him, directly to Mahoney's right, was Walter Munson, whose presence at this meeting this morning was a surprise to Mahoney. As chief embassy cipher communications man, Munson was more of a technician than an analyst or policy planner. He was the electronic whiz kid, if such a term could be used to describe a fifty-eight-year-old, stoop-shouldered man.

If there was one person in the embassy who looked, acted, and seemed older than Mahoney, it was Munson. And during the year Mahoney had been here, he supposed the two of them had not exchanged more than half a dozen words.

On the opposite side of the table, on Carlisle's right, was Darrel Switt, the CIA's chief case officer (the

James Bond of the operation) who worked very capably as the embassy's cultural affairs officer. He was a young man: long hair, drooping mustache, blue jeans, tennis shoes, corduroy sportcoats.

Next to him was Paul Bennet, Soviet historian for the embassy, in reality a CIA junior analyst, whom Mahoney hated with a passion. The twenty-seven-year-old kid, to hear him talk, had been everywhere, had known everyone, had thought every original thought, and could not be told a thing. He was good at his work, however, knew when to kiss ass, and, Mahoney mused now, would undoubtedly become the director of the CIA one day.

Finally, on Mahoney's immediate left, was George Congdon, the only man in the entire embassy with any sense, and with any hint of humanity.

Congdon, who was the CIA's chief political observer, and who worked in Mahoney's department under the guise of a trade mission specialist, was forty-two, had lost his wife the previous year to cancer, and had subsequently thrown himself into his work.

Despite his tragedy, the man still retained his sense of humor, and was forever poking fun at Mahoney, who was considered by most embassy staffers to be a hardass.

"Blood'n'guts Mahoney doesn't take shit from anyone except for Congdon," the embassy juniors said. And they were correct.

Congdon was smiling now at Mahoney, and half under his breath whispered, "Did the bad man disturb your beddy-bye, Wallace?"

Carlisle, however, began the meeting before Mahoney could reply.

"Lights have been shining at Two Dzerzhinsky Square since late last night. Looks like a convention over there," Carlisle began. "We confirm that the heads of at least three of their four Chief Directorates and five of the seven minor Directorates, have been called in. About three hours ago the individual staffs began showing up as well."

"You had no advance tickles on this one, Carlisle?" Mahoney heard himself asking.

Carlisle looked his way and shook his head. "None whatsoever. It just suddenly began happening last night. At first we sat on it, but as the activity increased we decided on this meeting."

"What the hell did you call me for?" McCann broke in. He looked angry.

Carlisle did not like the military man and it was obvious. "The heads of all five Soviet military services have also shown up," he said tonelessly. And he stared at McCann who, after a moment, fidgeted uncomfortably.

"How about the Kremlin?" Mahoney spoke up, but Carlisle continued staring at McCann a second longer as if to solidify his point.

"Business as usual," he finally replied, turning to Mahoney, and they all could almost hear the sigh escaping from McCann.

"Their foreign operations headquarters outside Moscow?" Mahoney continued.

"The same. Nothing unusual," Carlisle said.

"Tass? Izvestia? Pravda?"

"Nothing in the morning editions," Carlisle said somewhat peevishly. "Did you expect anything?"

Mahoney shrugged. As the chief CIA analyst for all Soviet operations, it was Mahoney's job to ask the surprising questions. His was a particular talent of coming up with connections where none seemed to exist. And he was very good at his job.

Munson spoke up after a short silence, directing his comments to Mahoney. "Mr. Carlisle called me in a few hours ago to look over the situation. Our sweeps of Lubyanka have come up with nothing. No unusual electronic activity."

Mahoney smiled at the naiveté. "Everyone is over there. Who the hell would they call?"

There were a few chuckles around the table, and Munson seemed offended, so Mahoney quickly added, "Maybe the fact their communications network is silent is in itself significant. Send the logs up to me after we finish here."

Munson, somewhat mollified, nodded and sat back, and Carlisle continued.

"One of three possibilities exist as I see it," he said, and everyone turned his way. "Number one, the most likely possibility, is something is happening or is about to happen in the Middle East situation. This is possibly a policy planning-session."

Mahoney shook his head. "The military chiefs of staff and perhaps some members of the Politburo would get together for that, not the entire KGB. You're talking about everyone all the way from personnel to covert affairs. External and internal security."

Carlisle ignored the interruption. "The second possibility has to do with the president's scheduled conference here in Moscow on Thursday."

Stewart Anderson sat forward at this, shaking his head. "We've been instructed to keep hands off that one," he snapped.

Technically, Carlisle worked for the ambassador and in his absence, Anderson. In actuality the CIA worked nearly independently of the politicos.

Carlisle turned to him. "Perhaps they are planning his assassination."

"That's insane," Anderson nearly shouted.

"Yes it is, isn't it," Carlisle said, and everyone around the table suddenly became very uncomfortable.

After another long silence, Carlisle again continued. "And the third possibility, the one we must turn to Mr. Mahoney for, is the least appealing since we have the least information."

Mahoney smiled. "The KGB is mounting some kind of an operation. A major operation. Unknown at this point."

"Exactly," Carlisle said. "I'm turning this operation, which is coded LOOK SEE, over to Mahoney, and I want the need-to-know list kept at an absolute minimum. I don't want to hear about this from the office scuttlebutt. If I do, heads will roll."

Mahoney pulled out one of his cigars, took it out of its aromatic wooden sheath, and began wetting it down with his tongue as Carlisle continued.

"Colonel McCann will feed to Mahoney all current Soviet miliary assessments. You'd better include personnel dossiers as far down the line as you can go. Funnel it through my office so that we can indiate on the list which staffers are over at Lubyanka this morning.

"Mr. Anderson, if you would be so kind as to supply Mr. Mahoney with the president's schedule and a list of who is coming along on this trip, I'd be most happy."

Anderson got up in disgust, and as he headed past Mahoney he nodded. "It'll be on your desk within the hour," he said and left the room.

"Munson will continue monitoring all Soviet communications and funnel that information—or lack of it—to Mahoney on an hourly basis." Munson nodded, and he, too, got up and left the room.

Congdon got to his feet a moment later and, completely ignoring Carlisle, held a light to Mahoney's cigar as he spoke half under his breath. "It's been quiet lately, but I'll get something together for you by noon."

Mahoney smiled and nodded. "Thanks. Maybe we can have lunch."

Congdon laughed. "Not unless you get rid of that goddamned cigar," he said and, without a glance at Carlisle, left the room.

Mahoney rose, cutting off Carlisle who was about to speak.

"Bennet, you and Switt can collate whatever data Carlisle's operation comes up with. I want it concise and to the point. No editorializing."

Bennet started to protest, but Mahoney had turned to Colonel McCann. "Colonel, if you and the others will leave us, I'd like to have a word with Mr. Carlisle."

McCann got up and without a word strode out of the conference room, leaving the door open behind him. A moment later Switt and Bennet followed.

"Close the door, would you please?" Mahoney called to Bennet, then he sat back down, put his feet up on the table and drew deeply on the cigar, which already had created a thin, blue haze in the room.

Carlisle stared across the table, obviously waiting for Mahoney to speak.

If there was one thing Mahoney had learned in his year working for Carlisle, it was that the man was not a fool, although at times he acted like one.

Carlisle was bright. Unlike Switt who had obvious ambitions for higher rank within the company, Carlisle always seemed intent on merely doing whatever job he found himself confronted with. He was a man, in effect, with blinders on. He saw neither right nor left when he was working, only straight ahead toward whatever goal he had set for himself and his staff.

In that, Carlisle was the exact opposite of Mahoney. As a senior CIA analyst, Mahoney had to have what might be called stereoscopic vision, a finely tuned peripheral sight that allowed him to see and feel apparently disconnected concepts that could be germane to an issue.

Simply translated, that meant Mahoney was, by his very nature, a suspicious man. Distrustful of everyone and their motives. It was his specialty.

Always distrust the obvious. Even when it comes down to the wire, never lose a sense of wonder: Is this really the way it is, or is it only supposed to appear that way?

Mahoney wondered now.

"What have you got going here?" Mahoney finally asked. Although he respected the man, he neither liked nor disliked him. Those were meaningless terms.

"Nothing more than appears on the surface, Mahoney," Carlisle said, his face straight, his dark gray eyes expressionless.

"Genuine concern?" Mahoney said, poking for a weakness.

"For the operation. *Nothing* more."

"And the presidential visit?" Mahoney asked softly. "How does that fit in?"

"Despite the melodramatics which were needed to keep Bennet and Switt on the track, I'm sure the Man's presence is a factor."

Suddenly alarm bells were jangling stridently in Mahoney's head. If a man acts uncharacteristically, look to see which of his values are being pressed to cause such an action, and you might find a clue to what he is thinking.

Carlisle continued, and Mahoney had the distinct impression that the man was like a poisonous snake, pressing close for the kill.

"Item," Carlisle said dispassionately. "The president is coming to Moscow in five days for a series of conferences.

"Item: The situation in the Middle East is rapidly deteriorating. The Arabs are getting ready to gang up on the Jews, only this time there's a rumble that Soviet-supplied nuclear weapons might be on the scene.

"Item: *Tass*, *Izvestia*, *Pravda* all had a field day when Nixon made the Moscow trip. Not so much as a one-line mention of President Forsythe's trip.

"Item: On a very early Sunday morning the KGB's downtown headquarters is lit up like a Christmas tree. Everyone and his uncle has come in."

Carlisle had been ticking the points off the fingers of his right hand, and now he switched hands.

"Question: Why no mention in the Soviet newspapers or their news agency of the president's visit?

"Question: Why was everyone called in at Dzerzhinsky Square? Or more importantly, why didn't they try to keep their meeting a secret? Why didn't they try to hide it, like they do everything else?"

"Like we would have done?" Mahoney asked quietly.

"Exactly," Carlisle said, and then he slowly got to his feet. A moment later Mahoney followed suit, flicking the thick, heavy, gray ash from the end of his cigar into the ashtray in front of him.

"I want to know what is going on over there, Mahoney," Carlisle said. "I want to know why. And I want it fast."

"Sure," Mahoney said casually, and he made as if to go, but suddenly turned back. "How did you tumble to this meeting so fast?"

Carlisle looked at him blankly for a moment. "Routine surveillance," he said and Mahoney left the room and headed back to his office with the uncomfortable feeling that Carlisle had been lying about that last part. Only he did not know why.

II

Sunday Afternoon

WASHINGTON, D.C. (AP) . . . Israeli Prime Minister Menachem Begin left Washington today for Tel Aviv vowing peace in the Middle East providing the Russians stopped supplying weapons to Saudi Arabia, Iraq, and Syria.

Begin had been in Washington for three days of conferences with Egyptian President Anwar Sadat and President Forsythe.

Sadat left earlier in the day for Cairo, claiming that a solution to the Middle East struggle was near.

The White House had no immediate comment on Begin's statement.

The huge gray stone structure on Dzerzhinsky Square stood squat and formidable against the almost impenetrable sheets of rain hurled at the building by a cold wind. The black stone statue of Felix Dzerzhinsky, father of the Soviet secret police, stood guard over the complex that was divided into two sections.

The older, smaller section, whose courtyard was separated from the wide street by a high stone fence, had before the Revolution housed the All-Russian Insurance Company. Now it was Lubyanka Prison. Lockup for political and artistic prisoners of the state.

The other, much larger, much newer section of the Dzerzhinsky complex, called simply "the Center," housed in its nine stories the headquarters for the Soviet secret police: the KGB. This section of the building had been constructed during World War II by prisoners of war, mostly Germans, and was serviced by nine pedestrian entrances and two underground parking ramps.

Last night and this morning there had been a steady flow of traffic into the parking ramps, while the pedestrian entrances had been fairly quiet. Nearly every window in the huge complex showed light.

Colonel Yuri Zamyatin stood in the busy eighth floor corridor of the Center looking out one of the heavily screened windows down at Ditsky Mir, the children's department store, and suddenly he remembered what he had forgotten. The vague thought had nagged at the back of his mind for more than a week now, until just this moment when he suddenly realized what it was.

The children's Easter break from school had come and gone without the usual presents from him. He had totally forgotten about it. And the children thoughtfully had said nothing to him.

He had been preoccupied with his work over the past few months, he told himself guiltily, and somehow he was going to have to make it up to them.

At the age of fifty-four, Zamyatin's life had been reduced to a single pair of constants. One was his children: Sandra, a rapidly maturing thirteen; Lara, still a sweet and innocent twelve; and his pride and joy, Aleksei, who was a curious eleven.

And the other constant was the Party: Father Lenin, Mother Russia, and the Komitet.

But it hadn't always been that way.

"Yurianovich," someone called from down the corridor, and Zamyatin turned as a husky young man, his arms loaded with thick file folders, rushed toward him.

The KGB was divided into four major divisions called Chief Directorates, and seven slightly less important divisions called, simply, Directorates.

Zamyatin and the young man heading his way were both officers in the Second Chief Directorate, the division of the Secret Service that oversaw industrial security operations, all the foreign embassies within the Soviet Union, tourists, foreign students and newsmen, foreign airlines and the few other foreign businesses allowed to operate here.

Within those subdivisions, Zamyatin had risen to the rank of KGB colonel and was in charge of the first six numbered departments in Political Security. His job was to watch over and, if possible, convert to informant status the personnel at all the foreign embassies in Moscow, except for the Chinese that had its own special department.

But at only twenty-seven, the young man who had called his name was of equal rank and had charge of the Second Chief Directorate's Seventh Department, which handled tourists all across the Soviet Union.

This disparity in ages yet equal rank and position was

a source of minor irritation to Zamyatin and an obvious source of pride to Stefan Chekalkin who nevertheless seemed to respect Zamyatin's age and wisdom.

"I looked for you in your office," Chekalkin said, out of breath. "When you weren't there, I figured you might already be up here." He glanced across the corridor toward the open doors of the rapidly filling Rally Hall, then looked back. "I was worried that I might be late."

"Do not worry, Stefan," Zamyatin said not unkindly. "We have a few minutes yet." He nodded toward the file folders. "I see you have kept yourself busy this morning."

Chekalkin beamed at what he took as a compliment. "I was here doing some homework when the call went out, so I had a head start."

Zamyatin smiled, reached out, and lightly tapped the bundle in Chekalkin's arms. "You know, if you stand up in there and read all of this, some of us might be buried before you are completed."

The young man blushed. "No,—no—it isn't that, Yurianovich," he stammered, and he looked down at the files. "My memory is not that reliable. If I'm asked a question I want the correct answer."

Youth, eagerness, and ambition were all deficiences in the Komitet, and yet without those qualities a man would not get very far. It was strange, Zamyatin thought, the tightrope they all walked. There was no net below, and if you fell off no one would bother to stop and pick you up.

It was a carefully designed system, he supposed, that came down to the survival of the fittest. But it had always been that way. It certainly had been during the war. It had continued that way afterward. The fittest managed to find housing one way or the other; to find enough calories each day to keep alive and healthy; to keep the balancing act between loyalty to the Party and a blind eye toward the purges going somehow, without falling off.

Chekalkin had recovered from his embarrassment and he stepped a little closer, lowering his voice to an almost comically conspiratorial level. "Have you heard yet what it is all about?"

Zamyatin shook his head. "Not a word since this morning when I came in and was told to have my department summary ready in time for a two o'clock meeting." He looked at his watch. "My department is summarized and it's nearly two; perhaps we should go inside."

A few other men had stopped to chat in the corridor, and when Chekalkin was certain no one was paying them any attention, he took Zamyatin's arm with his free hand and led him a few feet farther from the Rally Hall door.

"I heard that the entire Komitet is here this afternoon. That it has something to do with an incident at State University."

Zamyatin laughed. "Shame on you, Stefan. Idle gossip."

The young man reacted almost as if he had been slapped in the face. He reared back, his cheeks turning a beet red. "I . . . I didn't mean . . . "

Suddenly Zamyatin was tired of the little charade. Either Chekalkin was an absolutely naive fool, in which case the Second Chief Directorate administrator was a raving lunatic for promoting him so fast, or the young man was a control.

It was assumed that any officer at any given moment would be subject to a control, usually in the form of another officer sent to test efficiency and often loyalty. A control operation, and there were hundreds going on at all times, might take anywhere from a few minutes of seemingly idle conversation one afternoon, to a full-scale investigation that could take years.

But whether Chekalkin was a fool or a control, Zamyatin had had enough of him this afternoon.

"It may not have occurred to you yet because of your tender years, Stefan, but the Komitet wants neither children nor automatons," Zamyatin said evenly, careful to keep any trace of anger out of his voice. "It wants human beings. Men who are willing and able to use their brains in rational thought."

Without waiting for Chekalkin to respond, Zamyatin turned and stalked across the corridor into the nearly full Rally Hall.

Two guards wearing the armbands of Officers of the Proceedings checked his badge and number against a master list, then let him through. He found a place half a dozen rows back from the front.

The Rally Hall was just as its name implied; it was normally used to conduct May Day, Peace Day, October Revolution Day, and other special occasion rallies that were designed to pump up spirit and enthusiasm for the current five year plan.

It was a large room, laid out like a lecture hall with three sections of seats arranged in tiers that fanned upward and outward from a small stage in the front.

Zamyatin was normally a mild-mannered, very soft-spoken man, unaccustomed to such outbursts as he had directed at young Chekalkin, and it took him several moments to calm down before he became aware of the extraordinary nature of this meeting.

On the stage were seated the administrators of all four Chief Directorates, the seven subdirectorates as well as the operations chief for the entire KGB.

The audience of more than one hundred persons was composed of all the department heads, such as Zamyatin and Chekalkin, and a few section subchiefs.

He had never attended or even heard of such a gathering. Usually departments within the KGB were nearly autonomous. The system was set up that way to keep need-to-know lists at an absolute minimum. In fact, it was treason to ask information from any department other than your own without special permission from a Directorate chief or higher.

Now the entire officer corps of the Komitet was assembled in one place at one time, presumably for a single purpose.

Extraordinary.

The operations chief, General Mikail Barynin, a heavyset man with dark hair, dark brooding eyes under thick bushy eyebrows reminiscent of Brezhnev's came to the podium as the guards at the back of the hall closed and locked the doors. Half a dozen technicians who had been sweeping the walls of the Rally Hall with electronic detection devices nodded toward their officer who in turn nodded toward General Barynin. A moment later the lights dimmed, and the picture of an elderly man was flashed on the white plaster wall at the back of the narrow stage.

"Leonid Illyich Sakharov, Doctor of Physics, Professor of Laser Science, Moscow State University." Barynin's thick, rich Leningrad voice boomed through the hall without amplification.

Zamyatin sat forward in his seat. Sakharov. It was a familiar name and a familiar face. But he could not place the man.

"Professor Doctor Sakharov is considered to be *the* leading laser technologist in the world. Through his efforts have come laser advances in medicine, industry, and a dozen other areas including military application. On Professor Doctor Sakharov's shoulders rests the Soviet Union's world leadership in this science."

Sakharov's photograph was replaced on the wall with the projection of a map of Moscow. Moscow State University was outlined in red.

Without looking over his shoulder at the map, General Barynin continued. "At approximately 2300 hours last night, Professor Doctor Sakharov was taken from his office at Moscow State University. Two men identifying themselves as Fifth Chief Directorate officers from the Intelligentsia Direction were admitted to the university grounds by the gate officer at 2250 hours. The men were driving a Zil limousine, license unknown."

The map projected on the wall disappeared, and a moment later it was replaced with what appeared to be composite drawings of two men. Both of them heavyset and dark, but for the most part nondescript. They could have been any one of a hundred thousand Moscow residents.

"The two officers on duty at the physics wing of the university reported in their nightly logs that an officer with the proper Fifth Chief Directorate codes notified them at 2205 hours to expect two officers who would arrive to escort Professor Doctor Sakharov to the airport.

"The duty guards, whose descriptions provided the renderings behind me, confirmed that these men did indeed arrive at the physics wing at 2255 hours. At 2301 hours the two men left the building escorting Professor Doctor Sakharov. One of the two men removed from the building what is believed to be Professor Doctor Sakharov's briefcase."

The projected image of the two men flashed off the screen and the Rally Hall's lights came on. No one in the large room made a sound. All eyes were glued on the general.

Fully half the people in this room, Zamyatin mused, had never laid eyes on the famed chief of operations who maintained his office in the new building outside the city. The other half of this group, including Zamyatin himself, were almost awestruck by the man's presence. If Leonid Brezhnev himself had given this briefing, the audience would not have been more impressed.

Never had one man commanded so much respect since Joesph Stalin. And it was even said that Barynin had the power to turn Stalin down when the Soviet leader had ordered him to become the Party Secretary.

The man had preferred his job riding roughshod over the secret police, taking his place in the history books along with Dzerzhinsky himself, Menzhinsky, head of the old OGPU, Yagoda, who ran the NKVD until 1936, the infamous "bloody dwarf" Yezhov who was shot next door in the basement, and others. Stalin had deferred to his wishes, and Barynin, then only a colonel, was promoted to general, and appointed head of KGB operations, directly answerable to Yuri Vladimirovich Andropov, the Politburo politican who was named KGB chairman.

No one moved, no one coughed, no one talked in the large hall, and after a brief pause, Barynin continued.

"The Fifth Chief Directorate administrator assures me personally that his department has no knowledge of the events of last night. He assures me personally that his directorate in fact did *not* field such an operation involving Doctor Professor Sakharov."

The silence in the hall this time was a stunned quietness, and Zamyatin noted that the Fifth's administrator, General Losev, a man about whom he knew very little, sat on the stage with the other directorate administrators behind Barynin, immobile, his features rigid and chalk white.

What Barynin had said, in effect, was that the Fifth Chief Directorate was not above suspicion in this matter despite its administrator's assurances to the contrary.

"The facts are these comrades," Barynin's voice boomed through the Rally Hall. "Professor Doctor Sakharov is missing from his office at Moscow State University. He has not been seen at his apartment since he left for the university at 1100 hours Saturday. His whereabouts at this moment are unknown.

"Additionally, a device, portable in nature, one that Professor Doctor Sakharov developed himself, is missing from the university. This device, I am told, could easily be disassembled to fit into, say, a large briefcase and is capable of projecting a highly deadly beam of laser light. A beam that could easily penetrate a stone wall, several inches of lead shielding, and, most certainly, a man."

Again Barynin paused, and again the silence in the Rally Hall was absolute, all eyes rigidly fixed on the man before them.

"As of this moment," the general continued finally, "you may all consider yourselves under a full Center alert. This operation will be coded CLEAN SWEEP, and for its duration normal reporting chains of command will be suspended.

"Twice daily progress reports will be forwarded directly from each department chief to my office. I will have a staff set up to receive, collate, and respond.

"The primary objectives of CLEAN SWEEP are to find and recover Professor Doctor Sakharov and the laser device. Secondary objectives include the arrest of the planners of the operation, its agents, its methods, and, most importantly, its motives.

"I have imposed an absolute time limit on this operation of 1100 hours Thursday, that is, four days from now, by which time all objectives *will* be met."

Zamyatin's eyes narrowed in puzzlement. Such a specific moment in time; 1100 hours on Thursday. It had to be significant in itself. But what did it mean? He tried to think.

"There will be no restrictions of concept on this operation, comrades. Each department chief will assume for the duration of the operation, unless directed otherwise, that someone in his area of expertise, some person or organization, some group internal or external to the Soviet Union has Professor Doctor Sakharov and the laser device.

"Each department chief will make use of any and all resources within or without the Center to achieve the operation objectives.

"Absolute interdirectorate and interdepartmental autonomy will be maintained at all times unless specific operational objectives are cleared through my office.

"Funding is absolute for the duration. However, all requisitions will be cleared through my staff.

"All control operations are suspended for the duration unless cleared by my staff for a specific operational objective."

The general paused again, this time to stare out at his audience, and the effect was chilling. Zamyatin was certain the man's gaze was directed toward him and him alone. His eyes seemed to bore deeply, impressing the need for immediate action and absolute loyalty.

After what seemed like minutes but was actually only a few seconds, Barynin finished his briefing with the standard Center expression: "Comrades, we have work to do," and he marched off the stage through a back door, followed stiffly by the directorate administrators. The audience rose and began shuffling out of the Rally Hall, no one speaking a word or even daring to look at anyone else.

When Zamyatin was away from the press of the crowd he hurried down to Second Chief Directorate territory on the fourth floor, which looked toward Ditsky Mir and beyond it the huge Bolshoi Theater.

As head of the directorate's Political Security Service, Zamyatin was in charge of six numbered departments, each with the majority of its staff housed near the embassy it served.

At the Dzerzhinsky Square headquarters, Zamyatin

had his own small office that opened directly into a very large room filled with row after row of desks, manned mostly by data specialists and collators, officers whose specialty it was to collate data received from field operations into recognizable patterns.

He paused at his office door and looked out across the rows of desks, empty now on this Sunday afternoon.

Each department within the Political Security Service had a specific job. The First Department was charged with operations against the United States Embassy as well as the embassies of Latin American countries.

The Second Department worked on the foreign diplomats from nations of the British Commonwealth; the Third included the Federal Republic of Germany, Austria, and Scandinavia; the Fourth, all other western European nations; the Fifth, non-European developed nations; and the Sixth, non-European underdeveloped nations.

It was a huge operation, Zamyatin mused, one in which he was personally responsible for several thousand employees scattered all over Moscow.

The First Department alone was manned by a chief, two deputies, fifty staff officers, recruiters, plus scores of agent runners, and more than three hundred surveillance officers on permanent loan from the Surveillance Directorate. Its headquarters was located a few blocks away from the American embassy in a five-story building that had once been used as a warehouse.

The First Department in turn was divided into five sections, each with such specific tasks as the recruitment of U.S. Embassy personnel, the neutralization of any intelligence operations the Americans might mount from the embassy itself, and around the clock surveillance of any and all Soviet citizens who had any contact whatsoever with American embassy personnel.

It was a vast operation that would for the next four days have to be welded into a single unit.

Zamyatin went into his office and sat down behind his desk as he began to organize his thoughts. He would begin by calling in each department chief to outline objectives.

Something else intruded on his mind as well, however, as it had in the Rally Hall. Thursday, 1100 hours. Why the specific time?

General Barynin had run his career like he ran the KGB, on several levels at once. Official policy stated that an operation was never mounted with only one objective in mind when two objectives were possible; an operation was never mounted with two objectives in mind when a third was possible; and so on.

The objective in CLEAN SWEEP was to come up with the person or persons who planned and executed the kidnaping, their method of operation, and their motives, as well as Sakharov and the laser.

But 1100 hours Thursday? Was the general merely telling them that they had roughly ninety-six hours to accomplish their objective? Or was he telling them something else?

Zamyatin's gaze wandered from the Political Service Personnel Directory opened in front of him, to the framed photograph of his children atop the file cabinet by the door. The photograph had been taken by a friend two summers ago when he and the children had gone on a long-awaited vacation to the Caspian. The picture showed the children by the sea, building *dachas* in the sand. It had been a happy time. A truly happy time of togetherness.

Suddenly the date clicked, but he was certain of it only for a moment. Then his mind did not want to accept the possibilities it raised.

Thursday 1100 hours. It was the day and time the president of the United States was due to arrive at Vnukovo Official Airport. He had promised to take the children there to see it.

The president of the United States? Sakharov and a portable, deadly laser device? It was insane. Such thoughts were totally outside the realm of reality.

Zamyatin was suddenly very cold. He turned in his chair so that he could look out his window past Ditsky Mir toward the Bolshoi Theater ablaze in lights.

Were the date and time significant, or merely coincidental?

Zamyatin let his mind wander down that dark corridor. Assuming the date was significant, the laser device would have been the primary objective. Sakharov had been taken either as a decoy, as a smoke screen, or because his knowledge was needed to operate the device.

Given the device was to be used to assassinate the president, where would it occur? At the airport? During the drive through Moscow to the Kremlin?

General Barynin had said that the laser device could penetrate several inches of lead shielding. An armored limousine would offer no protection. The attack could come at any moment, from any apartment building, any rooftop. Silent. A pinpoint flash that only the victim might see if he were looking that way.

Ingenious.

But, and it was a big word, Zamyatin's role in CLEAN SWEEP was bounded by the assumption that someone within his area of expertise had Sakharov and the laser. That meant someone from one of the foreign embassies located in Moscow was planning to assassinate the American president.

Which included, Zamyatin thought with a sick feeling, the American embassy.

Could such a monstrous thing be possible, he asked himself, hardly daring to think such a thing let alone examine it in detail.

Could the Americans be planning to assassinate their own president? Could they use such an action to precipitate military retaliation on the Soviet Union? Was such a thing possible?

He turned back to his desk, and began telephoning his department chiefs one by one down the list, as a name kept nagging at the back of his mind.

John F. Kennedy.

III

Sunday Night

WASHINGTON, D.C. (AP) . . . The White House, in a brief announcement today, indicated that directly after his Moscow trip President Forsythe would vacation for five days at his Colorado Springs home.

Chief White House physician, Dr. William N. Morris, said the president was in generally good health for a man of his age, but did need the rest.

The vacation will be the first for the president since he took office 15 months ago.

Wallace Mahoney entered the second floor staff dining room, diplomat territory, and hesitated a moment just inside the doorway while he searched for a specific face.

The dining room, located in the front of the embassy

building, served mostly the diplomatic corps below the rank of assistant to the chargé d'affaires. The ambassador and his high-level staff ate in a small, pleasant room near the ambassador's office, and the CIA personnel, of which there were eleven including Mahoney, either ate out, grabbed a sandwich in their offices, or mingled in one or the other of the dining rooms.

Officially the Central Intelligence Agency did not work out of the American embassy, and therefore had no staff here. Unofficially everyone down to the lowliest typist in the steno pool knew that was a line of crap. But no one ever played the guessing game as to who was CIA and who was not. That was a sure method of guaranteeing a early rotation home with a bad service report. Moscow was grim enough without having to return home from a three-year assignment with absolutely no future.

A few people in the fairly crowded dining room noticed Mahoney standing by the door and they waved to him, but he merely returned the greetings as he continued to search for the specific face.

The regular embassy staffers had been told they had to work overtime, beginning this morning, to make ready for the president's visit. Part truth, part lie. It was true the preparations for a presidential visit fell heavily to the American embassy, but that could have been started sometime tomorrow or even Tuesday. The staff had been called in this morning to act as a cover for the sudden CIA activities.

Mahoney finally spotted the man he was looking for, seated alone at a table across the room. He ambled down the cafeteria line, poured himself a cup of coffee at the urn, paid for it, and then went across to the window table.

Dr. Clifford White, who was a Harvard professor of economics, looked up and peered at Mahoney through thick spectacles, a quizzical expression on his face.

"I see they even called you in today, Dr. White," Mahoney began pleasantly.

White, who was not yet thirty-five had the slightly bemused, open-mouthed look about him that marks most long-term Ivory Tower residents, and he squinted at Mahoney, obviously with no recognition on his face. "Yes," he said, his voice soft, almost effeminate. "Most unusual, Mr . . . ah . . . "

"Mahoney. Wallace Mahoney. I'm with the trade mission. May I join you?"

White continued to squint up at Mahoney for a moment, but then as if remembering his manners, indicated a chair. "Of course, it's my pleasure, Mr. Mahoney."

Mahoney sunk gratefully into the chair across the small table from the younger man. It was just past seven in the evening, and already the day seemed as if it had gone on for a couple of weeks, with every indication it would continue for a month or more.

Dr. White was ostensibly on a one-year study grant from Harvard to observe the Soviet economy at close hand. His real assignment, although neither he nor Harvard knew it, was to provide data for the likes of Mahoney. Data that would be funneled through CIA channels for assessment purposes. Strings had been pulled in the State Department, the bug was put in the Harvard Economics Department ear, and a few months later Dr. White was on his way.

So far he had provided only routine data, nothing more or less than had been expected. Once each week, White prepared a lengthy report on Soviet economic conditions that was to be sent back to Harvard. Of course, the report was included with the diplomatic pouch mailings. And of course it went via Mahoney's office where copies were made.

"Should I know you, Mr. Mahoney?" Dr. White asked.

Mahoney smiled pleasantly as he sipped his coffee. "We've bumped into each other briefly in the corridors, but I have not as yet had the pleasure of working with you. I do know something about you, however, or rather about your work."

"How interesting," White said, not returning the smile.

"Your monograph on Soviet consumer economics published last year I found highly interesting," Mahoney said, which was in part truth. The monograph, which Mahoney had read—but not until last month—was one of the reasons White had been selected for this assignment. When it came to Soviet economics, the man knew what he was talking about.

"And now you would like to work with me?"

"Not exactly," Mahoney said. "But I do need your help, if at all possible."

Dr. White's eyebrows arched, the action somehow irritating to Mahoney. "I'm afraid I'm quite too busy these days. I only have a few months left on my study grant and the work has been piling up."

"This would not take much of your time, Dr. White. A single morning. Perhaps tomorrow morning."

"Out of the question . . ." the younger man started

to protest, but suddenly the expression on his face changed. His eyes narrowed and his lips puckered slightly, as if he had suddenly recalled something distasteful. "I can't do a thing for you," he said and started to rise.

Mahoney forced his expression and tone of voice to remain conversational as he smiled up at the man. "I suggest you sit down and hear what I have to say, Dr. White. I'm sure you will find it most interesting."

"Not on your life," White said shrilly, his hands on his hips.

The effeminate gesture increased Mahoney's irritation, and he could almost feel his blood pressure rising, yet he forced his voice to remain calm. "Sit down, Dr. White, or I will sit you down."

A few others in the dining room were looking their way, and White glanced across the room, and then back down at Mahoney, his face indecisive. Mahoney started to rise and White quickly sat down.

"I know you, Mahoney," the man said, and Mahoney could see a trace of fear in his eyes. He smiled.

"From where?"

"Paul told me. Paul Bennet—he was at my home a few nights ago for dinner. He mentioned your name. You work for Farley Carlisle. You're a CIA man."

"And so are you," Mahoney said, regretting his lack of control.

The shock on the economics professor's face was instant and genuine. It was as if someone had told the leader of the Ku Klux Klan he was black. White began to sputter his protests, but Mahoney held him off.

"By tomorrow noon at the latest I'll need all the

current data that you will be using for your next weekly report. I'll also need you to extrapolate that data into a series of general parameters that might indicate current Soviet government expenditures."

Dr. White's face had turned a pasty color. "You've been into my weekly reports," he said. "You've opened my mail." Mahoney nodded. "That is correct. And until this point you've only gathered data. You've made no conclusions. We need your expert opinions now. Tomorrow at the latest."

"Impossible without further study."

"Nor will you have any further study unless you cooperate with me."

White jumped to his feet again, only this time he did not appear indecisive. He was mad. "You can't intimidate me. I know my rights. I'm a civilian. The ambassador will hear about this."

A number of people in the dining room were again looking their way, but Mahoney didn't give a damn any longer. Dr. White would have to be recruited. "The ambassador is not here today."

"What?" White said loudly.

Mahoney stared up at him. "I said the ambassador isn't here today. You'll have to see the chargé d'affaires—Stewart Anderson. He's upstairs in his office at the moment."

White looked imperiously down at Mahoney, flipped his right shoulder and laughed. "I'll do just that. This instant," he said, and he turned and stalked out of the room.

Carlisle would give him some static about his manhandling White, thus blowing the man's self-image about his position, and thus possibly his usefulness, but it could not be helped. White would not have cooperated otherwise, and conclusions were what they needed.

Besides, Mahoney thought, he had a lever now to use against Carlisle. Bennet, who was Carlisle's pet, had himself compromised the situation by shooting off his big mouth. It was Bennet who had led White astray, had told White that Mahoney was CIA and not merely a trade mission staffer.

Carlisle had been in and out of Mahoney's office all afternoon, along with a string of others, all the way from Munson with his as yet negative communications reports, to Switt, Bennet and even Colonel McCann whom Mahoney personally felt sorry for. The man had absolutely no business being in Moscow, and whoever in the Pentagon had handed him this assignment was probably either very stupid, or had a grudge against the man. And Carlisle's having included him in this morning's briefing was asinine.

The activities of this long day had tired Mahoney, and he sat back in his chair and went through the routine of lighting himself a cigar. It would take Dr. White about three minutes to get upstairs to Anderson's office and begin laying out his problem. Another couple of minutes would be spent hashing it out. Then Anderson would call Carlisle into his office.

Carlisle would be mad at first, but then seeing that there was nothing he could do about it, he would spend at least ten or fifteen minutes explaining the facts of life to the Harvard professor.

Mahoney could almost envision the scene. When Carlisle had finally run out of arguments to throw at White, arguments that would have proved totally ineffective, he would turn to Anderson, and in his flat, emotionless voice make a statement to the effect: "This man will be on a plane for the States within twenty-four hours. I want him quarantined in the embassy until then. We'll send someone around to his apartment to pick up his personal belongings."

At that point Dr. White would, of course, capitulate. After all, it was for his own country. And he was accomplishing tons of work while here. It would be a shame to let it all go down the drain.

And Mahoney. A bit gruff perhaps. Maybe even a bastard. But hell, when it came right down to the last analysis, the man was on our side.

"It wouldn't be as if I were a traitor."

Mahoney smiled wryly as his gaze wandered around the room at the others having their dinners. Why were any of them here in the first place? A visit to Moscow was perhaps understandable. To see the museums, to absorb the history that stretched back hundreds of years. But who would want to live and work here? The city was too grim, its people too preoccupied with survival.

As an intelligence officer, that was a stupid question. Moscow was rich with data. Clandestine information seemed to hang thick in the air. And it put everyone on edge.

Mahoney turned that thought over in his mind. Perhaps he was getting too old for this business. Perhaps he was done with it.

He had often thought about buying a small place in northern Minnesota, on a lake. A small boat with a trolling motor. Fishing in the morning when the wind was calm and the lake's surface was so absolutely smooth it looked like a fairy tale mirror, reflecting the pale blue sky, the yellow sun, and the ragged green borders around the shoreline caused by the reflection of the pine forests.

Once when he was a child he had spent the summer at Shultz Lake in northern Minnesota with his uncle Fred. Mahoney had only been eight or nine, and his Uncle had been in his early seventies. The cabin had been built thirty years earlier by his uncle before the man had his first bouts with the cancer that eventually would take his voice, then his life.

One morning they had risen early for a day of fishing. It was early summer, and not very many people had come up to the lake yet.

About an hour into the morning a huge northern hit Uncle Fred's line, and Mahoney could still vividly see the pole bent almost double, an expression of absolute joy and contentment on the old man's face as he huffed and puffed. And then the line broke.

His uncle Fred had slowly reeled in the line and then tested it with his hands. The string was rotted. It had probably been laying around in a fishing reel for ten years or more. And even as a young man Mahoney could see that his uncle Fred knew the rotted fishing line was a sort of symbol that his life was almost over with.

In the early days, when the man had come every summer to the cabin, he had kept up with such things as making sure there was fresh fishing line. But now such attention to details had escaped him. And Uncle Fred was like the rotted fishing line that had come to the end of its usefulness, could only lie around in the sun with no real purpose.

Mahoney had cried for the old man that morning. And by the end of that summer his uncle Fred had died.

Mahoney only rarely thought about his own mortality, but he turned it over in his mind now. When he died it damned well was not going to be as an old man trying to work some operation. Rather it would be on some northern Minnesota lake where he was told that the northerns were still hitting.

He shook his head, flicked the ash from his cigar, got up and headed toward his office. Dr. White would be ready to go to work in a few more minutes, and although an economic assessment of current Soviet government operations was a little thin as far as this operation was concerned, Mahoney was not worried. He had always worked thin.

What he looked for in such overall assessments were incongruities.

"Amass a body of facts, of data, and certain elements will always stand out as different from the others. Inconsistent. Incongruous. Apples, oranges, peaches, hammers, grapes, bananas.

"Look to the incongruities. When several of them are gathered, look to that data pool for conclusions."

It was as if a cold wind were blowing through his soul, and Zamyatin wanted to believe the feeling stemmed from the fact it was late, he had worked all day, and he was tired. But that simply was not true. He had never been less tired, and more awake than at this moment. The chill that burned deep inside of him came from something else. Fear perhaps?

By 8:30 all six of his department chiefs had crammed into his tiny office. By 9:00 P.M., he had briefed them all, had distributed copies of Professor Doctor Sakharov's jacket, the composite drawings of the two men who had snatched him, and the statements from the Moscow State University gate guard and physics wing guards.

The only thing he had left out of his briefing was his speculation about the significance of the due date: 1100 hours Thursday. If it was idle speculation, better to keep it to himself. If it had a basis in fact, it would come out. And at this moment Zamyatin was beginning to believe it already had come out.

Zamyatin stared across his desk at Major Boris Balachov, chief of Department One of Political Security Service. The man in charge of the department that watched over the American embassy.

Balachov was a young man, in his early thirties, who lived and worked under the name Leonard Skyles. His hair was cut in a Western style, his clothes were American imports, he smoked Marlboros, and his English was flawless New York, not the Oxford English that so many non-Americans spoke.

During the briefing in which Zamyatin had instructed his department chiefs to begin assembling all current embassy data, all the way from how much electricity and water each embassy was consuming, how often service employees did their jobs, to the latest microwave scans and telephone tap outputs, Balachov had made a simple statement that had completely stunned Zamyatin.

"They've been busy over the past twenty-four hours on Tchaikovsky Street."

Zamyatin had turned toward his First Department chief who was sitting back nonchalantly, but the man did not offer to amplify on his statement, and Zamyatin had cut his briefing short.

"Time and motion for outputs," he summarized his request. "If we know what they've been consuming, the hours they are spending, the personnel showing up, it might give us a clue not only to their activities, but the importance they are placing on those activities."

No one had offered anything further, and Zamyatin had dismissed them. As the others rose to leave, Zamyatin asked Major Balachov to remain, and now alone, Zamyatin was almost afraid to ask the man for more information.

He didn't have to. Balachov started without prompting.

"Barynin's due date is curious," he began. Even his Russian was somewhat flat, although he had never been out of the Soviet Union.

Zamyatin perched on the edge of his chair, barely daring to breathe. "You find it so, Major?"

Balachov took his pack of Marlboros out and offered one, but Zamyatin shook his head. Balachov smiled as he lit himself a cigarette and returned the package to his breast pocket. He took a deep drag, exhaling slowly.

"Sakharov and a laser device have been lifted from Moscow State by someone who our department must assume is external to the KGB. Someone from one of the embassies in town. But it must have been someone who knew the workings of our Fifth Chief Directorate well enough to fool the university guards. Not a big task in itself, but large enough so that I would rule out almost everyone we are charged with watching."

Zamyatin continued to hold his silence as he listened to the man.

"Coincident with that operation, the American embassy suddenly comes alive. Top level on down. Everyone is there. *Everyone.* Let us ask ourselves why."

"Why?" Zamyatin heard himself asking, his throat dry.

Balachov smiled. "The American president is coming on Thursday. The Americans are making ready for his visit."

Zamyatin shook his head. "They would not begin such preparations so soon. Not until tomorrow, perhaps Tuesday."

"Perhaps they are planning some in-house function. Such as a special briefing for the president, so they need time to make reports and summaries."

Again Zamyatin shook his head. "The diplomatic corps might sweat a few hours extra for that. But you said everyone had shown up."

"So I did," Balachov said, continuing to play the game of devil's advocate. "Perhaps they are preparing for some preliminary meeting with Comrade Brezhnev before their president arrives?"

"No," Zamyatin said softly. "Ambassador Leland Smith is out of the country. They would not make such a move without him."

"He is returning tomorrow?"

"No. Not until Thursday."

Balachov puffed on his cigarette for several long moments in silence before he finally nodded, almost sleepily. "No indeed," he said, and he stared across the desk at Zamyatin. "Nor would such diplomatic preparations require the presence of Farley Carlisle."

"Carlisle came in?" Zamyatin asked.

"The first. As far as we can determine, the call-up emanated from him."

Carlisle was well known in the KGB for his work in Portugal. The Komitet had managed over an eight-year period to place a dozen men at high levels of the government in Lisbon. In one year's time Carlisle had converted three government officials to informant status. One of them was a Komitet man, who was later found dead in his apartment.

It had been a brilliant operation on the American CIA man's part, and it had won the grudging admiration of field men everywhere.

The only reason Carlisle had been allowed to enter the Soviet Union under the guise of an assistant to the ambassador was that it was thought at the Kremlin that it was better to have the man in full view at all times. At least this way he would not come up with any further surprises.

Carlisle was a cold, dispassionate man. One with no loose ends to be compromised. Despite the fact the Lisbon center had tumbled to Carlisle's activities almost from the beginning, it had taken their people more than a year to get rid of him. He had no wife, no children, no vices, no secrets that could be used as a lever on him. He was clean. Almost inhumanly so.

The only reason Zamyatin, and therefore his First Department Chief, Balachov, knew anything about the man and about his activities in Lisbon was because he was under their personal supervision. They were charged with making sure he kept in one place, both hands on the table, so to speak. So Zamyatin and Balachov had been briefed about the man and his background two years ago when he had come to Moscow.

Since that time they had watched him with very special care.

"It would not be beyond Carlisle to engineer such a plot," Balachov was saying, and Zamyatin had to force himself away from his black thoughts.

"What?" he said.

"It's an imaginative plan. Worthy of Carlisle. Kidnap a Russian scientist and a Russian weapon. Assassinate the president in the presence of a planeload of American newsmen."

"Insanity," Zamyatin breathed.

"On the contrary. President Forsythe is not well liked. The Middle East situation has been effectively blamed on his meddling and interference, despite his capable work with Sadat and Begin. When that situation erupts he might be impeached. No, I think Carlisle's plan has merit. The American Joint Chiefs, the president's Cabinet, and even the National Security Council would not shed a tear if their beloved president were dead. On Moscow soil. Killed by Russians."

"Monstrous."

"No more so than Kennedy's assassination," Balachov said, sitting forward. "The American public still speculates. Hoover and the FBI? The CIA somehow connected with the Mafia? Perhaps Fidel Castro? And what was done in that situation? Do you forget the hapless Lee Harvey Oswald? The dupe who married a

Soviet girl? Who was known to have contacted our embassy in Mexico City? Do you forget those machinations, my dear Comrade Zamyatin?"

As Balachov spoke his voice rose louder and louder, and his eyes glittered like a hunter closing in for the kill. Like Carlisle, Balachov was clean. No wife. No family. Mother and father both dead. No vices or hangups. In fact, almost the perfect copy of Carlisle. Inhuman, but very, very good.

"This cannot be hung on Carlisle alone. There must have been others." Zamyatin said.

"Indeed," Balachov said triumphantly. "Many others. In Washington at high levels, I am sure, but more importantly to us, here in Moscow." He flipped open the briefing file and pulled out the composite drawings of the two men who had grabbed Sakharov.

"These are Russians. No mistaking it. Carlisle was given the go-ahead for this operation as long as a year ago, when the Middle East situation began to go all to hell for the Americans. They don't want another Vietnam. It was the reason Carlisle was sent here to Moscow in the first place. I'm certain of it.

"The Americans knew we had tumbled to his Lisbon operation, and yet they sent him here to Moscow. Curious. But in addition to Carlisle there must be Russians. Dissidents.

"Carlisle is running agents here and that will be my department's first step. We will cull through all contact sheets over the past year to watch for the repeaters. Those we will investigate fully."

"And then?"

"The information will be presented to General Barynin for his decision. That is policy. Not my field."

"How about within the embassy itself?" Zamyatin asked after a thoughtful silence. "Who have we got current?"

"An assistant cook in the staff dining room. He is from Tennessee. Our foreign operations got to him two years ago. His assignment to Moscow was a stroke of pure luck."

"No one else near to conversion?"

For the first time this evening Balachov seemed somewhat uncomfortable. "I'm afraid not, Comrade Zamyatin. Some progress is being made with a junior cipher clerk, but we are a long way away. I would hate to rush him for chance of ruining a potentially valuable convert."

Zamyatin was a loyal man. Home, government, mission. His home was his three children. His government, the State. And his mission, to protect his children and the State from harm.

He was at this moment a frightened man, however. Frightened of the implications of what he and Major Balachov had been discussing. It was a single man's assassination that had begun World War I. And it was the rise to power of a solitary figure that had brought about World War II. What would the assassination of an American president on Soviet soil do to the world situation? World War III, from which there would be no survival?

Perhaps the Fifth Chief Directorate had worked some kind of a plot, and indeed had kidnapped Sakharov and the laser. Perhaps Russian dissidents had for some reason kidnapped the scientist, to somehow strike back at the government they were so convinced was oppressive.

Perhaps any one of a dozen reasons could be found to explain Sakharov's disappearance. None of those speculations, however, were any of Zamyatin's concern. His mission was to first assume that someone within his area of expertise had done the kidnaping, and then try to prove it.

And at this moment, as distasteful, as deeply frightening as the possibility seemed, Zamyatin was being forced to assume that the Americans were behind Sakharov's disappearance, and that it somehow tied in with the American president's scheduled visit to Moscow on Thursday.

"What is your man in the embassy's code and schedule?" Zamyatin asked finally.

"The cook is Zeta-one, and he works six days a week, from ten in the morning until eight at night."

Zamyatin nodded. "I want his reports after each shift, the first report to include a summary of his conversion and information he has supplied from day one."

"Yessir," Balachov said, rising.

Zamyatin did not bother to get up. "I want your personal reports and assessments in my office every six hours, until this operation is completed."

"Yessir," Balachov said, and he waited for further orders, but when Zamyatin remained silent for several long moments, he gathered up his briefing files and his American raincoat and made to leave.

"Major Balachov," Zamyatin said softly, evenly. The First Department chief turned back slowly.

"Yes?"

"At this point our conversation has been one merely of speculation. It would not do for me to hear such rumors floating on the breeze. Do I make myself clear?"

Zamyatin was a mild-mannered man. Everyone who had contact with him knew that. But what only a few people knew, and Major Balachov was one of them, having seen Zamyatin's personnel dossier, was that at one time he had been, in Komitet jargon, a "hard man," a very hard man indeed.

"Yessir," Balachov said, subdued, and he meant it.

When Balachov was gone, Zamyatin stared at the closed door for a long time, lost in thought. The First Department Chief had confirmed his fears. At this point it seemed very likely that the Americans somehow were behind the disappearance of Sakharov and the laser.

But why? Was it really a plot to assassinate the president? Would they go that far again?

Zamyatin finally looked down at his desk and pulled a thick file folder toward him, then flipped it open to the first pages, which consisted of a series of photographs.

The first was of Wallace Mahoney, with the caption: "CIA senior analyst. U.S. Embassy Moscow. Trade Mission Office."

There were other pictures in the file as well. Pictures of Mahoney's wife Marge, and their two children, John and Michael.

John was a chemical engineer now in Los Angeles. Wife and three children. Michael was a scientist with the Forest Products Laboratory in Missoula, Montana. Unmarried.

Zamyatin flipped through the photographs and then began to ready Mahoney's dossier as his mind wandered backward in time. It had been more than thirty years since he had last seen Mahoney. But during that time he had managed to keep abreast of the man's career within the CIA.

With Mahoney, Zamyatin thought, there was perhaps a key to their problems.

Early Monday Morning

The larger of the three men sat in the driver's seat of the black Volvo station wagon. One of the others sat in the passenger seat while the third was in the back. All of them were nervous.

The rain that had fallen all across west central Russia had continued without letup through the weekend, making the dirt roads outside the city muddy quagmires, and the open fields a vast swamp.

Spring. Rain from the gods and mud from the devil. It was the Muscovites' plight.

The windshield wipers flapped back and forth. The Volvo's engine was running, but its lights were off. To the left off the road about three-quarters of a mile through a thin birch forest, and a final three hundred yards across an open field, was the west wall of Lubyanka Prison II. Lockup for 731 men and women who had all been found guilty of "parasitism."

It was a vicious, circular treadmill for Soviet writers and artists who did not play the game by the rules.

One got on the treadmill by openly speaking, writing, or painting contrary to the carefully laid rules of the Artists Union. Criticize the State. Doubt a Party leader.

Disbelieve a five year outlook. Publish in the West without the State censor's stamp of approval.

The treadmill turned.

The next position was the total denial of all publication or recreation rights. One could continue to write or paint, but no longer was a platform available from which to reach the people. No longer was income available from one's art.

The treadmill turned.

The next position, in reality, only affected those without money. And what writer or artist, except for a very few, had any money? If one had no means of income, no method of support, then the State would have to step in. Socialism. The State took care of its own. No one starved. No one went without shelter.

The treadmill turned.

If self-support was impossible so that the State had to step in, then by definition one was a "parasite" who lived off the honest efforts of the people, sucking the lifeblood from the veins of the working class. Illegal.

The treadmill turned.

A speedy trial before three impartial judges in an out-of-the-way suburb. "This court finds you guilty—*insert name*—of parasitism, and sentences you to five years at hard labor at—*insert prison name*."

The three men in the shabby car were all parasites, but that was not what was making them nervous this morning. They were frightened at the turn of events during the past months that seemed to be forcing them to make decisions they had never thought possible.

They were creators. Men of imagination. Men of the arts. Not violent creatures. The ends did *not* justify the means.

"And yet," someone had asked at the last meeting, "how else can there be even a shred of hope for us?"

The largest of the three men, a giant of a man physically as well as mentally, looked at the luminous face of his watch. "It is time, my friends," he said, careful to keep his voice soft although there was no one near to overhear him.

He shut the engine off, and the three of them got out of the car, standing their dark jacket collars up around their necks against the cold, windblown rain.

The other two men each carried a large ball of thick twine that they showed the larger man, and then they all held their breaths, waiting, listening for some sound from the prison, straining their eyes against the impenetrable darkness to catch at least a hint of the spotlights mounted on the prison guardtowers at each corner of the block-long wall.

But they could see or hear nothing other than the wind and rain sighing through the birch forest just off the road, and their own heartbeats.

The large man finally stepped down off the road into mud above his ankles, and the three of them worked their way very slowly, very carefully, and very silently toward the prison wall. To be caught here would mean more than a charge of parasitism with its attendent sentence of three to five years at hard labor. To be caught here like this meant treason: the penalty, death.

It took them fully three-quarters of an hour to make their way to the edge of the birch forest, and one of them involuntarily sucked in his breath as the faint trace of light flashed overhead from the spotlight on one of the guardtowers.

They all ducked down and at that moment were very close to giving up the entire insane plan, hurrying back to the car and going home.

Life is life. Let what will be, be. Mother Russia will endure.

But the large man's presence denied that escape for them. They would continue by dint of his will, his spirit.

They crawled out into the open field, the thick mud clinging to their clothing, weighing them down and making them incredibly cold. Nevertheless, in twenty minutes they had covered more than half the distance between the shelter of the forest and the west wall rising gray and ominous out of the night.

The two smaller men each handed the large man one end of their twine rolls, and then headed in opposite directions parallel to the wall, leaving the large man where he was.

One man was to be stationed opposite each corner of the west wall, connected to the large man in the middle by the twine.

When a guard came around a corner, the man was to tug once on the twine, signalling.

They had learned that there were two guards on this wall, who met at irregular intervals and places. Sooner or later one of them would be alone, opposite the large man's position.

Fifteen minutes after they had separated, the large man felt a single sharp tug to his right, and he tensed. A few moments later the twine leading into the darkness to his left pulled in his hand, and he settled back down from his half crouch.

He saw the guard to the left first, walking slowly, passing him without looking around, and finally disappearing in the darkness.

A few moments later the guard from the right appeared, passed the large man who crouched about twenty yards away, and then he, too, was lost in the night.

The large man moved a bit closer to the wall, and waited on his knees. The next time the two guards met, it would not be at this spot.

For twenty minutes the large man was alone with his thoughts. Alone. Cold. And somewhat frightened, he had to admit to himself. Frightened not only by what he was about to attempt to do, but by the consequences of it for his own soul, for his own personality. If one killed, for no matter what reason, was not one a killer? If you stole a loaf of bread to feed your family, weren't you nevertheless a thief?

There was a sharp tug on the twine in his left hand, and the big man tensed, waiting for a tug from the right. The seconds seemed to drag, but the twine in his right hand remained slack.

Finally he tugged sharply twice with both hands, the signal that it would happen now, and then crouched, his heart nearly hammering out of his chest.

The guard appeared slowly out of the rain, almost as if he were an apparition, and the large man crouched very low into the mud. In slow motion the guard came along the wall, closer and closer, the water dripping off his helmet making his raincoat shine. He did not look like a machine. He looked very human.

Then he was moving past where the large man crouched. One second. Two seconds. Three seconds. The large man eased himself to his feet, took a half-dozen careful steps behind the guard and then sprang with all of his considerable might toward the back of the figure.

At the moment of impact, the large man was surprised at how small the guard seemed to be. His burly arm curled around the guard's head, then he dropped backward and yanked with all of his might to the left. The guard stiffened, there was a sickening snap as his neck broke, and he released his last breath with a muffled sob.

The large man was on his feet in an instant, straining his senses for the other guard, or for an alarm. But all was silence except for the rain and the wind in the forest across the field.

He picked the guard up and carried him like a rag doll under one arm across the field in a loping, graceless run, toward the safety of the birch forest.

At best they would only have about ten or fifteen minutes before the second guard became curious about his partner's whereabouts. Perhaps another ten minutes of indecision before the alarm was sounded. And maybe another ten minutes before the road would be searched. Thirty-five minutes at the outside.

The large man did not stop at the edge of the woods, instead hurrying through the sparse, winter-bare trees, the tears streaming down his cheeks.

The other two were already at the road when he arrived and had the car started and turned around.

One of them began digging a shallow hole in the soft muck fifty yards off the road while the other helped the large man quickly strip the dead guard of his weapon, ammunition belt, identification, and finally his uniform.

They were finished in less than ten minutes, and a few minutes later the frail, half-naked body was dumped into the hole and covered.

The uniform, weapon, and other things went into the back under an old blanket, the three men climbed into the car, and they were gone as the rain seemed to increase in intensity.

It was just 4:00 A.M.

IV

Late Monday Morning

MOSCOW (AP) . . . A small group of Soviet dissidents calling themselves Activists for the Democratic Movement boldly picketed on Red Square early this morning.

The marchers carried signs that called for the immediate end to the harassment of Andrei Amalrik, author of the book *Will The Soviet Union Survive Until 1984?*.

The picketing was quickly broken up by Moscow Civil Police.

Neither *Tass, Pravda* nor *Izvestia* mentioned the incident.

"I've let my people go. We're done for the most part except for a few minor, last-minute details."

Mahoney looked up from his incredibly piled desk at Anderson who had just come through the door. For a moment his mind refused to leave the military dossiers McCann had finally dropped off a couple of hours ago.

Carlisle had checked off which of the Russian military high command had been at yesterday's gathering at Dzerzhinsky Square, and although that information did not really tell Mahoney very much he nevertheless found the dossiers interesting. Together they formed a fairly accurate picture of the Communist Party's struggle for world military leadership since 1917, and especially since World War II.

Anderson looked around. "How in God's name can you work in this mess?"

"I don't work in here," Mahoney laughed. "This is just a warehouse." He nodded toward a file in Anderson's hand. "Something more for me?"

The chargé d'affairs came all the way into the office and handed the file across the desk. "The president's finalized itinerary and the preparations we've made. It's all there."

Mahoney took the file from him and laid it atop a pile of dossiers that all but buried his telephone. "You said your people are done and gone already?"

Anderson nodded. "They're leaving now."

"Did you clear that with Carlisle?"

Anderson flared, but held his temper in check. "I don't work for Carlisle."

Mahoney smiled tiredly, leaned back in his chair, closed his eyes and rubbed the lids with his fingertips. "Sorry, Stewart, guess I'm just a little tired."

"I'm sorry, too," Anderson said. "We're all tired. And, yes, Carlisle did give me the okay to start winding down."

Mahoney opened his eyes. "When was that?"

"He left my office about twenty minutes ago. Asked me to drop my report off to you and then bring you along to a meeting."

"Everyone?"

Anderson shook his head. "No. Just Carlisle, you, me, and Congdon. The others have already gone or are going."

"No one said anything to me."

"He didn't want to disturb you."

Mahoney laughed. He suspected that Carlisle did not want to be confronted by the fact that Bennet had blown the whistle to Dr. White. Mahoney was sure that either the economist had mentioned his conversation with Bennet to Carlisle, or Carlisle had figured it out for himself. In any event, Carlisle knew that Mahoney was aware of Bennet's indiscretion.

"Have a seat, Stewart."

Anderson glanced toward the open door. "Carlisle wanted us upstairs right away."

"He can wait a couple of minutes," Mahoney said, indicating a chair that was less piled with files than the others in the small room. "Go ahead and put that stuff on the floor."

Anderson hesitated a moment longer before he finally removed the stack of file folders and laid them carefully alongside the desk on the bare wooden floor.

Carlisle's hold on everyone in the embassy seemed almost demonic at times. Anderson, Switt, McCann, almost everyone complained about him behind his back. But when the man called, they all jumped.

Despite this hold on Anderson, Mahoney was still convinced that the chargé d'affairs was a bright man more interested in doing a good job than promoting his own career. Moscow was an unusual place and it bred unusual attitudes and postures on its Western visitors, a phenomenon that Carlisle recognized and capitalized on.

"What do you think our friends in Dzerzhinsky Square are up to?" Mahoney asked softly, a slight smile on his face.

A startled look crossed Anderson's features, but a moment later he returned the smile. "Not assassination," he said. "Whatever can be said about them, stupidity is not among the comments generally heard."

"Agreed," Mahoney said. "But are you certain?"

"Come on, Wallace," Anderson said, sitting forward. "What the hell would it gain them? World War III? If this were Peking, or even Cairo, or perhaps Havana, I might be worried. But Christ, this is a civilized country with just as much at stake as us." He shook his head. "No. Definitely not assassination."

"What then?"

"If you really mean what else might they be up to, I haven't the foggiest. But if you mean why the coincidence between the Dzerzhinsky Square meeting, the president's scheduled arrival, and the sudden increase in the Middle East tension, then I think you're barking up the wrong tree. I think it is just a coincidence."

Mahoney kept his expression straight. "Stewart, in the last twelve hours Soviet surveillance of this embassy and its off-duty personnel has tripled in intensity. Additionally, Switt's overnight report indicates that a general roundup of all Soviet citizens who had had recent contact with this embassy—including people whose parties you have recently attended—has begun. Can you explain that?"

Again a look of genuine surprise and concern crossed Anderson's features. "I wasn't aware of that," he said softly.

"I take it you've felt no tightening of attitudes recently?"

"What the hell is that supposed to mean?" Anderson snapped angrily.

Mahoney just stared at him, and a few moments later Anderson's anger seemed to evaporate.

"You're asking me to do your job for you. What the hell am I supposed to say?"

"As far as you're concerned their sudden activity came out of the blue?"

Again a flash of anger crossed Anderson's face, and again it disappeared just as quickly. The man was young and relatively inexperienced, Mahoney thought, and yet he was fairly quick on his feet. One day, if he survived the political meat grinder that was the American diplomatic corps, he would be good. Mahoney doubted that Anderson was somehow pulling some little game with Carlisle. That thought had crossed his mind, but Anderson's attitude of genuineness and real concern about the situation was beginning to dispel Mahoney's supicions.

Always think the unthinkable. Look for the incongruities. Way back in Mahoney's mind there was still the hint that all was not as it seemed to be.

He sat forward and then slowly got to his feet. His legs ached. Anderson followed suit. "Sorry," Mahoney said. "I just had to cover all the bases."

Anderson still looked hurt. "I am working on your side."

"I know," Mahoney said, coming around his desk

and taking Anderson by the elbow. "Now let's go see what Carlisle has got planned for us."

Anderson stopped at the door and looked into Mahoney's eyes. "What do you think is going on, Wallace?" he asked earnestly.

Mahoney reflected a moment, and then slowly shook his head. "I don't know, Stewart. And that's as honest as I can be at this moment."

"Yeah," Anderson said, and together they went down the narrow corridor and took the elevator upstairs to the conference room just off Carlisle's office.

Mahoney came naturally by his suspicious nature because of his long and varied career within the intelligence community.

His background included U.S. Army G-2 during World War II in which he had worked at first as a cipher clerk and later as a messenger boy and near the end as an interrogator contacting pockets of SS resistance in the Obersalzburg. The last had been dangerous, but he had been young and had enjoyed it.

Those years had brought him his first contact with the Russians whom he had always been curious about as a people. And his service had scratched an itch, that had continued to grow as he got older, to learn what made people and their governments do the things they did.

He became an intelligence evaluator—as they were called in those days—when the Central Intelligence Agency was formed in 1947, and later, during the Korean Conflict, he became an analyst. Same job, same pay, different title.

His office after the fighting in Korea had been in a ramshackle tenement building in New York City. The routine in those days was childishly simple. Every morning the previous day's intelligence summaries based on Soviet newspapers, magazines, books, radio broadcasts, and agent data, would go out in triplicate with three of their people dressed as common workmen. They were supposedly three men in the slum building who were lucky enough to have jobs, and therefore not suspect when they left every morning and returned every evening.

Later, after much of the McCarthy paranoia had passed, and everyone realized that under every rock there wasn't a Communist waiting to subvert the government, the entire shooting match had moved out into the open, so to speak, down to the CIA's new building at Langley, just outside of Washington, D.C. The entire shooting match, that is, except for Mahoney who was fired.

It was a sloppy setup, but apparently no one had been watching very closely, because it had worked.

Out of a job for a few months, so the scenario was orchestrated, Mahoney ranged around New York, finally landing a position with the U.N. as a trade specialist. Later the State Department, in a supposed fit of genius, hired him, and in 1971, at long last, he had been shipped to West Berlin.

He had been promoted to senior analyst by the CIA and yet he still had his work as a trade mission specialist as a cover. From that moment he had been a busy man.

The work in West Berlin had been mediocre, but so had the intelligence data he had been funneled to analyze, so at Langley it was decided that it was time for bigger and better things. Namely Moscow. That was one year ago, and so far he had done well.

But that Monday morning he was still bothered because everything in the past twenty-four hours had happened so unexpectedly. Usually there was some kind of advance warnings, even slight warnings, that often only in retrospect told them something had been bound to happen. But for this there had been nothing.

The White Room, as it was called, was electronically clean. Except for that fact, however, it was like every other room in the American embassy. It was long and narrow. Cracked plaster walls. A barred, shuttered window at one end and the plain wooden door at the other. A parquet wooden floor that creaked, and a very low suspended-tile ceiling.

Mahoney and Anderson took their places at one end of the long conference table next to Carlisle and Congdon who had been deep in discussion.

When they had entered the room, Congdon had looked up, and for the briefest of instants Mahoney had the distinct impression that Congdon felt guilty about something. But then the moment passed, and Mahoney found himself wondering if he had really felt that at all, or if it was just his imagination and tiredness.

The conference table was bare except for a single ashtray in front of Mahoney's position. No one brought in any files or took any out with them. There were no notepads or pencils available, no blackboards, no recording devices. Everything that was brought in to these meetings was carried in a man's mind; everything that went out, left the same way.

Carlisle began the meeting.

"Before I ask for your preliminary analysis there are

a number of items you need to know to bring you up to date."

"Farley, why don't you cut the bullshit and get to the point? I'm tired and I want to go home to bed," Mahoney said. It was the first time Mahoney had ever called his boss by his first name, but there was no flicker of expression on Carlisle's face. Congdon, however, smiled.

"I've ordered LOOK SEE wound down. At least on the surface," Carlisle said, staring straight at Mahoney. "I've sent Anderson's people home already. They're done anyway, and they'd just be getting in the way."

Mahoney suddenly found himself not caring. He *was* tired, he thought. "In the way of what?" he asked nevertheless.

"I was rather hoping you would tell me that. But not yet. First I'll add to what you already know."

Mahoney waited for him to continue. When he got home he was going to have a nice, long, leisurely bath. And then Marge would rub his back. He might have a drink or two, and then he was going to sleep for about a year and a half.

"Langley came in on this six hours ago."

Mahoney sighed. "Then I'm off the hook."

"On the contrary, you're very much on center stage at the moment. They figure we're the closest to the situation, so they've agreed to funnel information this way."

Mahoney forced himself to be interested in what Carlisle was saying. And what the man was telling him was extraordinary. The CIA's home office people rarely let their field personnel blow their own noses without direction. "Spell it out, Carlisle," he said, sitting forward. "But without the embellishments."

"A number of curious things have been happening over the past twenty-four hours. Very curious things indeed."

"Such as," Mahoney prompted. He was beginning to lose his patience. He wondered what kind of an expression Carlisle would have on his face if someone were to throttle him.

"Such as the fact there has been a dramatic increase in KGB operations worldwide."

"What?"

"Coincident with the gearing up here in Moscow, the Soviet embassy in Washington has apparently pulled out all the stops. Their people from Detroit, Chicago, Dallas, San Francisco, and everywhere have suddenly tightened up. A number of them have dropped out of sight. Completely. Without warning. One minute they were there, under surveillance, and the next minute our people were left holding the bag."

"What else?" Mahoney was suddenly not liking this very much.

"The Soviet trade delegation to the U.N. has become incommunicado."

"There's more?"

"A lot more," Carlisle said, and it seemed to Mahoney that the man was almost enjoying this. "The Soviet embassy in Mexico City, their largest, looks like a circus. And in Berlin all the stops have been pulled as well. Every building we have there is under heavy microwave scan. Half our safehouses worldwide have come under surveillance. What was left of my own operations in Lisbon and Chile have been shut down."

"Which means they know about you."

"Which means they know about me and about a lot of other things."

Mahoney could hear the rain as a sudden gust of wind shifted against the shuttered window, and he shivered. Something big was going on. But what?

Dr. White had ended up a very cooperative soul, but for all his sudden, cheery goodwill he had been able to provide very little in the way of hard intelligence.

As far as could be determined the KGB had not done much of anything during the past months or even days to husband funds for such an obviously huge operation.

Normally, if the KGB was planning on mounting some major offensive, whether it be a secret war somewhere, the gear up of a new network, or even their favorite game—a one-time all-out push for data—a diversion of funds was begun as early as two months in advance. The indicators were subtle but detectable if you knew what to look for. A slowdown in production at a farm tractor factory in Minsk when farm tractors were desperately needed. A sudden, if miniscule, price increase in truck tires from Baku. A new ceiling imposed on oil imports.

From all across the Soviet Union the rubles were called home in tiny amounts from here and there, but totalling sometimes tens of millions.

The KGB was essentially the same as any other large organization; it had a budget. Overruns on the budget, overruns beyond its normal operating range, called for special funding.

No such special funding had been called for in this instance. That in itself was odd and made even odder by the facts Carlisle had just given. It cost big money to do the things he said the Russians were doing worldwide.

But maybe they were trying something new. Maybe they had taken a lesson from the Americans in deficit spending. Maybe.

Then there was Munson and his communications reports. Early this morning he had come to Mahoney with the last of the overnight logs, and he had seemed genuinely disappointed.

"People are coming and people are going. If I were them I would have hired a couple of traffic cops. But there has been no increase in their network communications, nor has there been any increase in their apparent power consumption. It's business as usual."

Mahoney had told the embassy's chief of communications to hold off on any further reporting unless the situation changed. He had not heard another thing from the man since then.

Bennet hadn't done a damn thing, and in fact had made himself scarce ever since Dr. White had blown the whistle.

McCann had brought the military dossiers in earlier, but had offered no comment.

Congdon had been strangely silent, offering up very little in the way of hard information except to cover the points that President Forsythe hoped to raise with Brezhnev on Thursday.

Which left Anderson and Switt. Anderson knew nothing. Or rather, Anderson had gotten no tickles as to what might be going on over in Dzerzhinsky Square. And Switt had only been able to provide the information that the KGB was watching the American embassy very carefully. But Switt had also mentioned that as far as he and his people could determine, the Russians were watching all the other embassies in town with the same vigor as well.

Mahoney brought his attention back to Carlisle who had been staring at him all the while, but there was no clue visible in his expression as to what the man was thinking.

"You mentioned sending Anderson's people home because they were getting in the way of something."

"Right," Carlisle said. "I'm sure you've seen Switt's reports. They're watching us pretty closely."

"Us and every other embassy in town."

"The others are not our concern. What concerns me is our posture. They took immediate notice that we were suddenly very busy. They also know about how long it takes to prepare for a presidential visit. Anderson said he was done with his work, so I had to cut it at that. To go on any longer would have been to hand them a message on a silver platter: *Hey there, we're running an operation. What would you like to know?*"

"So we're back to business as usual," Mahoney said.

"That's right. At least we are on the surface. But when and as intelligence data is gathered, it will land on your desk."

Mahoney offered no comment, and he was sure he could detect a slight note of impatience in his chief's eyes.

"I think we've covered everything," Carlisle said, turning to Congdon. "Anything to add?"

Congdon took a moment to answer, as if he was mustering up his thoughts into some kind of presentable order, which was unusual for the man. Congdon was known as the "hip-shooter," a nickname Mahoney himself had given the man.

"While the other slob is taking a bead, I can draw my gun and get a couple of shots off," Congdon had told him once, evidently proud of the tag. "You can usually scare off the cowards that way."

A lack of understanding of Carlisle's motives was in itself understandable; Carlisle had that kind of personality. But Congdon had been something of an enigma over the past twenty-four hours.

"I've got three things to add," he finally said, staring across the room neither at Carlisle nor at Mahoney.

Alarm bells began jangling along Mahoney's nerves. This was not the Congdon he knew. And as if in response to Mahoney's sudden concern, Congdon turned toward him and smiled.

"I'll be brief. I promise, Wallace. I want to go home to bed as badly as you do."

Mahoney was not reassured, but he nodded for the man to go on.

"Three points which Carlisle raised yesterday, and to which I can now add a little something," he began. "Number one: We assume the KGB is running some kind of an operation unknown to us at this point. It would be my guess they're after another data push like they did in '64 and again in '69 and '72."

Mahoney shook his head. "I've already dismissed that. In each of those instances they spent upward of twenty million rubles. Dr. White tells me there have been no diversions of funds in the past six months. At least none so obvious as to put them in the tens of millions range."

"Number two," Congdon continued as if he had

never been interrupted. "The Middle East situation is coming to a head, which is the reason President Forsythe is coming here on Thursday. Now, if I were the Russians, and if I were supplying the Arab bloc with say, tactical nuclear weapons, I would be worried at this moment that someone might know about it. So I would be mounting an operation to find out who knew just what."

"That one is a little thin, George," Mahoney said, smiling. "If that was the case, they'd be watching Israeli operations, perhaps Langley, perhaps the Arab countries themselves and, perhaps stretching it a bit, even us here in Moscow. But why the all-out push elsewhere? Like Mexico City. Like the other embassies here in town."

"As a diversionary tactic?" Carlisle offered. "A cover?"

"Rather expensive way to do business, wouldn't you say?"

Carlisle said nothing in reply, and again Congdon continued.

"Number three is the assassination of President Forsythe."

Anderson, who had remained quiet all that time, sat forward now. "Absurd," he said.

Congdon turned to him. "President Forsythe is *my* president as well as yours. And I am just as concerned for his safety as you are." He turned back to Mahoney. "Which is why I've prepared a twixt to send out on your recommendation, strongly urging the president to remain home."

"I'm finding that theory just as hard to swallow as the others," Mahoney said slowly.

"I don't like it either, but there it is," Congdon said, and he sat back in his chair with a sigh as if he were a schoolboy who had just finished reciting a long and difficult poem from memory.

"What then?" Carlisle asked. "We are open."

Mahoney took a very long time to speak, but if any of the others were impatient, they did not show it.

At this moment he was more tired than he had ever been in his life, but it wasn't that he had put in any more hours at one stretch than he had ever put in before. And it wasn't that he had been overtaxing his mind, at least not more so than on other operations. It was a combination of the fact that he was getting older—at this moment he felt more like ninety-one than sixty-one—and a series of doubts that had nagged at the back of his mind since Sunday morning's first meeting.

Carlisle. What the hell was going on with the man? Was he for real? Or was he pulling some kind of stupid, albeit dangerous, little game?

Congdon. What was eating him? He definitely was not himself at this meeting, nor had he been himself all through the night and early morning. One week ago Congdon would have been hounding him to slip out of the embassy for a couple of drinks. "Let's blow this pop stand and raise a little hell," was his favorite phrase.

Langley. What was going on at CIA headquarters that they were allowing such an apparently important operation to be directed from the American embassy in Moscow? Surely the foreign operations chief realized the unbelievably tremendous difficulties in maintaining secure communications with an Iron Curtain country. Just the increase in secure communications flow had to be like a Las Vegas neon sign.

And Soviet-supplied nuclear weapons in the Middle East? Had Congdon merely presented the scenario as a sort of an analogy? Was he merely guessing? Or was there some hard information floating around that hadn't as yet landed on Mahoney's desk?

In Mahoney's long career he had often been faced with the same choice he was faced with this morning. Play the guessing game with everyone else, or make an honest evaluation that covered nothing more or less than the known facts.

The first choice was the most creative. The specialty Mahoney was very good at. The art he was being paid for. But the second was a delaying tactic that usually provided him with a little more room to think.

He chose the latter.

"Subtracting all the knowns, and guessing at some of the other data," he began, and Carlisle sat forward, "I can only tell you what is *not* happening."

Anderson and Congdon both had blank stares on their faces, but Carlisle's expression was one of incredulity.

"I can only tell you that the Soviets have not geared up for anything covert. That is to say they seem to be watching, nothing more."

The room was deathly silent for a long moment, and then Carlisle slammed his open palm on the table. "Watching what, for Christ's sake?"

Mahoney smiled inwardly. He had gotten to the man. "Who the hell knows?" He shrugged. "I don't have enough data, and I certainly have not had enough time."

The range of emotions shifting across Carlisle's face for several moments was like a sunset. Purple rage changed to the reds of anger that changed to the violets and yellows of disbelief, and finally to the darkness of inscrutability.

Mahoney got to his feet. "If there is nothing more, gentlemen, I am going home to get some sleep."

"I have instructed every one of our people to keep moving on this one," Carlisle said with what Mahoney considered brilliant restraint under the circumstances. He got to his feet as well and escorted Mahoney to the door where they paused a moment. Carlisle spoke half under his breath so that Congdon and Anderson who remained seated at the conference table could not hear him. "I'm beginning to sweat, Mahoney. And when I sweat so do you and the others."

"The president's visit? Are you buying that?" Mahoney asked, because it seemed to be the question to ask.

"Yes," Carlisle said evenly. "But only because the president's assassination would be the most damaging of the three possibilities."

"Are you going to send out Congdon's twixt?"

"Not yet," Carlisle said. He studied Mahoney's face for a moment. "Go home and get some sleep."

"Right," Mahoney said, and without another word he left the conference room.

By the time he had stopped by his office to get his coat and had made his way downstairs, a car was waiting for him by the front door. Carlisle's doing. He signed out with the marine guard, went out the front door and hesitated a moment on the front stairs.

He had been cooped up inside for twenty-four hours now, and despite the cold, despite the wind and rain, the outside air was better than the closed-in atmosphere of the embassy.

He finally got in the back seat of the car and in a couple of minutes was deposited at the front door of his apartment building.

Like the American embassy, the apartment building Mahoney lived in would have been considered a ramshackle tenement slum in New York, Los Angeles, or Detroit. He had been given a choice of moving to the outskirts of town to a new building six months ago, but had preferred this building because of its central location.

He mounted the steps past the Soviet guardbox, nodded to the man inside, and entered the building. Just inside the door he stopped a moment. Every building in the Soviet Union occupied by a foreigner was assigned a police guard. Mahoney had gotten to know the faces of the guards assigned to this building, but the man outside this morning was new.

Switt had warned him about it last night, but it was disconcerting to see nevertheless.

He trudged upstairs to his apartment on the third floor, the ever-present stench of cooked cabbage in the air. This building housed no one but foreigners. Soviet citizens were not allowed to mingle this closely with Americans—or anyone else for that matter. Most of the people in this building were low-ranking American newsmen, a few Swedish and Danish correspondents, and one low-level diplomat from the Canadian embassy.

A number of the newsmen, especially the Americans, were of the philosophy: While in Rome do as the Romans, and while in Moscow eat cooked cabbage. The smell after twelve months of it nauseated him.

He pulled out his key, but the door was unlocked. He

silently cursed as he entered his apartment and closed and locked the door softly behind him. Marge was too trusting a soul. She could never be made to believe that any harm could ever come to her.

"What would anyone want with me?" her line went. "I'm just a dumpy old grandmother."

He could hear Marge in the kitchen, but he silently crossed the tiny, overstuffed living room and entered their bedroom where he took off his raincoat, and then entered the bathroom and hung it on the back of the door.

Several walls had been knocked out and a lot of paperwork juggled before the Mahoneys had been afforded the luxury of having their own bathroom in such an old building. It was accidental that the bathroom had been located off their bedroom, but all in all it was a luxury well within the station of the chief of the U.S. trade mission, whether the Russians knew that was a facade or not.

He took off his suitcoat, unstrapped his shoulder holster and pulled off his tie, draping them all over a chair in the bedroom. Back again in the bathroom he put the plug in the tub and turned the spigot on full hot. A moment later he could hear Marge calling over the noise of the running water.

"Who is it?" she shouted from the kitchen. "Wallace?"

"No, it's a burglar," Mahoney called from the bedroom as he took off his shirt. "I'm here to steal your bathtub."

Marge appeared in the doorway wiping her hands on her apron, her face beaming. "Do you want something to eat before you take your bath?"

"No, but I do want a drink. And you'd better make it a double. And then I want one of your back rubs."

She came in the bedroom to where Mahoney was sitting on the edge of the bed undoing his shoelaces and stroked his forehead. "You look tired, old man," she said softly.

He stopped what he was doing and looked up. "I am," he said. "And my legs hurt like hell."

She smiled gently, bent down and pecked him on the cheek, and then went into the bathroom. "I'll put some epsom salts in the water for you," she said over her shoulder. "You get undressed and get in the tub, and I'll get you a drink."

By the time he was undressed she had fixed his bathwater and had gone back into the kitchen to fix him a drink. Nude, he headed for the bathroom, pausing just a moment to glance at the photograph of his son and daughter-in-law, John and Elizabeth, and the three children. The photo had been taken nearly two years ago and had been sent to him and Marge while they were still in Berlin. The children were hugging a costumed figure of Mickey Mouse at Disneyland.

Mahoney smiled, went into the bathroom and climbed gratefully into the hot tub. Maybe in a few months they would arrange to leave Moscow for a few weeks. They needed a vacation. Maybe they could go to Los Angeles to see the kids. Michael could come down from Missoula if he wasn't busy, and make it a family get-together. He would have to remind Marge to write them a letter.

He lay back and closed his eyes, his thoughts about Marge, about the drink she was making him and about his sons and grandchildren instantly leaving his mind.

Instead he found himself going over the operation. The information that had been gathered so far was like a gigantic jigsaw puzzle. Somewhere there was the key piece, the corner, which would give him a start.

He never heard Marge come in with the drink, nor was he aware that she sat on the edge of the tub massaging his temples, watching him sleep, smiling sadly.

Something was intruding on his mind through his sleep, but gently, gently like a velvet hammer on a silk pillow. It was a face whose name he struggled to remember.

V
April 1945

They sat in a small room on high stools in front of a huge slanted table covered with maps. The windows, which had been shuttered, were open wide this morning letting in the fresh, sweet spring breezes and bright sunlight. From the other rooms in the large schoolhouse the sounds of people talking, field telephones buzzing, and papers being shuffled was constant. Mahoney wore a rumpled U.S. Army uniform with captain's bars on his epaulets. The young man seated next to him smoking a cigarette with a cardboard filter wore a Soviet lieutenant's uniform.

"We will have to penetrate their lines without our uniforms," the Russian was saying.

"Which is fine with me as long as we don't get caught."

Lt. Yuri Zamyatin looked up and smiled patiently, the gesture belying his youthful appearance. "It doesn't matter, Captain, what we will be wearing. To be caught is to die. The matter of uniforms is nothing more than an expediency."

"Against what?"

Zamyatin drew on his cigarette again and shrugged. "Civilians. *Luftwaffe. Waffen SS.*" He held his cigarette between his thumb and forefinger, the filter pointing inward toward his palm so that when he brought it to his lips his chin rested on the heel of his hand.

"Whatever," Mahoney said. He was tired. He turned back to the maps of southern Germany spread out on the table in front of them, and stabbed a finger at an area on the Austrian border. "Obersalzburg. General Eisenhower is worried about it."

Zamyatin turned to look, and he grinned. "The National Redoubt. We, too, have heard of it. But unlike your general staff, my commander takes little stock in rumors."

"I know," Mahoney said, looking into the man's eyes. "It's one of the reasons your forces will enter Berlin before ours."

Zamyatin shrugged again. "Which brings us back to you and me, Captain."

"Yes," Mahoney said.

Field Marshal Walther Model's German Army Group B, which was composed of twenty-one divisions from the Fifth and Fifteenth Panzer Armies, had been trapped in the Ruhr for eighteen days by the U.S. First and Ninth Armies which had joined forces at Lippstadt.

On the eighteenth day, when Model's army surrendered its thirty generals and 325,000 troops, the German western front had been effectively torn in two, leaving a 200-mile-wide gap for the First and Ninth Armies to head into Berlin.

By April 11, the Ninth Army had reached the Elbe River near Magdeburg, barely sixty miles from Berlin, but instead of continuing on into the German capital city, General Eisenhower ordered his armies to continue up the Elbe to meet with the Russians between Magdeburg and Dresden thus allowing the Russians to have a first crack at Berlin.

Eisenhower and most of the general staff at SHAEF, including his chief of staff General Bedell Smith, believed in the so-called National Redoubt, where Hitler and his remaining forces would gather on the Obersalzburg above Berchtesgaden to make a last-ditch stand. The alpine region could easily make an impregnable fortress where, rumor had it, the Germans would unleash wonder weapons and guerrilla trained SS troops to prolong the war indefinitely from bombproof underground bunkers.

Patton's army, which was closing on Berlin, had gotten word through its own G-2 that Hitler would be heading down to the Obersalzburg very soon. The questions were: When was the move going to be made, and more importantly, exactly where was the Führer going to set up his headquarters?

"A lot depends upon this," Mahoney's commanding officer had told him last night in Nuremberg where G-2 field headquarters for Eisenhower's armies was located. "If that mad paperhanger makes it south and sets up before we can nail him, or before we can cut him off, we're all of us fucked."

"How many other American-Soviet teams will be in on this?" Mahoney asked.

"There will be others, but you won't run into them," his C.O. told him, and he handed across a thin file folder that contained a single sheet of paper and one small, faded photograph. "They sent this over to us. You'll be working with Lieutenant Yuri Zamyatin. He's GRU but he's all right from what I'm told. Only twenty, but he's managed to keep out of the flap his bunch is having back home. I suppose if he stays out in the field long enough he'll be all right. Least I have him figuring it that way." The G-2 chief, older than Mahoney, salt and pepper mustache, deep blue understanding eyes, a slight stoop, shrugged almost apologetically. "He was the best we could get for you."

"Scraping the bottom of the barrel for me, are you?"

"No," the C.O. snapped. "On the contrary. Zamyatin is with the GRU's Western Fifth Division. The tops. Very good indeed. They've just moved into Vienna. You'll be flying over tonight in a Gooney Bird."

"Which means we'll be using Russian equipment for this mission?"

The C.O. shook his head. "I don't know," he said, looking into Mahoney's eyes. "You're the last of the bunch to leave. And you'll only be at it for a few days. A week, maybe ten days tops, and then we'll be calling you back."

"To where?" Mahoney aid, rising. "Berlin?"

The C.O. looked up at him. "No, right here. We're not moving. Ike said something about war trials or something like that." The C.O. stabbed a finger at Mahoney. "Keep *that* under your hat, Captain."

Mahoney smiled. "Nuremberg's the place. Should be interesting." And he left.

He had been flown across German lines the previous night, had been met at the airstrip outside of Vienna by the local Allied liaison, a British major, who showed him to a room in a small, undamaged hotel on the outskirts of town. In the morning he had been driven to Soviet Army General Staff Headquarters where he had been met by Zamyatin. They had had a cup of tea together, had exchanged views on when exactly the war would officially end, and then had gotten down to the mission's brass tacks of when, where, and how.

"I would like to leave this evening," Mahoney was saying. "We'll have to drive the back roads."

Zamyatin laughed. "I was told about that curious American expression—'back roads,'—but as I understand the definition, all the roads in this country are 'back roads.' "

Mahoney sighed deeply and stood down from the high stool he had been seated on in front of the map table. He looked at Zamyatin for a long moment and then glanced at the maps. They would have to cover a lot of territory in the next few days, and it was going to be a bunch of bullshit with a Russian comic in tow.

The thought of home crossed his mind. It seemed like fifty years since he had been to a baseball game. His dad and he had driven down to see the Cubs in a weekend doubleheader. They had driven back from Chicago, through Wisconsin, at a leisurely pace, seeing if they could somehow manage to hit one bar in every small town for one beer. They never even made it out of Illinois.

That was the last he had spent any amount of time with his father. The next year the war broke out and Mahoney had enlisted. Six months later his father was dead. A stroke, the doctors had said. But Mahoney knew it was a broken heart because the old man was too old to go back overseas. He had been a hot shot in France during the First World War. But now he was too old. And he could not handle it.

Zamyatin was staring at him, a sympathetic expression in his eyes. "I did not mean to make light of your orders, Captain," the Russian said.

Mahoney smiled and shook his head. "No . . . it's not that. I was thinking of something else."

"Yes?"

Mahoney shook his head again. "Nothing." He looked again at the maps. "I was told you would be supplying the equipment. Russian?"

"No," Zamyatin said. "We have a German car and some German civilian clothes. We will be airlifted well behind their lines to a point southwest of Linz. From there we will make it on foot to Lambach, which is a small town on the Traun River, where we will be met and given travel permits, the current issue ration stamps, and the car."

Mahoney had peered at the maps as Zamyatin talked, and he traced the route with his finger southwest from Lambach past the Atter See, over the Hollkogel Pass near St. Wolfgang, and from there south of Salzburg to Berchtesgaden itself.

"Beyond St. Wolfgang," Zamyatin was saying, "our work will begin."

Mahoney looked up. "The probable area extends that far east and north?"

Zamyatin shrugged. "I don't know. But you talk of the Obersalzburg and Berchtesgaden. That is the fringe of the area. We cannot afford *not* to be thorough, can we?"

Mahoney felt as if he was being made fun of, but he dismissed the impression as too obvious an assessment of Zamyatin's outward behavior. The Russian was much more complicated than that.

"No, we can't," Mahoney finally said.

They had spent four days together, working their way from Linz through the mountain passes to the Salzach River a few miles south of Salzburg. They drove only at night, hiding the car, a battered black Mercedes diesel, in the woods.

It was nearing dusk, and Mahoney stepped away from where the car was parked and walked back up the road on a narrow foot path that looked down on the city of Schellenberg on the Salzach. The Schellenberger Brücke, which crossed from Austria into Germany, looked new, or newly rebuilt, and obviously had carried much traffic.

Mahoney lit a cigarette, glanced back at the Mercedes where Zamyatin was asleep in the back seat and then stepped to the edge of the clearing in the trees. A few feet away from where he stood, the hillside plunged dramatically down and away, so that the town, the bridge, and the river were spread below.

In another time, he thought puffing on his cigarette, this panorama would be prime tourist stuff. The view was magnificent. Above him the sky was turning from a very dark blue to gray, and the clouds that had been incredibly white all day as they picked their way across the alpine sky, had turned pink. It all spoke of peace, but after nightfall, death would be waiting.

He turned that thought over in his mind. The last five nights were jumbled into a mass of data that seemed to form only two basic images.

The first image was of his wife. He could see her face in the face of each of the German girls he had bedded in the past five nights.

"The whores of a village are also the informants of the village. Look to them for information." It was almost axiomatic, he told himself.

The other basic image, the strongest of the two and by far the most distasteful, was of Zamyatin, and his methods of interrogation.

"The idea is to kill them in such a fashion that they willingly make deathbed confessions of their sins," Zamyatin had told him the first night out.

And although he was little more than twenty, Zamyatin was a master of the technique.

So far they had learned nothing about Hitler's plans for the National Redoubt. Nor would they, according to the Russian, because the plan was nothing more than rumor. Seemingly everyone had heard of the National Redoubt, but no one knew anything about it. The whores they had bedded, to whom they had paid very good money, wanted desperately to be helpful, but they knew nothing. And the men Zamyatin had carefully interrogated wanted to tell him what he wanted to hear, but they could not. Like the girls, they knew nothing.

Berchtesgaden and Hitler's Eagle's Nest was across the river and less than ten miles south. Bad Reichenhall was nearly the same distance to the west, and Salzburg was a little closer to the north.

The eighty or ninety square miles roughly bounded the area they were to search. Somewhere out there, Mahoney mused, finishing his cigarette, could be underground bunkers, ammunition factories, weapons and equipment dumps, and perhaps as many as a half a million troops. All of it was possible.

"But highly improbable," a Russian voice from behind him spoke.

Mahoney flicked the hot ash from the end of his cigarette with a fingernail, stripped the paper off the butt, rolled it into a tiny ball and threw it away from the path into the woods and then scattered the tobacco on the wind before he turned to Zamyatin who was urinating at the edge of the path.

"You're a mind reader now?"

Zamyatin zippered himself up then reached for a cigarette in his jacket pocket. "No, he said. "It is just that I was thinking along similar lines, my friend. We have been at this now four days—this will be the fifth night—and at last we have worked our way to the edge of what your orders call the 'target area.' "

"We Americans are filled with 'curious expressions,' aren't we," Mahoney said lightly, and Zamyatin laughed.

"Now it is your turn to become the mind reader," the Russian said, and he lit his cigarette with a flameless lighter. It was a cotton braid that ran through a brass tube attached to a flint and striking wheel. The cotton braid was pushed up near the flint, a couple of sparks ignited the cotton causing it to smolder, and the cigarette could be lit. The smoldering cotton caused no flash and when properly cupped with the hand could not be seen at any distance, even at night.

Zamyatin was a contradiction. For four days Mahoney had been trying to figure the man out, so far with little or no success. On the one hand he was a pleasant, gentle man with a fine sense of humor. He was a man who spoke of his homeland with great love and respect. He wanted very much for the war to end so that he could return home to rebuild his country; to find a girl and get married; to settle down with a few children; to have some kind of a future.

"We need more sanity in the world," he told Mahoney on their second night out. "*Con*struction, not *de*struction."

And yet on the other hand Zamyatin was a ruthless man. Perhaps the most ruthless man Mahoney had ever known.

The two attributes seemed, to Mahoney, to be mutually exclusive, like a Jekyll and a Hyde.

Zamyatin had joined Mahoney and he looked down at the bridge and the town below through binoculars.

"Even this far south there are no border guards on the bridge," he said after a time, and then he lowered the binoculars and glanced at Mahoney. "Perhaps we should become border guards?"

"Let's see," Mahoney said, reaching out for the glasses. Zamyatin handed them over and Mahoney looked through them. The bridge leaped up at him, and he followed the roadway halfway across until he came to the border guardhouse. The red and white striped border gate was raised and the guardhouse seemed deserted.

Mahoney followed the roadway across the bridge to the German side of the river, and shortly beyond the bridge the road curved sharply to the left. "There," he said, and he handed the binoculars back to Zamyatin. "Just across the bridge. The road curves to the south. We will wait there to pick up stragglers."

Zamyatin raised the binoculars to his eyes.

"If they are on that road," Mahoney said, "they can only be going to Berchtesgaden. It's perfect."

They waited until well after ten o'clock before they pulled the car back out onto the road, and, driving with only the blackout headlights switched on, they made their way down the mountainside to the town and across the bridge unchallenged.

The few people they saw on the way through the small town turned the other way when they passed, assuming they were SS or Gestapo agents on some mission to Berchtesgaden. "The less one knows about such things, the better off one is," the general populace had learned since the mid-thirties.

The lights on the bridge were out to avoid Allied air strikes, and not even the small red light that usually shined in border guardhouses was on. As they passed across the border, Mahoney had a strange sense of déjà vu, as if he had been here before; or perhaps he would be here soon under different circumstances. The fighting at this moment was concentrated mostly to the north, all eyes toward Berlin, so for the time being this area was deserted. Or at least it gave that appearance.

Mahoney was driving, and as they came off the bridge and started around the curve in the road, he glanced in the rearview mirror in time to see the flash of headlights some distance behind them.

He quickly shut off his lights, and a moment later

they were around the curve and out of sight of the bridge.

"Someone coming?" Zamyatin snapped.

"Looked like a jeep," Mahoney said. A hundred yards up the road, he pulled the car off to the side and set the parking brake but left the engine running.

They both got out of the car and Zamyatin, carrying a German submachine gun, quickly crossed the road and ducked down in the ditch out of sight as Mahoney, one hand in his pocket on the butt of a Luger, the other holding a flashlight with a red lens, waited by the car.

Within a couple of minutes a German army jeep came around the curve, its Volkswagen engine laboring under the strain of mountain driving, and Mahoney flipped on the flashlight and began waving it.

The jeep immediately showed down and Mahoney shouted, *"Halt! Halten Sie!"* as it got closer.

"Was ist?" someone shouted out the passenger window as the jeep pulled up at least twenty yards away. They were taking no chances.

Mahoney started toward the jeep, his shoes crunching on the loose gravel at the roadside. *"Dies ist einer Gestapso Grenze Kontrollieren."*

"Warum nicht auf der Brücke?"

"Saboteure," Mahoney said, coming to the side of the jeep. There were only two men in the little canvas-topped car. Both of them were very young, and both wore army uniforms with the insignia of second lieutenants. The one in the passenger seat was holding a machine pistol in Mahoney's general direction, but when he saw it was only one man in civilian clothes and apparently unarmed, he lowered the gun.

Mahoney pulled the Luger from his pocket and

pointed it directly at the young man's head. *"Raus!"* he shouted.

The young second lieutenant started to raise the gun, but Mahoney shouted again. *"Nein! Wollen Sie Sterben?"*

The German lieutenant hesitated a moment, and Mahoney again shouted for him to get out of the jeep. He wanted them out of the car before anyone else came along.

Zamyatin was suddenly on the sloping hood of the car, his machine gun pointing through the windshield at the driver. *"Raus!"* he shouted, his Russian accent thick.

The two young soldiers, their eyes suddenly very wide, their attention jerking back and forth between Mahoney and Zamyatin, slowly climbed out of the car. Mahoney took away their weapons and then headed them toward the Mercedes as Zamyatin quickly pulled their jeep off the road and threw its keys away.

Within a couple of minutes, the young German soldiers, their hands tied behind their backs, were seated in the back of the Mercedes. Zamyatin was covering them with the machine gun from the front seat while Mahoney drove.

Less than a mile farther along the highway, they found a narrow dirt road that led into the woods. Mahoney turned down that path and within a few yards they were lost to view from the highway.

"This is far enough," Zamyatin said, and Mahoney stopped the car.

One of the Germans struggled forward and tried to open the car door with his knee, but Zamyatin casually turned back from speaking to Mahoney and slashed the boy's cheek viciously with the front sight of the gun.

Mahoney got out of the car and opened the back door on his side. "*Kommen Sie*," he said gently to the young boy who looked up at him, tears streaming down his cheeks.

"*Der Russe . . . der Russe*," the young boy kept calling as Mahoney pulled him out of the car. He was frightened of Zamyatin. Already the stories had come from the front about how the Russians were treating captured Germans, both soldiers and civilians.

Mahoney had heard about it, but these two young soldiers had evidently heard the details. And unfortunately for them, he grimly thought, they were soon going to learn the brutal truth, the last thing they would ever know in their young lives.

He could feel the bile coming up his throat, bitter in the back of his mouth, and the young German boy evidently read the emotion from his eyes because he pulled away from Mahoney, and fell to his knees babbling incoherently.

Zamyatin had pulled the other young German out of the car, and he brought him around to the same side and threw him down on the ground next to his companion.

Mahoney gagged the young boy Zamyatin had just thrown down with a gray wool scarf from the trunk of the car, then tied both boys' legs so neither of them could run.

There was no other way, he told himself, straightening up and stepping back. This method of Zamyatin's was quick, efficient, and foolproof. If the boy he gagged knew anything—anything at all—he would be willing to tell it to them in a very few minutes.

Zamyatin handed the machine gun to Mahoney and

got down on his knees between the two young Germans. He told the one Mahoney had just gagged that in a few minutes he was going to ask him some questions.

"And I will want answers," Zamyatin said in German. "I will want no lies. None. Because if you lie to me, or even if I *think* you are telling lies to me, something very bad will happen to you."

The young boy's eyes were open very wide. Zamyatin turned to the other German who was still babbling, the drool running out from the corners of his mouth, and looked at him for several moments almost like a father might look at a naughty son. The next part happened so fast that Mahoney, who knew it was coming, was unprepared.

Zamyatin reached in his left coat pocket and withdrew a pair of pliers with which he grabbed the young German's tongue and pulled it viciously out of his mouth. From his right coat pocket he pulled a knife and in an instant had cut the German's tongue completely out of his head, the blood gushing and spurting everywhere.

A low animal growl escaped from deep in the boy's throat and then was cut off as he began choking on his own blood, his chest heaving spasmodically as he tried to clear his throat.

Calmly Zamyatin cut the boy's jacket and shirt exposing his chest and abdomen, and then he cut open the front of the boy's trousers.

"The truth," he said, glancing momentarily at the other German, and then he turned back and cut the boy's penis and testicles off and threw them unceremoniously aside.

Again Zamyatin turned to the other young boy.

"Remember," he said calmly, "I will want the truth."

Mahoney had turned away and was vomiting at the side of the dirt road as Zamyatin began cutting thin strips of flesh from the already mutilated body. From the abdomen all the way up to the neck, Zamyatin cut strip after strip of flesh from the wildly struggly boy, until finally there was nothing left except raw, bleeding meat.

Finally, mercifully, the boy's struggles ceased. He was dead.

Zamyatin turned to the other young German, whose eyes were staring fixedly at him, and removed the gag from his mouth.

"And now the truth, my young Nazi," Zamyatin said.

Mahoney, whose back was still to the grisly scene by the car, waited several moments for the questioning to begin. At this point the subject was usually very ready to answer any questions Zamyatin might ask. But this time there was silence, and Mahoney slowly turned.

Zamyatin was sitting back on his haunches next to the young German whose mouth and eyes were open wide.

"He's dead," Zamyatin said, shrugging his shoulders. "Heart attack, I think."

VI

Early Monday Evening

WASHINGTON, D.C. (AP) . . . Diplomatic relations were severed today between the U.S. and Saudi Arabia, Iraq, and Syria when those nations' ambassadors were recalled from Washington.

The White House had no immediate comment.

The announcement came this morning at about 11:15 A.M. (EST) in a joint communiqué delivered simultaneously at the United Nations and the State Department.

It had somehow become night again. Yuri Zamyatin sat straight in his chair, turned away from his desk and stared out the window of his office. The city was dark, or nearly dark, with only a few lights showing here and there besides the patterns of the few streetlights.

The rain was still falling although the mist had cleared with the dropping temperature. It would snow by morning, probably, either that or the rain would turn to ice, and they would have trouble with the power again.

Zamyatin was tired, but there was still something remaining for him to do this night before he could go home to his children, his bath, and his bed.

At fifty-four Zamyatin was in very good physical shape. Every day or nearly every day he worked out in the officers' gymnasium in the basement of the prison next door, and despite his cigarette habit, he could jog a mile or more without becoming seriously out of breath.

Part of this, he was certain, was due to the fact that he was a small man. He stood less than five-feet-seven and weighed around 165 pounds. He had not developed a paunch, nor had his face wrinkled yet. His hair had begun to turn gray at the sides, but his oldest daughter swore it made him look distinguished, not old.

"Papa, you look like a high Party Secretary now," his daughter Sandra had told him six months earlier when he had finally broken down to her insistence that he purchase a new suit.

When he came home from the foreign currency store, where he purchased the Finnish-made suit, his daughters immediately made him put it on, and they had hemmed the cuffs to the correct length, while his son Aleksei polished his brown shoes.

"Mama would be so proud of you," Sandra said, and she stood on tiptoes to hug him and kiss him on the cheek.

Aleksei had been too embarrassed to show any emotion, but Lara cried, and Zamyatin had been very touched and at that moment, closer to his wife, now dead eleven years, than he had ever been when she was alive.

He had read once that a person's capacity to love had little or nothing to do with the person he loved, but rather it had more to do with his own state of maturity and development.

The more mature you happened to be, and the more your life had developed, the greater was your capacity to understand and to feel compassion and therefore the greater your ability to love.

In the eleven years since his wife had died giving birth to Aleksei, Zamyatin had matured, had grown, had learned much of compassion, and subsequently was more in love with his wife, or the personification of his wife that he saw daily in his three children, than he had ever been when she was alive.

It was a dream world he lived in, he knew that. And he supposed it could be argued that he was unbalanced. It was his intense love that over the year had softened him, had ground away the rough edges from his personality, had transformed his energy and drive to softer, more refined pursuits.

The telephone on the desk behind him buzzed and Zamyatin turned slowly, pressed the correct button and picked up the receiver.

"Four-three-one," he said softly into the phone, giving only his office telephone extension number.

"Colonel, this is General Barynin's staff calling."

"Yes, comrade," Zamyatin said, stiffening slightly in his chair.

"You've been given the go-ahead to convene an action order board. Immediately."

"Yes, comrade. Will you require a minutes-of-the-proceedings annotation to the jacket?"

"That won't be necessary. We will want the proceedings taped, but not transcribed. The tape will be included with the jacket."

"Yes, comrade. Are there any other special instructions?"

"None," the caller said and rang off leaving Zamyatin holding the telephone to his ear, the dial tone humming flatly.

He continued listening to the tone for several seconds, using it as a point of reference while he went out of himself. It was almost as if he were sleepwalking, and yet he could turn around and look at himself as another person sitting behind his desk in the tiny, cramped office, stupidly holding the telephone to his ear.

The call from General Barynin's staff had not been unexpected. As a matter of fact Zamyatin had, by his own actions, precipitated the contact. And yet it had still taken him by surprise.

He slowly put the telephone down and fingered the stack of file folders in front of him on his desk. It was strange, he thought, how irrefutable facts of nature were sometimes surprising. It had something to do with a person's state of mind. How receptive one was.

A Japanese study on suicides had revealed that the last conscious thought a person had before certain death was surprise. A man jumped off a tall building in a depressed state of mind. The fall brought with it fear, a certain perverse curiosity, and in some, even a summing up of life's foibles. But at the moment of impact, it was surprise. Surprise that this then was the end. That it was about to be final. That there were no longer possibilities of second thoughts.

The study had been based, of course, on case histories of suicides who had failed. Unfortunates who had somehow survived their attempts.

Zamyatin had precipitated a course of action, had begun a chain of events, and at this moment he was surprised, much the same as a suicide was surprised.

He sighed tiredly, picked up the phone, and dialed an outside number. A moment later the Center security operator answered.

"Your call, comrade?"

Zamyatin gave the operator the outside number he had just dialed. "First department chief."

"Authorization?"

Calls to telephones outside of the Center could be made only by department chiefs or above. Each department chief was issued an authorization calendar each month. Zamyatin's calendar was opened to the proper date and he read the corresponding code, which was unique to the date and to him personally.

"Alpha-seven-seven-one-baker."

A moment later the telephone clicked, and his call went through. Major Balachov answered it on the first ring.

"Yes."

"Need you home for an A.O. conference at 1900 hours."

"Right," Balachov said and hung up.

Zamyatin held the button down on the telephone for a full minute until it rang. He released the button.

"Four-three-one," he said.

"Confirming," Major Balachov's voice came softly over the line.

"Nineteen hundred hours," Zamyatin said, then he hung up. He made three other calls, these all within the

Center, one after the other, and then he sat back again in his chair and stared out the window at the city below him. In forty-five minutes the conference that had been authorized by General Barynin's office would begin. In forty-five minutes his decision would either be confirmed or denied. And if confirmed, the considerable might of the Komitet would be used as a gigantic lever stretching from Moscow to the United States and back again.

December 20, 1917, was the key date. On that day the Council of the People's Commissars established the *Cheka*, the All-Russian Extraordinary Commission for Combating Counter-Revolution and Sabotage, with Felix Dzerzhinsky as its chief.

Dzerzhinsky was an austere man whom many considered absolutely merciless. He had come from a Polish family of aristocratic background and therefore knew well, and could use to great advantage, the powers of command.

The People's Commissars had established the *Cheka* originally as nothing more than an investigative body. A detective agency, so to speak, that would watch over the backlash of lawlessness that follows revolution.

But under Dzerzhinsky's hands the *Cheka* became much more than that. Its avowed purpose became the extermination of all opponents to Communism, with powers of execution without trial.

The terror had begun.

Zamyatin slowly got to his feet and, moving closer to the window, leaned forward, placing his forehead on the cool glass. His breath fogged the window in front of his eyes so that he could not see outside, but it didn't matter to him. He closed his eyes and tried to marshal his thoughts, to justify what he was doing.

In its little more than four years of existence the *Cheka* grew from a tiny nucleus of ruthless men to an organization of more than 31,000 zealots. Virtually every aspect of Soviet society was controlled from such divisions as the Secret Political Department, which watched over the general population; the Special Department, which watched the military; and other units that watched transportation and communications, newspapers, religion, concentration and labor camps, and even Soviet citizens who happened to be abroad.

But with the end of the civil war, and with the firm establishment of Communist power, the *Cheka* was abolished. It had become too much of a good thing. In its place, on February 6, 1922, the State Political Directorate, known simply as the GPU, was founded as a subordinate division of the People's Commissariat of Internal Affairs: the NKVD.

From the very beginning, Zamyatin thought tiredly, his life had been nothing but a series of trade-offs. The war had to be fought, so don't get married and have children until later. The war had to be ended swiftly, so become efficient and ruthless.

He opened his eyes, and the lights from outside were soft and blurred through the fogged glass.

"If you work for us," Zamyatin's first chief had told him, "the rewards will be great, but every aspect of your personal life will be under constant scrutiny. Our country is too young, our aims too high, to risk having traitors among us."

A trade-off.

"Colonel Zamyatin, we were able to save your son's life, but not the life of your wife. I am sorry," the doctor had said.

A trade-off.

"Comrade Colonel, I am afraid that because you are a good man we will have to call on your time to a much greater degree than might be wished for. We cannot allow your transfer. Your children will learn to understand."

A trade-off.

In 1923 the GPU became the OGPU, or the Unified State Political Directorate and was detached from the NKVD for administrative reasons.

Of course, all of those changes were mostly window dressing, because Dzerzhinsky himself continued to control the State Security apparatus until his death in 1926 when he was succeeded by the equally tough Vyacheslav Menzhinsky.

Under the new leader the OGPU flourished with an innovative network of informants that honeycombed every aspect of Soviet life.

Menzhinsky died in 1934, and Stalin reorganized the OGPU into the GUGB—the Chief Directorate for State Security—and again made it a part of the NKVD, which itself rapidly became the primary organization.

The NKVD not only controlled the State Security Service, it also controlled the conventional police, the border guards, the internal troops, and a new host of concentration camps for political criminals.

Until this point, however, there was still one segment of the Soviet population that had managed to defy total control: the peasantry. It was the same segment of the population that had defied the earlier control of the czars. And it was to this task that Stalin set the considerable resources of the NKVD under the direction of Menzhinsky's chief deputy Genrikh Yagoda.

Yagoda slaughtered peasants by the thousands, but failed to control them. And two years later, in 1936, Yagoda himself was tried and found guilty of insufficient vigor in the task and was shot. His replacement was Nikolai Ivanovich Yezhov, a man just over five feet tall who truly earned his nickname, "the bloody dwarf."

Zamyatin finally turned away from the window, withdrew a handkerchief from his breast pocket and rubbed his eyes. He gathered up the stack of file folders from the center of his desk and, squaring his shoulders, headed out the door of his office.

He did not want to do this, but the move was logical. It was correct. It would accomplish the purpose he had been assigned.

Most of his staff was still there, and would remain at their desks until he dismissed them, and a few of the men looked up as he crossed the large room toward the corridor door. No one said anything to him. He had a look in his eyes that precluded any comment from a subordinate.

In 1936, with Yezhov's appointment to head the purges, the Soviet State Security apparatus evolved in a series of stunning, dramatic, and oftentimes bloody transformations.

Tens of thousands of artists, Jews, Catholics, peasants, doctors, military men—men, women, and children from all walks of life—were systematically murdered.

"The Communist Sate must be pure. The purification process merciless."

By 1941 the NKVD under the leadership of Lavrenti Beria was controlling so much of the Soviet Union, its responsibilities so great, that the GUGB was again detached from its parent organization, and the State Security Service was renamed the NKGB, the People's Commissariat for State Security.

In 1946 the NKGB was elevated to the status of a government ministry in charge of State Security. The NKVD, also elevated to ministry status, was charged with handling internal affairs.

One year later, in 1947, the Soviet government finally began to look outward from its own borders, especially toward the United States. And its first clandestine operations were begun under a new, independent department: the Committee of Information, known as the KI. The cold war had begun.

The KI took over many of the functions of the NKVD and NKGB. Until Stalin's death in 1953 several administrative changes were made in the three security organizations until March 13, 1954, when the present-day KGB was formed.

Beria had been shot as a spy, as were many of the other State Security leaders. And under Krushchev, Malenkov, and Molotov, the KGB took over nearly all the functions of all its predecessor organizations, with virtually hundreds of thousands of employees in nearly every country in the world.

But basically nothing had changed. The KGB was as ruthless as its parent organizations. Its leaders acted as surely and as terribly as their predecessors. Only now there had come to the service a certain sophistication, a certain pervasive organization.

The Second Chief Directorate's staff conference room was located on the fourth floor of the Center in a tiny, square cubicle. A single light globe hung from the plaster ceiling over a cheap wooden table around which were positioned a half-dozen chairs. The dirty, cracked plaster walls were unadorned except for a small portrait of Lenin, and the single window was covered with a fine wire mesh. The same wire mesh was also embedded in the ceiling, walls, and floor, and was charged with a high frequency, low voltage that served as an antisurveillance measure. The door, similarly protected, was locked.

The room was, in the parlance, clean.

The conference technician, a young second lieutenant, had arrived moments earlier and had set up a tape recorder that was encased in a steel box with remote controls. Without that protection the only sounds that could have been recorded on tape would have been the electronic interference coursing through the steel mesh.

Zamyatin sat at the head of the table. To his right was Major Balachov, who still wore his wet raincoat, and Valentin Stanislav Kuzin, who was Zamyatin's chief analyst, and second in command of the Second Directorate's Political Service Division.

Across the table from them was Major Portini Pavlovich Yashchenko, from the First Chief Directorate's Executive Action Department V.

Everyone in the room was nervous in Major Yashchenko's presence.

The technician donned a set of earphones, pushed the record buttons on the table machine, and then nodded his head slightly. Zamyatin began tiredly.

"This is a Second Chief Directorate, Political Service Division, action order conference. Classification, most secret. Key line, urgent. Operation, CLEAN SWEEP."

He looked at the others, but no one said anything as they waited for him to continue.

"Convening at 1900 hours, conference room four-one-three. Present are, Zamyatin, Yuri Petrovich. Colonel, Political Service Division." He nodded toward Kuzin, who, in a low-pitched, gravel-throated voice, gave his name, civilian rank, and position.

Kuzin went back a long way, even beforc Zamyatin himself, and yet he had never begrudged Zamyatin's promotions.

"I don't want administrative responsibilities," Kuzin had told him years ago when Zamyatin's first daughter was born. "But you now with a child to consider, you need the new apartment and increased rations."

Kuzin had never married, although at one time he had been a tall, square-shouldered, handsome man.

"It's my voice," he laughed, the sound much like two boulders grating together just before an avalanche. "Old women take pity on me. Middle-aged women are ashamed. And the young girls are frightened."

Zamyatin had learned from a man who knew Kuzin from a few years after the Revolution, that his vocal cords had been all but completely destroyed when he had eaten some black bread that had been left in a back alley behind a Moscow hospital that treated high Party officials.

Kuzin had been starving to death, and had not even tasted the rat poison in which the bread had been soaked until it was too late. Several hundred starving people had died in the hospital's efforts to control its rat population.

After Zamyatin had learned that, he was able to understand and appreciate Kuzin's often-repeated answer to the question: Were the post-Revolution days tough?

"More people than rats died in those days," he would growl.

Balachov was next, and he gave his name, rank, and position within the Second Chief Directorate, and all of them held their breaths as Yashchenko spoke his name, rank, and position for the tape recorder.

The man was a mystery. It was the one word that described nearly every aspect of him.

Yashchenko was huge, standing well over six-feet-six, and weighing, Zamyatin estimated, at least 280 pounds. But there was no fat on the man. His arms were like gigantic battering rams, his legs like pillars of stone, his body like a gigantic statue and his neck and massive head merging into a single solid unit atop his soccer-field-sized shoulders.

Yashchenko, the Second Chief Directorate chief once told Zamyatin, cried at poetry readings and was a habitué at the Bolshoi, yet he rode roughshod over the Executive Action Department V, the department within the Komitet that engineered and carried out assassinations, kidnapings, and other *mokrie delas*, which was the terminology for actions in which blood would probably be spilled.

Yashchenko, despite his size, had a pleasant and somewhat cultured voice that was never raised in anger. And yet he had probably murdered more people than any other man presently employed within the Komitet.

Zamyatin had once been a hard man. Yashchenko held that title now.

"If we are to implement your action order, Colonel," Yashchenko said respectfully, "we must first begin the conference."

Zamyatin looked up out of his thoughts and nodded. "Yes," he said, and he opened the first of the file folders in front of him. For an instant he wished he had never remembered Mahoney's name. But he had. And there was nothing to do for it now.

Action orders were just that. An order for a specific, one-time action, such as the blackmail of a foreign newsman, or an assassination, or the sabotage of some particular target.

Each action order was supported by three things: first were pertinent documents, such as the intended victim's complete dossier; second was a record of all inter-and intradepartmental discussions; and lastly was an analysis of the necessity for such an action and a prognostication of probable results.

"Major Yashchenko," Zamyatin began, resigning himself to it, "I will first outline briefly the steps which have led to these proposed action orders, and then we can go over everything in whatever detail you may require."

"Fair enough, Comrade Colonel. Please continue."

"Number one. Operation CLEAN SWEEP activities have uncovered excessive activity over the past thirty-six hours at the United States Embassy here in Moscow.

"Number two. Those activities were and are being directed by the CIA chief of station Farley Carlisle, under the guise of routine preparations for the American president's visit here on Thursday.

"Number three. It is our studied opinion that the Americans indeed may have engineered the kidnaping of Professor Doctor Sahkarhov and the laser.

"Number four. It is further our studied opinion that the Americans may—and, Major, I must emphasize the word *may*—be planning the assassination of their own president on Soviet soil.

"Number five. It is finally our opinion that the Americans plan to place the blame for the assassination of their own president on us.

"And number six. The possibility for the conversion of a high-ranking CIA employee within the embassy exists. If this were accomplished within the next twenty-four to thirty-six hours, the American plans to assassinate their own president could either be stopped or converted for our own use."

Kuzin and Balachov were unmoved by Zamyatin's summation, which was not surprising since Kuzin had analyzed the data that Balachov had supplied.

But Yashchenko had not blinked an eye. Either the man had no soul, or he was harder than even Zamyatin had given him credit for being.

"There is more than one action order?" Yashchenko finally asked.

"Two of them," Zamyatin answered.

"They are to be used as a lever to convert your target?"

"Yes."

The big man thought a moment. "And these are internal or external?"

"External," Zamyatin said carefully. "In the United States."

"I see," Yashchenko said pleasantly. He looked across the table at Balachov, who fidgeted somewhat uncomfortably under the man's gaze. "And Major Balachov. I would assume your department's routine surveillance turned up point one. Is that correct?"

"Sunday morning we noticed an increase in activity. All of it apparently stemming from Carlisle himself."

"And this did not occur on Saturday morning, or even Saturday afternoon, *before* the kidnaping occurred?"

"That may not have been necessary," Kuzin's voice rasped.

Yashchenko turned his almost hypnotic gaze toward the older man. "And so?"

"If the Americans kidnaped Sakharov, and the possibility seems valid, they could have planned this months ago, their sudden activity on Sunday morning nothing more than the final stages or perhaps the aftermath of their action."

"But not merely a reaction to our own sudden activity?" the Department V chief asked softly, turning to Balachov.

"I don't understand," Balachov said, and Zamyatin could see that his Department One director was not only nervous, he was lost.

But Yashchenko was patient. "Your job, Major, is to watch the American embassy. Do you understand that there is a man who is your counterpart? A man watching us?"

Balachov nodded uncertainly. "Switt."

"Just so. And do you further understand that very early Sunday morning, when activities are normally at their minimum here, our entire upper echelon leadership was called in?"

"The Americans detected that activity and had to meet to figure out what we were up to," Zamyatin said. He was tired, but he wondered if his weariness was not just a mental trick to insulate him from a task he considered exceedingly distasteful.

"Yes, Colonel."

"We thought of that, but our primary directive is one of assumption. Assume that someone from our area of surveillance has kidnaped Sakharov and the laser. The Americans are the only ones in Political Service Division who fulfill the requirement. Do *you* understand that, Major?"

"Yes, Colonel," Yashchenko said straight-faced.

"And do you further understand, Major, that your presence here is merely advisory in nature to your department?"

"Yes, Colonel," Yashchenko said, still with the straight face.

Zamyatin stared at him for a long moment before he continued. "Very well," he said. "Point one, excessive activities at the American embassy. Any question?"

"None."

"Point two, the activities are of an intelligence

nature because of the presence of Farley Carlisle. Question?"

"Yes," Yashchenko said. "Is that confirmed information?"

Zamyatin nodded toward Balachov.

"Yes it is, Major. We have a low-level embassy staffer who confirmed the information for us."

"A State Department employee, or a physical plant staff member?"

"A cook, actually," Balachov said. He sat back. "Someone from your own directorate converted him some time ago in the States."

"Don't play silly little word games with me, Boris Aleksandrovich," Yashchenko said, leaning forward slightly.

Balachov blanched. "I am sorry, Major . . . I did not mean to . . . that is . . . "

"Points three, four, and five," Zamyatin forcefully interrupted. Yashchenko looked his way but said nothing. "The Americans kidnaped Sakharov and the laser with which they will assassinate their own president when he arrives here in Moscow on Thursday. The laser, from my understanding, is powerful enough to do the job. Professor Doctor Sakharov would be found dead at the controls of the device, thus proving to the world that the Soviet government engineered and carried out the assassination."

"Insanity," Yashchenko said softly, but Balachov had recovered enough to challenge the assessment.

"Not so," he said. Yashchenko looked his way and was about to speak, but Zamyatin interrupted again.

"Enough," he said. He was sick to death of the entire affair and wanted nothing more now than to end it and go home to his children. Soon it would be their bedtime, and he wanted to have some time with them first. "It *is* insanity. But so was the Bay of Pigs. So was the Cuban blockade. And certainly so were the assassinations of the Kennedys and of King. We are not here to judge rationality. We are here for an action order conference."

For the first time Yashchenko and Balachov both seemed to realize that their squabble with each other was all recorded on tape, and both of them seemed somewhat contrite for it.

In a way Zamyatin felt some pity for Balachov, who had done a very good job over the past few years. But the man's career would be finished within a dozen months. Yashchenko was not a man to treat roughly unless you had the rank or the position. Balachov would learn that the hard way, because he had neither.

"This insanity, as you term it, Major Yashchenko, if true, must at all costs be stopped. To that end I personally will attempt to convert the CIA employee I mentioned earlier. Through that man we will learn about their plans."

"Shall we know his name?" Yashchenko asked respectfully.

"Wallace Leonard Mahoney," Zamyatin said. "He is the CIA's senior intelligence evaluator—they call them analysts."

"Yes," Yashchenko smiled. "And the action orders?"

Zamyatin flipped open the two thin file folders which were both marked with a red action tag. In each folder was a single document, the action order itself, which required the signature of an officer grade thirteen or higher. Zamyatin was a fourteen. He signed both documents, closed the file folders, and handed them across the table to Yashchenko. Then he gathered up the supporting documents in two other file folders and handed them to Yashchenko as well.

"The tape will go with these jackets," he said. "But the entire package will have to first be cleared through General Barynin's staff before the authorization number and budget line are assigned. I will count on you to expedite that, Major."

"Yes, Colonel," Yashchenko said, making no move to open the files.

Zamyatin got to his feet but did not move away from the table. "Mahoney has two children. One of them, named Michael, is a plant pathologist with the Forest Products Laboratory in Missoula, Montana. He is not married, and as far as archives knew, he lives alone." Zamyatin took a deep breath and closed his burning eyes against the harshness of the single light.

"Mahoney's other child, John, is married to a woman by the name of Mary. They have three children, Carl, John Junior, and Cindy. All quite young. They live in Los Angeles, California, where John works as a chemical engineer for Monsanto."

And now it came, Zamyatin thought. A picture of his own three children flashed through his mind. "I want John, his wife and three children, and Michael picked up and held. And I want confirmation of that action within twenty-four hours."

"Excellent," Yashchenko said, smiling.

Zamyatin was suddenly sick, but he held himself in check. "Then if there is no further discussion, comrades . . . " he said, pausing a moment.

No one said anything, and he nodded to the recording technician who switched off the tape recorder then jumped up and unlocked the door.

Without a word to anyone Zamyatin strode out the door, went back to his office where he dismissed his remaining staff, got his coat, and left the Center alone, thoughts of Mahoney's children and grandchildren intermingled with thoughts of his own children hammering through his head like a dull but insistent headache.

Monday Evening

Leonid Sakharov opened his eyes, and a light bulb encased in a wire cage on the ceiling above him slowly swam into focus. It had happened like this how many times before? Twice? Three times? Four times?

His stomach was rumbling, and he closed his eyes again against the glare, trying with all his will to maintain his consciousness. His biological time clock had emptied the food he had eaten. He had slept. Now he was hungry again. Six hours, perhaps eight. But he could not remember how many times he had eaten since the two men had taken him away in the car.

He opened his eyes again, slowly swung his legs over the edge of the cot he lay on and attempted to sit up. A wave of dizziness and nausea swept through him, and he slumped down on his side, his feet just touching the bare concrete floor.

It was a problem of focus. One part of his mind dispassionately examined the situation. He had been cut off from the outside world in the tiny, windowless room for twenty-four hours or more. He no longer had the change from morning to afternoon to night to focus on.

Pi, the ratio between the circumference of a circle and its diameter. A transcendental number. Approximately 3.14159.

Sakharov tried to make his mind work on that problem. The square of *pi*. One . . . carry the eight. Five times nine is forty-five, add the eight makes fifty-three, carry the five.

At sixty Sakharov was a gnome of a man, barely five feet tall, stoop-shouldered, thinning, stark white hair, bulbous nose, sagging jowls. But his mind was almost as sharp as it had been when, as a young man, he had entered the mathematical physics department at the Soviet Academy of Sciences, and his intuitive genius was sharper because of his experience.

As one part of his mind worked on the problem of squaring *pi*, another part of him catalogued his body. He was hungry. He was dirty. And deep inside his gut his bowels were rumbling. He had always had problems with diarrhea, but at this moment the pressure against his sphincter muscle was growing. Soon he would have to relieve himself.

As he slowly, patiently, carefully worked out the problem, a digit at a time, he could feel his mind coming back to the present, assigning some reality to his situation.

Finally he sat up and opened his eyes, an almost beatific expression on his features.

"*Pi*," he said aloud. "The square of *pi* is 9.8695877281."

The room he was in was tiny, barely ten feet on a side, furnished only with the cot and across the room, a toilet without a seat or a lid. The walls were bare concrete relieved only by a metal door on one side and a small ventilating grille high near the ceiling on the opposite side. The floor was bare concrete as was the ceiling with its single, caged light bulb. He felt that he was underground, perhaps in a basement.

Saturday evening he had been working late at the university when the telephone call came. Two men from the People's Ministry of Science, a euphemism for the KGB's Directorate T, would be coming for him. It was a matter of utmost importance that had to be discussed. Utmost military importance.

Sakharov raised a hand to his mouth. They had come for him. Had taken him away in a car. As soon as they had left the university grounds the man who sat with him in the back seat had placed a cloth over his nose and mouth. It had been chloroform.

He shook his head slowly. When he had wakened for the first time, he had found himself here in this room, lying on the cot, still in his topcoat, hat, and shoes.

But why?

Suddenly it came to him. It was as if a veil had been lifted from in front of his eyes and he could see again. Suddenly he knew exactly why they had come for him. Why he was being kept prisoner in this place.

"Mayn Got," he said softly in Yiddish, and he lay all the way down on the cot.

Sakharov had, all of his life, kept three secrets that until this very moment he had been sure no one knew anything about.

The first was that his name wasn't really Sakharov, it

was Zakhreim. He was a Jew. He had managed to change his name during the confusion of the war.

The second was that he hated the Soviet Union, what it was, what it stood for, and what it was doing to his people. All these years he had been living a lie. Too timorous to speak out.

And the third was that for some time he had been funneling information to a scientific friend of his who was a professor of physics at the Polytechnic in Zurich. At least once a year he was allowed out of the Soviet Union to meet at the Zurich Congress of Light Physicists. Each year he and his friend collaborated on their studies.

Sakharov had never defected, despite his feelings about the Soviet Union, because he was a frightened man. Frightened of the KGB which had ears everywhere. He also remained in Moscow because his friend in Zurich said he was more valuable to their science where he was.

But now he was not so sure his secrets were indeed secret. He was a prisoner and soon, he supposed, the interrogation would begin.

He had no family. His parents had long since died. He had never married. Had no brothers or sisters that he knew of. No cousins or aunts or uncles. Most of them had been killed by the Germans during the war.

There was no one except for himself, and a few colleagues and students at the university. But they would not raise the alarm. One did not raise such alarms in the Soviet Union.

Alone. He was alone.

Sakharov could feel his legs trembling, and he began to cry like a frightened baby as he urinated in his trousers. Across the room was the toilet, but he could not even raise his head that far to see it.

After a time he let himself go completely, babbling like a complete idiot as a hot gush of semi-liquid rushed from his bowels, soiling his trousers.

VII

Monday 11:45 P.M.

MOSCOW (AP) . . . The Communist Party newspaper, *Izvestia*, this evening accused the U.S. of engineering a massive buildup of arms in Israel and Egypt.

Quoting from unnamed sources, the newspaper labeled the arms buildup as "a clear act of aggression against neighboring Arab countries."

Kremlin sources available to Western news media neither denied nor substantiated the story, but *Izvestia* is generally regarded as an accurate indicator of Party thinking. . . .

Ever since the war, whenever Mahoney awoke from a nap or a long sleep when he was troubled, he did so instantly and without moving until he was sure of his surroundings. He opened his eyes now and the room was dark.

It had been noon when Marge had awakened him, helped him out of the tub, helped him dry off and led him into the bed. He had slept without moving since then.

The rain still pattered against the window, and across the room he could see Marge sitting in an easy chair. She was knitting.

"Did the embassy call?" he asked softly.

Marge looked up, a small amount of light from somewhere glinting on her glasses. "Did you sleep well, my darling?"

"Yes."

"No one called," she said, putting her knitting in the small wicker basket by her feet. "And if they had I would not have awakened you."

"What time is it?"

"Nearly midnight, I think. I've been knitting. Your sweater is almost finished."

"With the leather patches on the sleeves?" He could see her smile.

"Yes, Wallace, with leather patches on the sleeves. And pockets for your matches."

Mahoney let his muscles, which had tensed when he woke, loosen, and he sighed deeply. He had dreamed about the war. But the images he had seen were not clear, and he had spent his dreamtime struggling to get a better view. Zamyatin, the Russian he had worked with more than thirty years ago, had been there and so had Carlisle. They had been working with each other, doing something to someone. Children, he thought now, it had been.

"I wrote two letters while you were sleeping. One to John and the other to Michael. I told them that we would be coming home for vacation in a couple of months, and that you wanted to have a family reunion. Los Angeles would be best."

"June will be too hot in Southern California," he said. "Let's make it Montana."

"I haven't sealed the envelopes yet, so I can change it. I thought you might want to add something."

In Mahoney's long intelligence service career, whenever things began to go sour he developed a nervous tic in his right eyelid. That eye was twitching like crazy now, but he had no conscious idea why.

"Marge," he said.

"Yes, Wallace?"

He hesitated a moment. "I love you, do you know that?"

"Yes," she said simply.

He closed his eyes. "Do you remember when John was little, and we lived on C Street in D.C.? We were as poor as church mice?"

"What made you think of that?"

"This place. And before this, Berlin. And all the other places all the way back to C Street."

"I've never complained."

He smiled to himself. "No."

"My mother told me long ago that for the love of a man a woman should never complain."

"This is the last assignment, Marge. This time I mean it."

She laughed, but not unkindly. "Were you dreaming about Minnesota again?"

He pushed the covers back and sat up in bed, swinging his legs over the edge. "No. But I was thinking about it the other day. We've got plenty in the bank. I'll cash out my retirement fund, and we can buy a little house on a lake."

"And a boat so you can go fishing in the morning?"

"Yes," he said. His legs were throbbing. "And a screened-in porch so you can sit and enjoy the evenings without getting bit up by mosquitoes."

"I'd like that."

He got to his feet and grabbed for the bedpost for support. It was the goddamned weather. Cold. Damp. Whenever the weather was like this his legs hurt so badly he seriously thought about amputation. The service doctor had told him that someday his varicose veins would be impossible to live with. Then they would have to be stripped. But that would lay him up for at least a year.

He would live with the pain just a little while longer.

Marge had gotten out of her chair, and she came across the small room and helped him walked slowly into the living room. Movement tended to loosen his leg muscles and ease the pain somewhat. It was something they had been doing for several years.

"We're going to have the service doctor fix your legs first," she said as they walked around the tiny living room. "Let the company pay for it. And then you can go on medical recuperation leave, and when that's over with you can tell them you are retiring."

Mahoney looked down at his wife and laughed out loud. "Mrs. Mahoney, I do believe there is a bit of the bargain-hunting Arab coming out in you."

She laughed, too. "I've had a good teacher."

Mahoney stopped and pulled his wife to him and hugged her. Their laughter had served to ease his tense mood. "You're a beautiful woman."

She parted from him and looked up into his eyes. "Are you going back to work tonight?"

"Yes," he said softly. "But we have time."

Without a word they walked arm in arm back into the bedroom, where they parted and went to their own sides of the bed. Mahoney slipped off his shorts and Marge took off her housecoat and pulled her nightgown over her head.

They climbed into bed and held each other closely, Mahoney kissing her neck and behind her ears. She had always loved it when he did that, and now that their lovemaking occurred so infrequently, she seemed to enjoy it even more than before.

Like their daily lives together, which stretched backward thirty-nine years, their love was soft and gentle and slow, yet was in a sort of abbreviated code: each word, each gesture, each touch loaded with meaning and shared experience.

He kissed her breasts which had sagged with age, but he did not see those ravages of time. Instead he saw a woman, a sexual creature, whom he loved with all his heart and soul.

She touched and caressed him the way he enjoyed it most, and when he was ready he entered her, gently and with much feeling.

Sex had always been a very special expression of their love for each other, and it was no different this night. Mahoney, for those few minutes, forgot every other aspect of his life: his children, his job, everything except his love for his wife.

Afterward, they kissed deeply and parted without speaking, words, at this moment, unnecessary for them.

Marge used the bathroom first, and when she was finished she came back into the bedroom. She had put on her nightgown and housecoat again.

"Do you want something to eat before you go to work?"

He got up from the bed. "Just a sandwich and a very large bourbon." He went to her and touched her cheek with the back of his right hand. "Love," he said, and he went into the bathroom to clean up, shave, and get dressed.

He was through in the bathroom in ten minutes, and when he came back into the bedroom he quickly strapped on his shoulder holster and .45 automatic, slipped on his suitcoat, then went into the kitchen where Marge had poured him a bourbon in a large glass and made him a liverwurst sandwich. He sat down at the small table, drank deeply of the straight whiskey and began eating his sandwich.

"Did you mean it about retiring?" she said as she puttered with a few dishes at the sink.

He looked up at her. "Yes," he said between mouthfuls. He took another drink, the whiskey warming his insides.

"Will you be late again?" she asked. During their long marriage she had never asked more than that despite his odd hours and frequent long absences. In the old days it often happened that he would leave for work one morning and not return for two weeks without a word to her. When he would return they would pick up the threads of conversations that had been begun the morning he left as if nothing out of the ordinary had happened. She knew what he did for a living, but she never questioned him.

"Probably," he said, finishing his sandwich and then his drink.

He got up and went into the living room where he took his raincoat and hat from the closet and put them on. When he turned around she was standing in the kitchen doorway.

"You'll be walking to work?" she asked.

He nodded, and she came across the room to him and pulled up his collar and buttoned the top button of the coat. "Don't catch a cold, old man," she said.

He kissed her on the cheek. "I won't," he said, and he turned and left the apartment, tromping slowly down the stairs, the pain from the varicose veins finally fading from the exercise and the whiskey.

Outside the front door of the building, the Soviet guard in his little guardbox looked up from the newspaper he was reading as Mahoney paused and stared at him. The light in the tiny structure lit the back of the man's head, throwing his face into shadow, but Mahoney was certain he had never seen the man before.

"*Dawbrih y vyehchehr*," Mahoney said in Russian.

"Good evening, sir," the guard answered in English.

Mahoney continued to stare at the man for a few moments longer, trying to catalogue his features for future reference, and then he turned and went down the steps and headed in the cold rain toward the embassy four blocks away.

"You stupid sonofabitch, one of these days you'll turn up dead," Carlisle had told him eleven months ago when he learned that it was Mahoncy's habit to walk to the embassy from his apartment.

That was when Carlisle was new in Moscow, and he

had tried to convince Mahoney either to take an apartment with most of the other staffers in the embassy itself, or have a car come for him every day.

Mahoney had flatly said no to both suggestions. "It's like trolling for a very smart catfish," he had told Carlisle later by way of explanation. "If I'm nailed, we'll know that they understand I'm something more than a trade missionary. If I make it, they either have not tumbled to me, or I'm doing nothing worth a damn to hurt them. Either way when I get to my office safely each time, I work just a little harder to shove it to them."

The wind was blowing, driving the rain into his face as he walked, and he pulled up his coat collar closer around his neck and pulled his hat down lower over his eyes.

Mahoney was an orderly man. An organizer. A planner. In the morning his routine never varied. Socks and shoes then trousers. Clean the teeth, then shave. T-shirt, shirt, then tie.

Work was the same, and each day he spent these few minutes of walking organizing his thoughts for the coming problems.

At this point there was not enough data for him to draw any conclusions about what had been, and still was as far as he knew, happening in Dzerzhinsky Square.

But that in itself was his first clue. There was no financial data indicating any big push. And according to Munson there had been no significant increase in communications. Which meant either that the Russians were simply doing their spring housecleaning; rounding out paperwork, updating files at all levels, running control operations on their own personnel; or they had finally gotten cagey and were working on a deficit spending budget. If the latter was true, it would be something totally new for the Soviet government. New and very dangerous, because it would mean that henceforth everything the Komitet did would be done in the financial blind as far as the CIA was concerned. There would be no advance tickles on anything, only after-the-fact evaluations.

All along, that had been the CIA's little secret, even from their British, French, and West German friends. The Russians were naïve when it came to things financial, and had somehow never tumbled to the fact they wore many of their deepest secrets on their financial sleeves for everyone to see.

The streets were totally deserted, and the only light came from an occasional second- or third-story apartment window. Mahoney stopped at the first corner. The embassy was two blocks ahead to Tchaikovsky Street and then one block left. To his right, about one block, Old Town Moscow began, the area of the city unofficially off limits to Western tourists. It was an area of the city that dated back to pre-Revolution days, of old, unpainted and yet ornately carved houses, of French and Italian influenced brick buildings. Here were no modern expanses of glass and steel and smooth concrete: by day the most charming part of the city; by night the darkest and most brooding. But it was as if the Kremlin wanted to keep this section of Moscow a secret: a skeleton in its closet; an old cousin it was ashamed of.

About half a block from his apartment, Mahoney had picked up a single set of footsteps behind him. He had concentrated on his thoughts, allowing only one part of his mind to listen to the soft slap of shoe leather against concrete. He had stopped at the corner as if deep in thought, and the footsteps behind him had also stopped.

Now he stood thinking as he lit a cigar, his blood racing as it had years ago in Germany.

He threw the match away, took a deep breath and turned right down the narrow side street that led into Old Town. As he walked through the shadows he threw his cigar into a doorway so that the glowing tip would not give him away, and then quickly stepped into the next doorway, loosening the buttons of his raincoat as he moved silently on the balls of his feet.

Whoever was following him had not yet rounded the corner. Mahoney withdrew his .45 military automatic from its shoulder holster.

It was highly unusual for a company intelligence analyst to carry any kind of a weapon. They were the office sloggers, not the case officers. But Mahoney was from the old school and had always carried the gun.

"'My beefy hog leg," he called it. "'Can't hit the side of a barn with the goddamned thing, but when it goes off it sure scares hell out of anyone in the vicinity."

A small man in a dark raincoat and dark hat pulled low came around the corner about thirty feet away and stopped. Mahoney could not make out the man's features, but he could see the unmistakably Russian cut of the coat.

He raised the .45, snapped the slide back bringing a live round into the chamber and cocking the hammer, the noise itself almost like a gunshot in the quiet back street.

"A little closer," he said softly in Russian.

The man stiffened and hesitated a moment. Mahoney

raised the gun so that it pointed directly at the man's chest. He could not miss from this distance. The man would be dead with one shot, and within five or six minutes Mahoney could make it on foot to the embassy where he would be safe.

"*Edyetyeh syodah*," Mahoney repeated.

"Your accent is terrible, Mahoney," the man said, slowly withdrawing his hands from his pockets and moving forward. "But then you never did speak the language well."

The voice was soft, cultured, obviously Russian but with a heavy British accent.

He stopped about five feet from Mahoney and tipped his hat back. "There is no need for the weapon. I am alone and unarmed."

Mahoney slowly lowered the gun and eased the hammer back to safety. "Zamyatin," he said. "Yuri Zamyatin."

"That is right," Zamyatin smiled, moving closer and holding out his hand.

Mahoney pocketed the gun and took the Russian's hand.

"It has been a long time since the war, my friend. I did not know if you would remember or recognize me."

"I could not forget," Mahoney said, and he could hear the disapproval in his own voice although he had not meant to sound that way.

"Those were ruthless times."

"Peopled by ruthless men."

"Yes," Zamyatin said almost sadly.

Mahoney studied the man's face in the dim light for several long seconds, neither of them speaking. He had aged considerably since the war. His hair had started to turn gray, and his features had lost their cragginess. The most striking change in the Russian that Mahoney could see, however, was in his eyes. In 1945 they had been bright, flashing, very intense. But now they seemed deep, gentle, and very understanding.

"May I walk along with you?" Zamyatin said almost apologetically as if he did not want to intrude into Mahoney's thoughts.

"What do you want with me, Zamyatin?" Mahoney asked evenly. This, of course, had not been a happenstance meeting.

Zamyatin shrugged. "To reminisce perhaps about the war. To discuss our respective futures."

"We have nothing to say to each other."

"Yes we have," The Russian quickly contradicted. "I'm a colonel now," he said more slowly. "In charge of the Komitet's Political Service Division." He smiled. "It is my job, my old friend, to watch your embassy. Watch you and your assistant Congdon, and your boss Carlisle, who did an outstanding job in Portugal."

Mahoney reached for his .45 and was about to withdraw it again, when Zamyatin laughed.

"I am unarmed. I am alone. No one has followed me. No one knows I am here. You may search me if you would like. And afterward we can run the rabbit to elude a tail. But we must talk. Out here. Away from any ears. Your people's or mine."

This was a setup. Mahoney could feel it through Zamyatin's apparent sincerity.

So they had tumbled to him after all. Him and Carlisle and Congdon. Probably Bennet and Switt were known as well. Perhaps they had gotten it from the microwave scans that had been going on for the past several years. Perhaps there were other listening devices besides the one found in the fifties behind the U.S. seal in the ambassador's office. Perhaps someone from within the embassy had sold out.

Perhaps a lot of things, Mahoney told himself. But it was no perhaps that Zamyatin was here now, wanting to talk.

"Your people have been busy in Dzerzhinsky Square," Mahoney said.

Zamyatin smiled tiredly. "And so have your people in the embassy."

"Our president is coming on Thursday."

Something flashed across Zamyatin's eyes, and Mahoney felt a chill rise up his back, the hairs on his neck standing on end.

"I know," the Russian said. He took Mahoney's left arm, and they started down the street, deeper into Old Town. "Years ago, just after the war, my wife and I lived down here. Not too far from where we are at this moment."

"And where do you live now, Colonel?"

Zamyatin glanced up at Mahoney. "I have a wonderful apartment not too far from Kutuzovsky Prospekt where Comrade Brezhnev himself lives."

"Do you have children?"

"I have three marvelous children. But my wife is dead."

"I'm sorry."

"She died eleven years ago giving birth to our only son, Aleksei."

"Are your children well?"

"Yes," Zamyatin smiled. "And anxiously awaiting our holiday. We plan to go back to the Caspian."

Mahoney stopped and looked into Zamyatin's eyes. "The war *was* a long time ago, Yurianovich. Then came the cold war. And Korea. Then Vietnam. Detente. And now your dissident trials and my president's hopes for world peace and human rights."

"Let us not forget your race riots or your jailed draft evaders."

Mahoney continued as if Zamyatin had not interrupted him. "You and I are from opposite sides of the world. Opposite ideologies. Opposite goals."

"Yes, my friend, but you are now operating in my country."

"Only to better defend my own."

Zamyatin seemed to weigh those words carefully in his mind, and before he replied a look of infinite sadness came over him. Mahoney was moved almost to reach out and touch him.

"The war changed us all in this country, my friend. But the changes were much greater afterward."

"And you?"

"And me, perhaps, most of all."

"You say you came to me alone. And you want to talk without fear of being heard. What do you want?"

"Let's walk," Zamyatin said, and again they moved arm in arm down the narrow, deserted street, the rain seemingly colder and more intense.

Mahoney kept his right hand in his coat pocket, his fingers curled around the butt of the .45, part of his mind listening for something, anything behind them. During the war Zamyatin had been a ruthless man. Perhaps he *was* telling the truth, and he indeed had changed, softened. But Zamyatin also had been a very careful man. Mahoney doubted if that had changed. In all likelihood he had become more careful, which meant that every detail of this meeting had been meticulously worked out, every word painstakingly orchestrated in advance.

But why?

"I need your help," Zamyatin said as they neared the end of the long block.

Mahoney didn't break stride. "I'm listening, Colonel."

"Something quite extraordinary happened late Saturday night."

"I gathered as much," Mahoney said dryly, and Zamyatin looked at him.

"I'm not playing a game with you."

"I'll be the judge of that."

"No one knows I am contacting you."

"Yet," Mahoney said sharply, and Zamyatin started to protest, but he cut him off. "A colonel in the KGB, Political Services Division, who obviously knows my habits, contacts me on the street in the middle of the night after his organization has operated full blast for almost forty-eight hours."

Zamyatin said nothing, and Mahoney continued.

"This colonel knows not only of me, but he claims knowledge of others whom I work with. Which means Soviet surveillance of my embassy amounts to much more than mere observation. Perhaps even a double agent within the embassy itself. Low level. Maybe a janitor, or a cook, or even a minor staffer who got in over his head at one time or another."

"Already you have enough information to seriously hamper my division's operations. Enough information to have me shot as a traitor."

"Exactly," Mahoney said, pulling his arm away from Zamyatin's. "Which leads me to speculate on what kind of an operation you are attempting to work on me at this very moment."

Mahoney pulled his hand out of his pocket and suddenly spun Zamyatin around and quickly frisked him. Zamyatin did not move, and when Mahoney was finished he smiled.

"No weapons, no tape recorder, no transmitting device."

Mahoney searched the building fronts and roof line for any kind of a sign—a careless face in a window, the glint of metal from a rooftop parapet.

"And no long-range listening devices," Zamyatin said. "We can walk anywhere you would like except your own apartment or embassy."

Mahoney looked deeply into the man's eyes, but all he could detect besides an almost too obvious sincerity was perhaps a slight trace of fear.

"What do you want, Zamyatin? Are you defecting?"

Zamyatin laughed. "I am not a man who would want a life of constantly being on the run. I am not mobile. I have three children."

"What then?" Mahoney snapped. "What do you want from me?"

"Help."

"You already said that."

"Saturday night, near midnight, Professor Doctor

Leonid Sakharov was kidnaped from his office at Moscow State University by two men who identified themselves as Directorate T officers."

"Scientific and technical operations."

"Exactly. But no such operation was authorized or carried out."

"The two men were imposters?"

"Yes."

"We'll come back to that," Mahoney said after a moment's hesitation. "Meanwhile, who is Doctor Sakharov?"

"The leading laser scientist in the Soviet Union. The one man who has contributed more to military weapons laser research than any other man in the country."

"And he was snatched—just like that?"

"Just like that, Mahoney. We do not keep all of our scientists under lock and key on military installations."

What Zamyatin was telling him was extraordinary, almost too extraordinary. "How did you get involved?"

"The entire Komitet is on alert. Our orders are simply to find Professor Doctor Sakharov."

"And me?" Mahoney asked. At this moment he had absolutely no idea what was coming, but whatever it was it would be big. Zamyatin was suddenly nervous.

"Whoever snatched Sakharov also took a portable laser device. It is small enough to fit into a briefcase, and yet powerful enough to be used as a weapon. A very effective weapon. Long-range. Silent. No real defense against it."

"An assassination," Mahoney said. "Brezhnev is the suspected target?"

Zamyatin shook his head. "If that were the case I

would not be contacting you. I would be fighting you with everything at my command."

"Aren't you now?" Mahoney said, but the words were a cover for his surprise.

"No. I'm trying to enlist your cooperation." Zamyatin reached out and touched Mahoney's arm. "I'm sincere, my old friend, in my request for help."

"Make your point."

"The entire Komitet is on alert. Worldwide. No limitations. The operation, to find and recover Sakharov and the laser device."

Mahoney was about to interrupt, but Zamyatin held him off.

"Find and recover Sakharov and the laser by 1100 hours Thursday."

For several long moments Mahoney just stared at the Russian who had suddenly become agitated. The deadline was the significant factor, the one point of information that Zamyatin had seemed overly intense about.

Suddenly it fell into place. Chillingly so, and Zamyatin evidently read the recognition from Mahoney's face.

"Yes, my friend. There may be an attempted assassination. But not of Brezhnev. Of your own president. Here in Moscow on Soviet soil as he steps off Air Force One Thursday morning."

Mahoney pulled his gun from his pocket as he stepped back away from Zamyatin. He pulled the hammer back and pointed the gun at the Russian. "You are coming with me."

"Don't be a fool, Mahoney," Zamyatin said. "If I was pulling an operation on you, why would I tell you what I have?"

"I don't know, and that's what worries me."

"I need your help. And you need mine. If you pull me in now everything will be ruined. Neither one of us will be able to do a thing to stop it."

Mahoney looked at Zamyatin who held one hand out in a gesture almost of supplication.

"How is this operation being budgeted?"

"I don't have that information, nor am I interested in it."

"What do you want from me? Specifically."

"One of two things is happening," Zamyatin said, lowering his voice. "First the kidnaping was arranged by a Soviet group—for what reason, I do not know."

"To assassinate my president. You've already said it."

"But why? No Soviet citizen in his right mind would do such a thing."

"We are not talking about sanity," Mahoney started to say, but Zamyatin cut him off savagely.

"The other possibility—the one more likely—is that this operation is being carried out by your own people."

"For what reason?"

"Our little war is based on such coups, Mahoney. Your president is kidnaped or assassinated in Moscow. Think of the repercussions against us. Your president is not a popular man in your country, but his death blamed on us would be brilliant."

"We would not kill our own president."

"What about Kennedy?"

Mahoney almost shot the Russian at that moment, but something made him hold back. This was all like some sort of horrible dream. At their last meeting

Congdon had suggested the possible assassination of President Forsythe. But as a Russian operation. The situation in the Middle East was coming to a head. President Forsythe was coming to Moscow to speak with Brezhnev about it. Meanwhile the prophets of doom were already saying it was too late. That war, perhaps even nuclear war, was inevitable between the Arab bloc countries and Israel. Translated, that meant a nuclear war between the Soviet Union and the United States fought in the Middle East.

Who would gain by the president's death? The Russians because they hoped to gain the upper hand in the confusion? The American military because it hoped to use the president's death as an excuse to fire the first shot? Or was it some individual Soviet group who objected to President Forsythe's interference on the human rights issue?

None of it made any sense, but all of the possibilities were viable. And meanwhile Zamyatin stood here asking for help.

Mahoney once again let the hammer back to safety and pocketed the .45. The relief was visible on Zamyatin's face.

"You will help?"

"Perhaps," Mahoney said.

"If it is a Soviet group, I will find them," Zamyatin said. "If it is an American operation, there will be indications of it at your embassy. If that is the case, you must stop them. None of us wants a repeat of the Kennedy business. It would surely mean war between our two countries. A war from which none of us would survive."

VIII

Early Tuesday Morning

WASHINGTON, D.C. (AP) . . . President Forsythe today told leaders of the Congress at a meeting in the White House that the U.S. would continue to supply conventional arms to Israel and Egypt.

Speaking to the majority and minority leaders of both houses, the president warned that nuclear weapons would "at all costs" remain out of the Middle East situation, but that if either Israel or Egypt requested more help, the U.S. would cooperate.

Mahoney rated an office that was, because of the nature of his work, only slightly smaller than the ambassador's. Mahoney's sweatshop, as it was called, was stuffed floor to ceiling with shelves crammed to overflowing with books, magazines, newspapers, boxes of newspaper clippings, and maps of every size, shape, and description.

The overflow from the shelves was stacked on every available chair except the one behind Mahoney's desk, on top of file cabinets, atop a library table, and finally on the floor.

Mahoney did his "data collection"—as he called it—in this room, but for his serious thinking he removed himself to the embassy's English language library where, behind the last stack in a row of a dozen free-standing shelves, he had a windowbox seat that overlooked a bare, graveled courtyard beyond which was a brick wall.

Usually no one disturbed him here in his think tank, but had they this morning they would have found an uncharacteristically mean and intolerant soul.

The dawn had come, finally changing the black, starless sky into a dark gray, sunless one. The previous night the temperature had risen slightly so that the rain, now falling in earnest, had not frozen after all.

Mahoney was angry. Not so much at anyone in particular but at the circumstances that had brought him to his present state of mind. In whatever direction he looked, incongruities abounded.

He had been busy for the past six hours, first downstairs in the archives, then later in the embassy apartments, and now he had only one step left. But first he had to think it all out, sort everything into recognizable patterns so that he could deal with the raw data.

The Handbook, page 171, paragraph three: "It will be the duty of the analyst to assemble collated data itself into Patterns of Recognizable Reality (PRRs). (See appendix C-IIIa for further PRR definitions and examples.) The PRRs then become the basis upon which Real Time Actions (RTAs) will be recommended. In all events, PRRs of sufficient credibility will be required in support of any RTA."

Mahoney had arrived at the embassy around 1:30 A.M., had signed in with the somewhat surprised marine guard at the front entrance, and had gone immediately to his office.

He had taken out a pad of paper from his desk drawer and written down all the possibilities that he could think of:

POSSIBLE PRRs

I. Assassination of President
   a. A Soviet KGB plot
   b. An American CIA plot
   c. A plot by unknown Soviet group
II. Other operation
   a. Unknown KGB operation (worldwide?)
   b. Unknown CIA operation (objective?)
   c. combination
   d. presidential
   e. unknown group

Immediately Mahoney had crossed out c. and d. under the second heading as highly unlikely. The CIA and KGB had no basis upon which to run a joint operation, nor would the president of the United States be able to run such an operation without the cooperation of everyone, or nearly everyone in the Moscow embassy.

Which left the possibilities of assassination of the

U.S. president by the KGB, the CIA, or an unknown group, or some kind of an intelligence gathering operation by the CIA, KGB, or that unknown Soviet group.

Carrying that line of thinking another step further, Mahoney listed in his mind only the known happenings of the past two days.

First, the entire upper echelon of the KGB had met at Dzerzhinsky Square. That was a fact confirmed by too many people for it to be a setup. Switt, Bennet, and even Munson himself had lent their confirmation and therefore credibility to the fact.

Second, the CIA staff here at the embassy had met twice, activity here had increased, and Langley had given its go-ahead for a locally run operation coded LOOK SEE. These were solid facts witnessed by Mahoney himself.

Third, Yuri Zamyatin had contacted him in the middle of the night on the street with his startling revelations, and request for help. Zamyatin's appearance was definitely a fact, but what the man had said was at the very least, suspect.

The weak link at this moment, then, was the information Zamyatin had passed to Mahoney.

Weak links were to be strengthened or disregarded, so the handbook read. And at that point Mahoney had nothing else to go on, so he descended into the bowels of the embassy building to the archives themselves.

In almost every other American embassy, this section was called recordkeeping, or data storage, or filing. But here at the Moscow embassy the area that took up most of the basement of the large structure was called archives.

Archives was run by a ferret of a little man named

C.W. Dobbs who felt it was the embassy's prime duty to keep records. And since Dobbs was of the firm belief that each and every scrap of paper stored here was his personal property, it followed that the embassy itself was operated for, by, and because of him.

"This is holy territory," Dobbs had once told Congdon who had been in the habit of leaving files laying around and worse: during a cross-matching search, replacing documents in the wrong jackets.

Congdon had tried to argue the point that files were to be used, and Dobbs had immediately marched upstairs to the ambassador's office with his complaint.

Congdon had been called on the carpet, because not even the ambassador himself crossed C.W. Dobbs, and it had provided the embassy wags with several days of delicious gossip.

Standing at the locked, steel-mesh gate that barred the way, Mahoney felt like an intruder. A single light bulb lit the small space between the elevator door and the gate, beyond which Mahoney could see the counter from which Dobbs and his four assistants serviced what he called his "customers."

Over Dobbs's objections, night and weekend duty officers had the key to archives for emergencies, and the man who had come down the elevator with Mahoney unlocked the gate, reached inside, and flipped on the lights that illuminated the entire vast, cavernous basement that was crammed with row after row of file cabinets, shelves, and large cases that contained maps, aerial photographs, and other larger than file-sized documents.

The whine of the air conditioners that always ran was the only noise.

"I won't envy you in the morning Mr. Mahoney,

when C.W. comes in and finds out you've been messing around down here,'' the O.D. said, smiling.

''I'll be sure to lock up when I'm done,'' Mahoney said as he brushed past the O.D. and went immediately around the counter to the indexing files.

Mahoney never heard the O.D. leave as he began searching the files for references to Zamyatin, Political Services Division, and KGB Second Chief Directorate Activities.

The latter two headings in the index were followed by a long series of reference numbers that Mahoney copied on a blank piece of paper he found atop the file cabinets, while Zamyatin's name was referenced with the personal dossier code and index number, and was cross-referenced to the Political Services Division file, the Second Chief Directorate personnel jacket, and two others; one dated 1945 and the other, 1956.

In three and a half hours, his coat off, tie loosened, and shirt-sleeves rolled up, Mahoney had a fairly clear and complete picture of Yuri Petrovich Zamyatin.

The man had been born on October 10, 1924 in Rzhev, a town of a little more than 50,000 people northeast of Moscow on the Volga.

His parents had been workers for the Rzhev State Riverboat Works after the Revolution, and yet Yuri had somehow managed to finish school and was sent to Lomosov University in Moscow on a State grant where he studied world political science and history.

The wartime years in his personal dossier were cross-referenced to a jacket in the GRU file, and from those records Mahoney began building a picture in his mind of a man who was ruthless not by nature, but strictly by training.

The *Glavnoye Razvedyvatelnoye Upravleniye*

(GRU) was formed in the spring of 1920 as the chief intelligence directorate of the Soviet military general staff. And its history was inextricably tied with that of the KGB's.

At that time Dzerzhinsky's *Cheka* was the chief Soviet secret service apparatus, but for military intelligence the *Cheka* was almost brilliantly ineffective.

In April of 1920 the Polish army attacked the Soviet Union, getting as far as the Ukraine before being pushed back. Dzerzhinsky's *Cheka* convinced Lenin—erroneously—that the Polish people were ripe for revolution, and Lenin ordered an all-out attack.

The *Cheka* had been terribly wrong, however, and the Red Army was annihilated. Consequently Dzerzhinsky himself assigned Yan Karlovich Berzin to head up what was called the Cheka Registry Department responsible for gathering military intelligence as a specialty.

Eventually the Registry Department became the GRU, an adjunct to the general staff, responsible for gathering strategic, tactical, and technical military intelligence.

But from the beginning the GRU's history was one of ruthlessness, rivalry, and bloodshed.

Stalin himself encouraged much of the rivalry, so that at times the GRU extended its operations well beyond military intelligence. During the latter half of the '20s and into the '30s the GRU operated networks of illegal agents in foreign countries that did not diplomatically recognize the Soviet Union. In whatever country a Soviet embassy was denied, the GRU operated.

Just before World War II, a series of purges cleared the GRU of many of its ablest officers among those who happened to be at home. GRU officers in the field, however, managed to survive so that during the war the GRU did operate with some degree of efficiency and, at times, even brilliance.

It was during the latter half of World War II that Yuri Zamyatin was assigned to GRU activities in Austria as a second lieutenant. It was then, in 1945, that Mahoney had been sent on a mission with the young GRU officer.

After the war, in 1947, the GRU was submerged into the KI for a time, and Zamyatin, by then a first lieutenant, was permanently transferred out of military intelligence and into the State Security Service, so that in 1953 when the KGB became a full-fledged ministry, Zamyatin's career was well on its way.

The 1945 cross-reference in Zamyatin's file told Mahoney little more than he already knew about the operation that he and Zamyatin had carried out against the Obersalzburg area, although it felt strange to see his own name in a file connected with a Russian intelligence agent.

There were still other cross-references to KGB Second Chief Directorate activities in Zamyatin's personal file, but Mahoney set those aside for the moment to look through the cross-reference for 1956, more specifically the fall and winter of that year. The time of the Hungarian Revolution.

Yuri Valdimirovich Andropov, who until recently had been the director of the KGB, in 1956 was the Soviet ambassador in Budapest. It was at that time that Imre Nagy had headed the Independent Hungarian government.

Andropov's maneuvers that year were brilliant, and in part were among the reasons he later was chosen to head the State Secret Service.

First, Andropov convinced the Hungarians that the Soviet government was willing to negotiate withdrawal of the troops that had been there since the war.

Next, the man worked in secret with János Kádár to set up a puppet government backed by Soviet tanks.

And finally, Andropov invited Hungarian Defense Minister Pal Máleter and his staff to a banquet on November 3, at which time all of the Hungarians were arrested and many of them, Máleter included, were shot.

Mass arrests and executions swept the country, led by Lieutenant General Oleg Mikhailovich Gribanov, who was then chief of the KGB's Second Chief Directorate. One of his principal aides was Captain Yuri Petrovich Zamyatin.

The other cross-references from Zamyatin's personal dossier only made brief mention of his name in connection with the Second Chief Directorate, which was not surprising in view of the fact he had worked so well with that directorate's chief in Hungary. But there were no extensive details about the man's work since that time and only very little about his personal life.

On December 5, 1963, he had married Sandra Pogin, a girl of twenty-three from Leningrad. In 1965, a daughter named Sandra was born. In 1966, they had another daughter, Lara, and in 1967 Zamyatin's wife died giving birth to their only son, Aleksei. Since that time Zamyatin had not remarried and had refused on four separate occasions to give up his children for State adoption.

He was a devoted father.

Mahoney took no notes other than one-word reminders of what was contained in each file, jotted after its index number.

After he had returned all the files to their respective niches, he again returned to the index cabinets and looked under the heading Sakharov, Leonid, Scientist.

There was only a one-line reference to that heading, and in the glare of the overhead lights Mahoney stared at it for a long time. The reference consisted of nothing more than three sevens and a date in 1968, which meant the file was on the active list and had been so since 1968.

Sakharov was an agent, or was at least a source of information for Western interests, and had been for more than ten years. Subsequently his file was kept in a closed section that could only be tapped under the ambassador's authorization, or by special request of the CIA chief of station.

(It was curious, Mahoney thought, sitting at the library windowbox staring down at the courtyard, that a man whose file was on active should be the one kidnaped. Very curious indeed.)

He had finished in archives at a little after five o'clock, had locked up, returned the key to Finch, the O.D., who had made another petty, but somehow irritating remark about C.W. Dobbs's probable wrath, and had gone upstairs to the west wing of the building and woke Congdon from a deep sleep.

Congdon, like most embassy staffers, found it easier to maintain an apartment within the embassy itself. When he had come to his door he had seemed surprised at first, then slightly irritated that his sleep was disturbed, and Mahoney thought he somehow seemed guilty. It was the same impression Mahoney had gotten at the meeting they had had with Carlisle earlier.

"I only need a couple of minutes of your time,

George,'' Mahoney said, entering the man's apartment and sinking down wearily on the couch.

Congdon shut the door and sat down in an easy chair across from Mahoney. "Couldn't this have waited for a decent hour, Wallace?''

Mahoney shook his head. "What's the matter, George?''

"What the hell do you mean, what's the matter,'' Congdon snapped angrily. "It's five o'clock in the goddamned morning.''

"Carlisle has gotten to you, hasn't he.''

Congdon just stared at him, and Mahoney had the unsettling feeling that he was looking into the eyes of a stranger.

"I need an assessment out of you,'' Mahoney finally said. Congdon he would have to deal with later, and yet, once made, that decision seemed wrong to Mahoney. Wrong. But he could not put his finger on why.

"At five in the morning?''

"Yes, goddammit, at five in the morning. Or two. Or midnight! I need some help!''

"Go home to bed,'' Congdon said tiredly.

"What do you know about Soviet deficit spending?''

Again there was a blank look in Congdon's eyes.

"Are you listening to me?''

"Yes,'' Congdon said in a small voice.

"What is it?'' Mahoney said gently. "What has Carlisle done to you?''

Congdon shook his head. "Nothing. Nothing at all.''

"What part are you playing in LOOK SEE, George? What has he done to you?''

"Leave it be," Congdon said, sitting straighter in his chair and looking across at Mahoney as if he was seeing the man for the first time.

"Is it LOOK SEE, or your relationship with Carlisle?"

"What about deficit spending? What do you want to know?"

If Zamyatin had been correct in his assessment of the situation, there was not time to pick up the pieces during the operation, Mahoney thought. If Congdon was to be a casualty of the battle, then he would have to wait until the fighting was over before the medics could be called.

"Are the Soviets capable of it, and have you seen anything to indicate such a shift in policy?"

Congdon seemed to ponder the question for a moment before he answered. "I take it this is in relation to LOOK SEE. Evidently our good Dr. White didn't give you shit to go on."

"Right on both counts."

"Then my answer is yes and no. Yes, they are capable of deficit budgeting. Any five-year-old child who borrows against next week's allowance is capable of it. But no, I've not seen any signs of it. Their oil setup in Krasnodar is already in big trouble, and the fiscal year doesn't end for more than two months. They'll cut back production before they'll deficit dip into next year's budget."

"Could that mean a ruble call-up for secret funding?"

Congdon was shaking his head. "Maybe a few rubles are floating around free, but, goddammit, that could only explain Moscow. For anything outside the

Soviet Union they need Western currency backup. If you've got nothing from White, there's nothing I can add."

Congdon. The first incongruity besides Zamyatin's story itself.

Bennet was next on Mahoney's list, and it had been quarter to six before he had finally roused the man and had been reluctantly admitted to his apartment.

Unlike Congdon, Bennet's belligerence was not tinged with guilt. It was plain and simply pure dislike, so Mahoney took off his kid gloves.

"I'm just here for a couple of bits of information, Bennet, and unless I get complete cooperation you'll find yourself rotated back to the States within twenty-four hours."

The man was dressed only in his shorts, but he had not been asleep. Mahoney was certain of it.

He started to protest, but Mahoney cut him off. "Your little indiscretion with Dr. White was your undoing. If you want me to go to Carlisle with it, I will."

Bennet turned white but said nothing. They stood facing each other just inside the door of his apartment. Beyond Bennet, Mahoney could hear someone moving in the bedroom, and suddenly a number of things fell into place for him.

"When we're finished you can tell Dr. White that I'm sorry I disturbed you two."

Bennet looked on the verge of collapse, and for a moment Mahoney was almost sure he was going to have to hold the man up. But he recovered enough to ask what Mahoney wanted.

"What do you know about Doctor Leonid Sakharov?"

Something flashed across Bennet's eyes but was gone in an instant. "He's a scientist. A laser physicist, I believe. Moscow State University."

"Who's running him?"

Bennet had a blank look. "What do you mean?"

"He's an agent, or at least a source. Who is running his operation? Who does he report to?"

"I haven't the slightest idea what your talking about."

Mahoney took a step forward, a menacing tone in his expression. "Central Intelligence Agency officer found to be a homosexual. Won't go too good on your personnel file, Paul. And it would look even worse in the *New York Times*."

Bennet's lips curled into an animal snarl. "You think you're so fucking great, *Mr*. Mahoney."

"Paul . . . what is it?" Dr. White appeared naked in the doorway from the bedroom.

Bennet snapped around, and in an instant the economist realized his blunder and nearly leaped back into the bedroom.

"Who is running Sakharov?" Mahoney asked again.

Bennet turned back and looked like a cornered animal.

"I don't know," he said, shaking his head. "I swear to God, I don't know. I don't know anything about it."

"What do you know about Sakharov? I want everything."

"I gave it all to you. Jesus Christ, Mahoney, you've got to believe me. All I know is that Sakharov is a laser scientist. He goes to Geneva once a year to a scientific congress. That's all."

Bennet. Another incongruity.

Darrel Switt, the resident case officer, had been Mahoney's last stop shortly after six o'clock, and he had been up, dressed and waiting.

"I expected you'd show up here sooner or later," Switt said as he admitted Mahoney into his impeccably furnished apartment.

Switt was a bachelor and the only hardship he ever complained about here on his Moscow assignment was the fact he could not live with a woman.

"Can't bring any of my girlfriends from the States here with me; the old man frowns on it. And the Russians would just love for me to move in with a *dyehvushkah*," he had explained once.

Mahoney liked the young man and expected no resistance from him this morning although he was somewhat surprised that Switt knew he was coming.

"Congdon called and said you were on the rampage this morning. Figured you'd come knocking on my door."

Switt showed Mahoney into his kitchen and offered him a cup of coffee. "Real honest-to-God American coffee," he announced proudly.

Mahoney laughed, and for the first time that morning allowed himself to relax slightly. "Why not," he said, and he sat down at the small table as Switt poured the coffee.

"You're working on LOOK SEE, I assume," Switt said.

"You assume correct. What do you know about Yuri Zamyatin?"

Switt smiled as he set Mahoney's coffee cup in front of him and then sat down across the small table.

"Colonel Yuri Petrovich? Head of the Second Chief Directorate's Political Services Division?"

Mahoney nodded.

"Not much. Have you checked downstairs in archives?"

"This morning."

"Then you know about as much as I do. He was a tough bird once upon a time from what I understand." Switt sipped his coffee, a touch of curiosity in his eyes.

"If you looked in the files then you know that I was on a mission with him during the war."

"Yup. So what has Yurianovich been up to these days that's bothering you?"

"I was hoping you could tell me that."

"Sorry, Mahoney, no can do. Zamyatin is a mystery man, or I should say a deskbound bureaucrat. Lives just off Kutuzovsky Prospekt with three kids. A widower."

"Nothing more?"

Switt shook his head. "Nothing more."

"How about his department?"

"Do you mean his entire department or just the American embassy section?"

"Us," Mahoney said, blowing on his coffee.

Switt shrugged. "It's common knowledge that Major Boris Balachov, alias Leonard Skyles, runs the factory a couple of blocks down the street. They watch us and we watch them."

"But lately there has been an increase in activity."

Switt nodded. "Not really unusual, though. Every couple of years or so they shake the tree to see how many good Soviet citizens were crawling out on a limb to visit with us. They usually come up with a few." Switt lit a cigarette. "In a month or so there will be a spate of trials out in the suburbs. Might even be one or two big ones."

"How closely is Zamyatin's apartment building guarded by his own people?" Mahoney asked nonchalantly, but the question stopped Switt short.

"Come again?" the younger man said softly.

Mahoney put down his coffee and looked at him. "How many Soviet guards are assigned to Zamyatin's building?"

"None," Switt said. "What have you got in mind?"

Mahoney smiled tiredly and shook his head. "Not a thing. Yet. I'm just on a fishing mission this morning." He got to his feet. "Thanks for the coffee."

"My pleasure," Switt said absently.

Mahoney started to leave, but Switt stopped him. "The atmosphere has gotten a little too thick in here this morning for my liking. Would you mind thinning it out a little?"

Mahoney turned back. Switt was a good man, but like all case officers worth their salt he had the irritating habit of poking his nose into everything. "Need-to-know" as a guideline was anathema to them. "Yes, I would mind," he said, and he turned again and let himself out.

Back in his office Mahoney had initiated a Real Time Action jacket, including in it all the information he had gathered so far that morning. Then he had removed himself and the file up to the library where he had remained for the past forty-five minutes.

He looked at his watch. It was nearly eight o'clock. By now Carlisle was in his office. And by now word had spread among those in the know: Mahoney is on the warpath.

He got up from the windowbox seat and with a last

glance at the dismal day that was just beginning for most of the staff, headed upstairs.

The thought of Zamyatin's wife dead these eleven years flashed across Mahoney's mind as he avoided the elevators, busy at this time of the morning, and trudged slowly up the three flights of stairs.

He wondered how like Marge the woman must have been. It was something he had always wondered about every woman. How did she compare to Marge as a wife, as a bed partner, as a companion. Every woman he had ever met, or had ever heard about, came up second best to Marge.

But Zamyatin's wife had borne him three children. Devoted, no doubt. Dutiful children who loved their father. When Zamyatin had mentioned them last night the pride was evident in his voice.

He was taking his children to the Caspian for a holiday, he had said. It was a curious coincidence that Mahoney and his wife were also planning a holiday soon with their children.

Carlisle's office was a small, barren cubicle totally devoid of any personality. A double window, barred and screened, overlooked the Moscow Zoo that was around the corner from the front of the embassy, and the room was furnished only with a large wooden desk around which were set several chairs, a half-dozen file cabinets against one wall, and a combination horizontal file and sideboard along the opposite wall.

Carlisle did not seem surprised when Mahoney knocked and came in, but he rose from where he was seated behind his desk and indicated that Mahoney should sit down.

Mahoney slumped down in a chair, his legs throbbing from the climb up the stairs, and carefully laid the RTA jacket with its three diagonal red stripes on the edge of the desk.

Carlisle glanced at the file but had the good grace not to say anything until Mahoney offered his explanation.

"Early this morning, shortly after midnight, a high-ranking Soviet KGB officer contacted me on the street about a block from my apartment," Mahoney began. For an instant he had a second thought about what he was going to do, but he pushed it aside. A job had to be done. Expediency was the cultured word. Ruthlessness was the less kind definition.

"Colonel Yuri Zamyatin," Carlisle said. "Dobbs is raising hell all over the place this morning. The man was up here a few minutes ago with a list of every file you indexed." He held up the sheet of paper on which Mahoney had written the index numbers. He had forgotten it downstairs.

"I'll apologize when I'm done here," Mahoney said.

"Don't bother. I already took care of it." Carlisle sat back in his chair waiting for Mahoney to continue.

"He asked for my help."

"Really," Carlisle said, and for an instant Mahoney had the impression that the man knew what was coming. But he continued.

"He told me that a laser scientist was kidnaped from Moscow State University late Saturday night, and that the entire KGB from the top brass on down are engaged in an all-out manhunt."

"And he wants our help?"

"Along with the scientist, a portable laser device was also lifted from the university. It is Zamyatin's fear that the device will be used on Thursday morning to assassinate President Forsythe."

Carlisle snapped forward. "What?"

"Zamyatin believes the assassination is imminent. And may be the work of someone here in the embassy."

Carlisle laughed, the sound thin and absolutely devoid of humor.

"He mentioned your name and position, Congdon's name and rank as well as my own as senior analyst, which means there is a leak somewhere here in the embassy."

Carlisle's lips compressed into a thin line, but he said nothing.

"Number one," Mahoney said. "I want a class six review of every single personnel file from the ambassador on down to the janitors. And I want it done within the next twelve hours. I want my back covered if I'm going to crawl out on a limb."

Carlisle nodded but maintained his silence.

"Number two. I want a twixt sent this morning to the president informing him of what is happening here, and advising him that a second twixt has been prepared and will be sent to the head of the Secret Service Protective Forces Division. If nothing is settled here by 10:00 A.M. Thursday the Secret Service Presidential Protection Act will be enforced, and Air Force One will be ordered to return home."

Carlisle offered no objections, although Mahoney could had sworn that the man had no intention of complying with the last part.

"Three," Mahoney said and looked directly into Carlisle's eyes. "The laser scientist, Leonid Sakharov, is on a triple sevens active file downstairs. He had been since 1968. I want that file."

"You will have it within the hour," Carlisle said softly, no surprise, no emotion whatsoever in his voice.

"And four," Mahoney said, picking up the RTA jacket and handing it across to Carlisle. "All the supporting documents are there. I'm going to run an operation on Zamyatin. I want his three children picked up."

Carlisle held the file in his fingertips, almost as if he were afraid of contaminating his hands. "This is a risky business. If this were Washington, or Lisbon, or even Berlin, I might—"

Mahoney savagely cut him off. "Do you think I like playing these fucking little games, Carlisle, you heartless sonofabitch? Do you think I like this?" Mahoney got to his feet and, placing his closed fists on the desk, leaned forward so that his face was only inches from Carlisle's.

"I want his children picked up and brought here to the embassy. I want it done no later than six o'clock this evening, and if so much as one hair on those children's heads is disturbed, I will personally see that you are shot as an inept cocksucker."

Mahoney backed off, and Carlisle reached up with one hand and straightened the knot in his tie.

"Is there anything else?" he asked calmly.

Mahoney glared at him for a moment. "I hope to God, Carlisle, that I never find out this has been nothing but a setup. Because—"

Carlisle interrupted him angrily. "I don't like this any better than you do, Mahoney. But I've had about all your prima donna crap I'm going to take!"

"Tell that to your pet, Bennet, and his boyfriend,

Dr. White," Mahoney snapped, and he turned and headed for the door. Halfway out the door, Mahoney stopped and turned back. "You will be covering my back, Carlisle. I'll expect you to be there every time I turn around."

Carlisle said nothing, and Mahoney brushed past a startled junior staffer just coming down the narrow hall and headed back downstairs to his office.

An instant scenario flashed through Mahoney's mind that upset him even more than the kidnaping he had just asked Carlisle to carry out. It was of him and his own family years ago. Marge was much thinner then, and more stylish than now. John was twelve and Michael was six. They were on vacation. Cape Cod. The kids were playing in the surf with a small rowboat.

Mahoney could clearly see the rowboat tipping over. Marge going after the boys. Slogging through the water. The surf over her head. She could not swim.

Somehow he had managed to save them all. He had saved his family. It was a father's natural instinct.

A picture of Zamyatin flashed through his mind.

A father's natural instinct.

IX

Tuesday Noon

WASHINGTON, D.C. (AP) . . . President Forsythe today denied Soviet charges that yesterday's series of Strategic Air Command exercises were in reality a "thin disguise" for bringing the U.S. strike force up to alert status.

"It would be dangerous to assume such," the president said answering the charges published today in *Izvestia*.

"And it would be even more dangerous to respond with any kind of countermeasures," the president added.

First Chief Directorate territory was downstairs on the second floor of the Center. Zamyatin got off the elevator and stood to one side across the busy corridor from the executive dining room doors, his stomach rumbling not so much from hunger as from nervousness.

Very early that morning he had gotten off this very same elevator. Had hurried down the nearly deserted corridor to the Executive Action duty officer's cubicle where he had handed the startled night man an Action Order Kill form.

He had held his breath foolishly waiting for the explosion to come, but the young first lieutenant had merely shrugged, logged Zamyatin's time in and shoved the single page document into the Telefax machine that would distribute the order to the proper departments as well as record it downstairs in the computer.

Zamyatin had stared at the man who finally looked up.

"Will there be anything else this morning, Comrade Colonel?"

Zamyatin shook his head, turned on his heel, and went back upstairs to wait for the storm to break.

At eleven o'clock it had come when the head of the First Chief Directorate himself had called to invite Zamyatin to lunch at noon.

He was exactly on time. Zamyatin took a deep breath, crossed the corridor and entered the executive officers' mess, which was a large room with an uncracked plaster ceiling, warm wood-paneled walls adorned with several paintings, and soft, luxurious carpeting. The only reminder that this room was within the Center and not some exclusive restaurant was the wire mesh over the four large windows.

The head of the First Chief Directorate, General Sergei Anatolevich Ganin, was a kindly-looking old man: white hair, roly-poly cheeks, a red, smiling face, and flashing gold-capped teeth.

He was seated alone at the head table, and when he saw Zamyatin by the door he stood up and beckoned.

What worried Zamyatin was that he knew absolutely nothing about the man. Not rumor, not legend. Nothing. Merely that the man was chief of the KGB's most powerful and feared directorate.

"Yurianovich!" General Ganin boomed. "I am pleased that you could join me."

A number of men in the dining room glanced idly toward Zamyatin who had made his way across the room, but then they went back to their meals.

"I am honored, Comrade General, that you asked me to join you," Zamyatin said.

General Ganin was beaming as if he was genuinely pleased to see Zamyatin, and he indicated a chair. "Sit. Please sit down. I have taken the liberty of ordering for us. I think you will be pleased."

Zamyatin took his seat across the table from General Ganin, and a moment later two young men in long white aprons came with a wheeled serving cart laden with food and a bottle of red wine. One of the men uncorked the bottle and poured first for the general and then for Zamyatin.

"It is *Khvanchkara*, the best of the Georgian reds," General Ganin boomed heartily as he held up his long-stemmed wine glass to the light.

The two young men quickly and efficiently laid out several silver serving dishes of caviar, smoked salmon and sturgeon, several kinds of thinly sliced meats and cheeses, a bowl of cut fruit, and a small tureen of borscht, and then they were gone.

Still smiling broadly, General Ganin held up his

wine glass for a toast. "To operation CLEAN SWEEP," he said. "A successful completion."

Zamyatin's hand shook when he raised his glass, but he managed the toast. He had known exactly why General Ganin had called him for lunch, but being confronted under these circumstances was somewhat unnerving.

Three men came into the dining room talking loudly, and they took a table by one of the windows. Zamyatin was suddenly aware of the other sounds in the room: the silver clinking against dishes; the indistinct snatches of conversations; and through the wide kitchen doors behind him the pots and pans rattling. They were soothing sounds. Not urgent. Sounds of normalcy, if that word could be applied to any room in the Center.

General Ganin was watching him, and when Zamyatin looked up from his wine he got the distinct impression that he was about to hear some bad news. The instant the feeling began he tried to shake it, but it persisted.

"I was really quite surprised this morning," the general said conversationally as he dished up some of the salmon and a large dollop of caviar onto his plate.

Zamyatin said nothing, nor did he make a move to serve himself any of the food. He twirled the wine glass, holding the stem between his finger and the thumb of his right hand.

"Try some of the caviar, Yurianovich," the general said. "I doubt if your officers' mess serves anything quite so fine."

Zamyatin still made no move to help himself to the food. General Ganin laid his knife and fork down precisely where they had been placed when the table was set. Gone suddenly was the general's jovial expression; his eyes now held a cruel, calculating look.

"As you evidently learned from the overnight log, your action order was delayed."

"Yes, Comrade Director," Zamyatin said, keeping his voice even. "As point-of-origin officer I was informed."

"Your request this morning to kill that action order came as quite a surprise to us. Yashchenko especially was surprised. He asked me to have a word with you."

"I have an explanation, comrade," Zamyatin said. Guilt. That was the force upon which the entire Komitet was run.

"Indeed," General Ganin said. "I would be most interested."

Guilt drove some men into working harder to accomplish the goals set out for them, whereas guilt drove other men, weaker men who could not do their jobs, into confession. Cleanse your souls, sinners against the State. Expunge from your very existence all but steadfast devotion to the Party and its ideals.

"Mahoney is a very capable intelligence officer. A man whose career spans more than three decades."

"But he is not an expedient man," the general interjected.

"No, nor is he ruthless," Zamyatin said.

General Ganin held both of his hands palms down in front of him on the table as he stared at Zamyatin, waiting for him to continue.

"He is a man who when pushed will fight back. Swiftly and with much force. But he also is a man who can be led."

"And you are the one to lead him?"

Zamyatin inclined his head slightly. "Yes, Comrade Director. Because of our past association I believe I can. Because of my understanding of Mahoney as a reasonable man I believe I can convince him to help us."

General Ganin seemed to be weighing Zamyatin's words very carefully, but beyond that, very little else could be told from his expression.

The man had begun his career during the war as did many officers of his present status. Those who survived the purges tended to go in one of two directions: either up the political ladder in the Party heirarchy, or up the ladder in the State Secret Service. In either direction the structure was like a huge Egyptian pyramid with a greatly elongated peak. The base was massive and heavily supported. The pinnacle was tall, the positions near its peak immensely powerful.

Men who were strong enough, shrewd enough, expedient and ruthless enough to survive the climb to the pinnacle had to be extraordinary individuals to begin with. But in their climb upward they seemed to gain strength and depth rather than lose it from the weariness of the climb.

General Ganin was very near that pinnacle, and near the height of his power, and he was now very much like a high tension wire. Emanating in all directions from his office, the power served his purposes, ran the motors that operated the State. And like a high tension wire the man was exceedingly dangerous to the unsuspecting fool without the proper insulation.

Zamyatin at this moment felt like an ignorant savage whose bare hand was reaching out to touch the wire.

The sparks were already beginning to arc his way.

"I won't ask you if you have already contacted the man," General Ganin said slowly. "Nor will I ask the substance of your conversation."

Zamyatin held his breath.

"Suffice it to say that you are a capable officer who knows his job well and whose career has been nothing short of illustrious. But this morning you made a mistake."

Zamyatin noticed that the rain which had let up for a short while this morning had started again.

"Your original action order was quite brilliant, almost elegant, but this morning's request to kill the order was nothing short of a pang of conscience."

General Ganin looked down at the food on his plate, selected a fork with care, flaked off a small piece of the salmon and raised it to his lips.

"Nowhere in the world, not even in Paris, is the food like this," the general said, his eyes half-closed as he savored the tiny bit of fish. "Are you sure you won't join me?"

Zamyatin shook his head. "No, thank you, General. I have no appetite."

"It is a shame," the general said, wiping off his fork with his linen napkin and then setting it back in its place beside his plate. "I have a curious shortcoming in that I simply cannot eat alone." The general shrugged. "Silly, actually, but I can't help myself."

"Shall I withdraw the kill order?" Zamyatin heard himself asking, but it was as if the general had not heard him.

"Conscience, Yurianovich. Do you know what it really is?"

"The ability to distinguish between right and wrong and then feel remorse if we do wrong," Zamyatin said impulsively. He felt very close to the high tension wire.

The general laughed. "Quite a naive view for a man of your experience and intelligence." He shook his head. "No, my dear Comrade Colonel, you are not correct. The implication you give depends upon a concept of absolutes. Conscience is nothing more than an awareness of oneself in relationship to his own social order."

Despite himself Zamyatin was intrigued. The general was a philosopher.

"Murder in our society is generally punished. It is a negative. Not right or wrong, merely negative. If we commit murder the feeling that we have done something against our society's rules is a pang of conscience.

"But consider a south sea island where for a man to see a woman's bare feet is considered taboo. If you or I—unknowing of the islanders' taboos—observe a woman's toes, we would suffer no pangs of conscience."

"And the business with Mahoney?" Zamyatin asked softly.

"Let us remain with the south sea islanders for a moment where to see a woman's breasts, on the contrary, is of little or no importance. Let you or I see her breasts and we may become red in the face. A pang of conscience." The general leaned forward. "But an unnecessary pang of conscience because our behavior was well within the laws of that island's customs."

"There are no universal rights or wrongs?"

The general shook his head. "No, Yurianovich,

which is an oftentimes difficult lesson for a man to learn."

Zamyatin just stared at him.

"I have withdrawn your request to kill the action orders. Mahoney's children and his three grandchildren have been picked up and are at present being held." The general flicked an invisible crumb on the tablecloth next to his plate. When he looked up into Zamyatin's eyes he seemed genuinely sad.

"What we have devised, perhaps the CIA will devise as well. Yours was and is a very good plan. So we have taken your children into protective custody until this matter is settled. We do not want the Mahoneys of the world to touch them."

For the first time in a very long time, since his wife died, he realized, Zamyatin felt fear as a palpable, solid, dark thing. "Where are they?" he asked, the words half choking in his throat.

General Ganin waved him off. "It is of little consequence. They are safe and are being well cared for. It is a holiday for them, actually. As I understand it they are having a good time."

Anger began to build inside of Zamyatin, replacing the fear at least temporarily, but the general knew what was coming and he shook his head.

"Do not do anything you would later regret. Your children are safe, as are Mahoney's children. You may assure him that they will remain safe as long as he deigns to cooperate."

Zamyatin just stared at the general.

"Let me hasten to add that when Thursday comes and goes without incident, all will return to normal. There *are* rules to this business after all. We do not want to involve a man's family, or else none of us would be safe."

Faces in the busy corridor and then in the elevator were a blur to Zamyatin, and he was suddenly very cold although he repressed the urge to shiver.

Eleven years ago it had been nighttime. He had been working late here in the Center when the hospital contacted him.

"There have been some complications with your wife's pregnancy, Comrade Zamyatin," the doctor said. "She is asking for you."

Colonel Morozov, whom everyone called grandfather, had offered his car and driver, but because of a late winter snowstorm it still took them nearly forty-five minutes to make it across town to the hospital.

"Good luck, little Yurianovich," Morozov had called to Zamyatin who ran up the broad steps, through the heavy doors and down the wide corridor.

The doctor was waiting, his surgical mask hanging loosely around his neck, his gown blood-spattered. He was smoking a cigarette.

Zamyatin stopped several feet away from the doctor, and he suddenly knew that he was too late.

"Sandra!" he shouted. "My Sandra!"

Stefan Chekalkin stood at the open elevator doors staring at Zamyatin. "Yurianovich?" he said.

Zamyatin blinked, his mind snapping back to the present. He realized he must have called out.

"Is there something the matter?"

Zamyatin shook his head as he stepped off the elevator and brushed past the young man. Without a word he hurried down the corridor to his office, but he could feel Chekalkin's eyes on his back until he rounded the corner and entered his operations room.

Most of his staff was here busily at work, and the noise of dozens of typewriters clacking, and as many voices speaking into tape machines created a din that under normal circumstances Zamyatin found soothing. But at this moment the noise seemed to be too loud and too sharp for his ears that were suddenly ultrasensitive.

He hurried across the room, acknowledging none of the greetings and entered his office, slamming the door behind him.

Major Balachov was seated in the chair next to Zamyatin's desk, and he looked up.

"They said you would be back soon, so I decided to wait," Balachov said.

Zamyatin went around behind his desk and sat down. Balachov, like Chekalkin in the corridor, had an odd expression on his face.

"What do you want?" Zamyatin asked.

Balachov looked startled. "You asked me to report after lunch. You called this morning."

This morning. It seemed like a million years since the children were getting ready for school. They must have taken them from school, or perhaps on their way to school.

"Is there something wrong?" Balachov was saying. "Are you sick? Shall I call a doctor?"

Zamyatin looked at his staff officer. He wore the same clothes he had worn yesterday and the day before. His soaked raincoat was draped over one of the other chairs and it was dripping onto the floor.

"Take that miserable raincoat out of here and hang it someplace else," Zamyatin snapped harshly.

Balachov sat immobile for a moment, but then he jumped up, grabbed his raincoat and went out the door. When he returned he had a sheepish look on his face.

"I'm sorry . . ." he started to say, but Zamyatin cut him off.

"Number one. I want a floating seal put on the U.S. Embassy. I'll pull officers and surveillance people off other details for you. Set up as many command posts as you need to cover every direction."

"How far out do you want it extended?"

"I want the coverage absolute," Zamyatin said. "I'll expect implementation within the hour. No movements in or out of the embassy are to be interfered with. However, any person who leaves the embassy will be tailed no matter where he or she goes, no matter how long they are gone, and no matter the expense."

"Security?"

"This time I don't care if we are spotted. I merely want to know where everyone is at all times."

"Any exceptions?" Balachov asked.

"Two," Zamyatin said. "Your cook, Zeta-one. Whoever was responsible for running him will now be responsible for his activities."

"And the other?"

"I am taking the responsibility for Wallace Mahoney," Zamyatin said and reached for Mahoney's dossier.

"I know the man," Balachov said. "Are we running a specific operation on him? Anything I should know about?"

Zamyatin ignored the question. His anger, which at first had tended to blur his thinking, was now making him see everything in sharp perspective. Thursday at 1100 hours it would be over.

"I will be pulling in every legman I can get my hands on for the duration."

"We can handle this without . . ." Balachov began, but again Zamyatin cut him off.

"Every person coming out of the Unites States Embassy will be followed. In turn, every place any embassy person stops at will be thoroughly checked out."

Balachov looked stunned.

"If a man comes out of the embassy and stops at a tobacconist's shop a legman will be detailed to check out the shop. If a man takes an airplane somewhere, the clerks and baggage handlers all will be investigated. Am I making myself clear?"

"It's a mammoth operation, comrade," Balachov said, the words barely audible. The man was obviously completely shaken.

"Indeed," Zamyatin said. "We must know minute by minute what every single person who has any contact with the embassy is doing while off embassy grounds."

"Someone will lead us to Sakharov and the laser?" Balachov asked.

Zamyatin nodded. "We will continue this operation until the president of the United States arrives safely or until Sakharov and the laser are recovered."

Balachov fumbled in his breast pocket for his package of cigarettes, but suddenly Zamyatin felt the need to be alone.

"Get out of here," he said softly.

Balachov looked up, startled. "Comrade?" he said uncertainly.

"You have a job to do," Zamyatin said, holding his voice even against the strain building up inside of him. "Get to it."

"I . . . " Balachov started to speak, but then he jumped up. "Yessir," he said. "How shall I handle the reporting?"

"I don't want reports. I want results. Bring me Sakharov and the laser and the people responsible."

"Of course, comrade," Balachov said. He looked at Zamyatin for a few seconds, then turned and went out the door, closing it softly behind him.

Zamyatin stared at the closed door for several minutes, then slowly swiveled his chair around so he could look out his window. The rain was coming down so hard now that he could not see anything outside except for indistinct blurs.

The view out the window perfectly matched the condition of his mental state.

The operation must have been simple. One moment the children would have been standing at the corner waiting for the school bus. The next moment a black limousine from the motor pool downstairs would have pulled up, and two men would have gotten out and hustled the children into the back seat.

The license plates identified the car as official. No one would have questioned the action. No one.

At this very moment his children were probably in some room in the Center. There was no logical reason for General Ganin to deny his request to see his children.

Zamyatin blanked that thought out of his mind as best he could the moment it occurred to him.

"Logic," the general would say, "is nothing more

than a panacea of the proletariat. Or more accurately, the tool by which the ruling class maintains the status quo."

Every cause produces one or more effects. Every effect is the result of one or more causes.

The effect: The action order to kidnap Mahoney's children and grandchildren was carried out. The cause: General Ganin's override of Zamyatin's request to kill the action order.

The effect: Zamyatin's children were placed in protective custody. The cause: On an order from General Ganin. "We do not want the Mahoneys of the world to touch them."

The effect: Zamyatin's children were being held incommunicado from their father. The cause: Superficially, General Ganin's orders. But why?

The effect was General Ganin's order. But what was the cause of such an order? Zamyatin's children were now safe from the Americans, but they were also being insulated from their own father.

Zamyatin turned and reached for the phone on his desk, but then withdrew his hand. Did he want to hear the reason, or did he already know?

For nearly thirty-five years he had worked for the State. Thirty-five years of convoluted logic ran through his brain.

Although the operation may be distasteful, the protection of the State transcends normal moral considerations.

No one had ever said that out loud. But surely, Zamyatin's confused mind cried out, there were men who thought it. Who believed it.

If the State is not an entity in itself, but rather is made

up of the individual, then immoral individual acts of definition reduce the State to an immoral condition.

"Morality as a measure of rightness or justice is just as naive a view as yours on conscience," General Ganin would say.

Zamyatin laid his head down on his arms on the desk and wept: for the State, or actually his concept of the State; for the Komitet and what he had done and become in its name; and most of all for his and Mahoney's children.

Late Tuesday Afternoon

A thin man in his early thirties wearing the uniform of an army major, showed the guard at the Vnukovo Official Airport administration building his identification and was allowed through.

Looking neither right nor left, the man strode down the long corridor into the airport security wing, and entered a door marked SECURITY ADMINISTRATOR.

Inside the plain office the Vnukovo Chief of Security, an army captain, was waiting, and he jumped up and came around from behind his desk, offering his hand.

"Comrade Major, we were expecting you."

The major made no move to accept the man's hand, and after an embarrassed moment, the captain indicated a chair.

"Won't you sit down?"

"I will need free access to the control tower until

Thursday, at which time I will need free access for myself as well as my aides.''

The security administrator, a large man with a pockmarked face, looked startled. ''Major?''

''Is something in what I said not clear?''

''I don't understand,'' the captain said. He was clearly flustered. ''I was told to expect you here for a security conference. You are providing an additional security detail for Thursday?''

''That is correct,'' the major snapped.

The captain went around behind his desk but did not sit down. ''Then, begging the Major's pardon, I am the security administrator here. As I understand it you have been assigned to me.''

The major took two steps forward, yanked the telephone off the captain's desk and thrust it at the man. ''If you have the stupidity to challenge my orders, telephone your superiors for confirmation!''

The captain shrank back from the telephone, the tone of his voice suddenly placating. ''I am sorry, Major, I didn't mean to question your orders.''

''In that case notify your security detail. I wish to visit the control tower at this time.''

''Yessir,'' the captain snapped, and he took the telephone from the major, dialed a number and a moment later spoke into the phone. ''Major Boris Azarov has authorization to visit the tower. He'll be up in a few minutes.''

The captain hung up the phone, then reached inside a desk drawer and withdrew a plastic security badge that he handed across the desk to the major. ''When you leave the facility, drop this off at the main guard post. It will be there whenever you need it.''

"And my aides?"

"How many will there be?"

"Two."

"Badges will be waiting for them at the main guard post Thursday morning."

The major stared at the captain for a moment, then managed a very slight smile. "Your cooperation in this matter will not go unnoticed, Captain," he said.

The captain beamed. He came around his desk and again held out his hand. "It is my pleasure, Comrade Major," he said, but the major had turned and was out the door before the words were out of the captain's mouth.

The major hurried down the corridor toward the heavy steel door at the control tower entrance which was guarded by two men both armed with automatic weapons. As he came closer, the two guards came to attention, and he could feel the sweat rolling down from his armpits.

It had been close in there with the security administrator. But the man was indeed stupid, his actions reflexive, not thought out.

A man in an army major's uniform could not be lying. He *had* to be who he represented himself to be. Behavior other than that was unthinkable.

The guards at the steel door saluted when they saw the security badge the major had clipped to his tunic pocket and one of them opened the door.

"You may go directly up, Major," the one holding the door said.

Without breaking stride he nodded at the men, went through the door and calmly took the stairs two at a time, the heels of his highly polished black boots ringing loudly on the metal treads.

At the top of the stairs, four stories above the ground level, was another metal door. A button was set in the door frame. The major took a deep breath and pushed the button. A moment later a man in an open-necked white shirt and light gray trousers opened the door.

"Come in, Major—we were told to expect you."

The major entered the control tower and the man closed the door behind him.

"Will you require anything, Major?" the man asked.

The major did not turn around, instead he moved slowly forward to look out the large bay windows facing east, toward the official aircraft parking apron. "No," he said. "Go back to your work. I'll only be a minute."

"As you wish, comrade," the man said, and he went back to one of the radar consoles along the far wall.

Several other men in the large room had looked up from their radar scopes and glanced at the major, and then went back to their work.

The American Air Force One jet would land on the main east-west runway and then would taxi to the official parking apron directly below. The boarding steps would be placed in position, the door would open and the president of the United States would step out into the open.

The major took a package of cigarettes out of his breast pocket, lit one and inhaled deeply.

He stared out the windows for several minutes. It would be simple, he thought, studying the layout below. Almost too simple. He finally turned around, quickly surveyed the room and the men busy at their equipment, then moved toward the door, stopping long enough to put out his cigarette in an ashtray atop one of the equipment consoles.

"Will there be anything else, comrade?" the man in the white shirt asked, getting up from his console and coming across the room.

"Not at this moment, thank you," the major said, and he left the control tower.

After the door was shut, the chief controller picked the half-smoked cigarette butt out of the ashtray and held it up so the others in the room could see it.

"The major has power. He shops at the exchange store. I'm sure he gave our captain a good time."

The others laughed. "What kind of cigarette is it, Vladimir?" one of them asked.

"It is a Marlboro. American, I think."

X

Tuesday Evening

MISSOULA, MONTANA. (AP) . . . Three men who apparently burglarized the Forest Products Laboratory near here burned to death this evening in the crash of their automobile that ran off the road during a high speed chase by a Montana Highway Patrol unit.

"The bodies were burned beyond immediate recognition," the Missoula County coroner said. But one of the men was believed to be an employee of the FPL.

Both men wore nondescript clothing: jackets but no ties, aging raincoats still wet from outside, and tired hats with brims pushed back and misshapen.

They sat at a small table near the front window at the Crystal Cafe across Kutuzovsky Prospekt. The five-piece band that had been on a break for the past twenty minutes began to play again, making any kind of normal conversation all but impossible.

The club, which was quite famous in Moscow, was full for a Tuesday evening, and the room was dark and smoky and smelled of wet clothes, cheap Russian cigarettes, and cabbage soup—the specialty of the house.

"I thought you would feel safe here," Zamyatin said, leaning forward. He nodded toward the band across the dance floor. "They are not very good, but they are loud. Impossible to filter out completely."

"I find it difficult to believe you're here on your own," Mahoney said.

Zamyatin just looked at him but said nothing. After awhile Mahoney turned to watch the several couples gyrating on the small dance floor. They looked as if they were having fun. But it was too hot in here for him. He longed for a breath of fresh, cool air.

Marge had called from the apartment at about six o'clock, her voice bright and cheerful over the line.

"An old friend of yours stopped by just a little while ago," she bubbled, and Mahoney's breath caught in his throat.

"Who was it?"

"He wouldn't give me his name. He was a Russian. Said you were friends from the war."

"A small man? About fifty?"

"That's him."

"You let him in the apartment?" Mahoney said incredulously.

"No . . . no," Marge continued brightly, unconcerned. "He refused to come in. Just said he wanted to get a message to you."

Mahoney looked up at his office door, closed, and he felt an itch between his shoulder blades. "What was the message, Marge?"

"You're to meet him at the Crystal Cafe at eight o'clock."

He was being used. He could feel the signs all around him, and he didn't like it, especially when it came to involving Marge.

"Listen to me, darling," he said.

Marge started to say something but then hesitated. Evidently she had detected the note of seriousness in her husband's voice.

"I want you to lock the apartment door and let no one in tonight. Do you understand me? No one."

"Yes . . ." she said uncertainly.

"I'll probably be late, so don't wait up for me."

"Is there something wrong, Wallace? Something I should know about?"

Mahoney continued staring at the door. In all the years they had been married she had never once asked him that kind of a question. There was trouble and it hung thick in the air.

"It's nothing. Just routine. But I will be busy and I don't like leaving you alone, especially since you've developed the habit of leaving the apartment door wide open for anyone to come in."

She laughed. "Piffle! Who'd want an old lady like me?"

Mahoney cut her off savagely. "Goddammit, Margery, do as I say!"

"The door will be locked, Wallace," she snapped. "And don't ever swear at me again."

"I'm sorry," Mahoney said, the itch between his shoulder blades intensifying. "I'm sorry," he said again. "I'll be home as soon as I can."

"Take care, old man," she said and hung up.

Mahoney held the phone to his ear for a moment, holding his breath, and then he heard an almost inaudible click, after which the dial tone buzzing in his ear increased slightly in volume.

He hung up the telephone, sat back in his chair, took out a cigar and went through the routine of lighting it, savoring for the moment his solitude, the quiet of his office and the rich aroma of the smoke.

The door opened, and Carlisle came into the room. There was a look of triumph on his face.

"Two and a half minutes from your office," Mahoney said, his voice flat. "You must have taken the back stairs."

Carlisle smiled, came across to the desk, removed some file folders from a chair, laid them on the floor, and sat down. "Actually, the elevator happened to be there and waiting. I was downstairs in communications."

"Is Munson in on this?"

"No," Carlisle said, staring directly into Mahoney's eyes. "I had one of the technicians set it up for me."

"Is my apartment bugged as well?"

Carlisle nodded.

It was time to bail out, Mahoney thought, the decision sour in his gut. Or at least back off a few paces to get a better look.

"Don't worry, Wallace, we're watching your place. Marge will in no way become involved in this."

Mahoney snapped forward in his chair. "So help me God, Carlisle, if she is . . . if for one minute you think that she'll be used in any fashion . . . as bait, as the front-runner . . . for any reason . . . ." He let it trail off.

"Despite what you think of me, I would not do anything like that. Never."

"I don't believe you," Mahoney said, the anger that had suddenly boiled up inside of him subsiding. "You are an expedient man, Carlisle. Nothing is sacred to you."

Carlisle said nothing for a long time, and Mahoney was aware of the rain beating against the window behind him. He was cold.

"This is the big one," Carlisle finally spoke, his voice soft. "LOOK SEE, starts to pay off."

"Not me," Mahoney said. He had done a lot of thinking this afternoon, and since Marge's call his brain had gone into high gear. Each time his thoughts seemed to be turned around in a circle he came back to one name. Congdon. Somehow the man was a key. Something had changed in Congdon over the past few days and Mahoney was certain that Carlisle had had something to do with it.

But why? Why? Why had Carlisle bothered to sit on Congdon? What did Congdon know or suspect that made Carlisle take that action?

Mahoney thumbed through a stack of file folders on his desk, coming up with the originating officer's copy of the Real Time Action folder he had initiated earlier today. He flipped it across to Carlisle.

"I'm canceling this," he said, and Carlisle looked genuinely startled for just a moment.

"You evidently thought this over carefully and have come up with a good reason."

Mahoney had to turn away momentarily. In fact, there was no good reason for withdrawing the RTA jacket against Zamyatin's children except one. He turned back to Carlisle.

"Decency. But I don't expect you to understand that."

Carlisle smiled, this time almost sadly. "For a man of your age, Wallace, you are terribly naive. We're the good guys with the white hats, and they're the bad guys with the black outfits. Right?" He leaned forward, and Mahoney felt a flutter in his gut.

"Let's just step back a way, Mahoney. Let's say up to an orbiting space station. Just far enough so that we can see the entire earth spread out below us." Carlisle shook his head. "No lines down there indicating borders. Minnesota isn't colored green to distinguish it from the blue that is Wisconsin or the orange that is Canada.

"You can't even see the people down there, just the land and the water and the clouds. There are no bad guys. Just as there are no good guys. Just people who believe in slightly different things. We are talking here about nothing more than a difference of ideological opinion.

"Push a button and something happens. Push another button and something else happens. But before you start pushing buttons all over the place you first make sure you know exactly what you want to happen."

Mahoney leaned back in his chair and closed his eyes

as he pulled deeply on the cigar, drawing the warm, sweet smoke into his mouth.

Carlisle continued.

"The early Romans killed the Christians because they were threatening a way of life. The Huns killed the Romans because they felt civilization was threatening their way of life. The Germans killed Jews partly because Hitler was a madman, but also partly because the German nation needed some kind of a rallying point to mobilize for world domination. It was a national fever. If Hitler could have laid the blame for the defeat in World War I and the terrible depression that followed on the Poles, or on the Armenians, or on the black man, he would have done so."

"You're a sick man, Carlisle," Mahoney said softly.

Carlisle continued unperturbed.

"The German people did not stop Hitler. The Russians did not stop Stalin. The American people did not stop the slavery of the 1700s and 1800s, or the exploitation of the Irish and Chinese laborers who made the railroads, or the black man's plight in the '50s in the south, or the killings at Kent State. At least not until the time was ready. Not until whatever advantage that had to be gained had been accomplished."

Mahoney opened his eyes. Carlisle was staring at him, a slight sheen of perspiration on his forehead. He looked agitated.

"I'm not a sick man, Mahoney. I am a realist. Without the persecution of the Christians, the Catholic Church would not be alive today. Without the murder of the Jews, Israel would not have become a nation. And without the exploitation of cheap slave labor in the

United States, we still would be an uncleared, underdeveloped nation. Those are facts, Mahoney, not diseases."

"And now LOOK SEE," Mahoney said.

"It's nothing more than that. An operation to look and see what the Russians are up to. If it's assassination, then we stop it. If it's an information gathering drive, we feed them a little false information. But hard-won false information, and gather a little data of our own."

"What else?" Mahoney said, his voice a monotone.

"There's a lot more," Carlisle said. The light that had been in his eyes earlier was gone, and he had reverted back to his old, inscrutable self. "But first I want your gun."

"Why?" Mahoney asked, but he realized he did not really care.

"It is a factor I don't want introduced into this operation. There will be no shooting. No front line troops. No heroics. Just information gathering."

Mahoney reached beneath his jacket and pulled the .45 out of its shoulder holster and handed it across to Carlisle, butt first. Carlisle took the gun and stuffed it in his coat pocket.

"Zamyatin's three children have already been picked up. Switt set it up and it went without a hitch. They're here right now in the embassy, a little frightened, but they're calming down."

Mahoney's gut tightened.

"We picked up Michael in Missoula, and John, his wife, and the three kids in Los Angeles. Everything was explained to them. They're safe."

It was as if a volcano had gone off inside of Mahoney

and all he could see was Carlisle's face which seemed to be leering at him from down a long tunnel. Mahoney leaped forward across his file-laden desk, knocking his chair over behind him, reaching for Carlisle's throat. The man had pulled back, however, just outside of Mahoney's reach.

"They're all right!" Carlisle shouted.

Mahoney regained his balance and came around the desk as Carlisle, who looked definitely worried, backed toward the door.

"Jesus Christ, man, listen to reason! The Russians were about to grab them! We got to them first! They're all right, I tell you! They're safe!"

Mahoney stopped short. Carlisle had his right hand in his jacket pocket.

"What did you say?" Mahoney asked, his voice soft but very even and controlled.

Carlisle was shook. "I said they are safe."

"I mean about the Russians."

A little color began to return to Carlisle's cheeks. "We've had your children under surveillance ever since you were assigned to Moscow."

Mahoney advanced a step farther. He could see Carlisle's hand in his right coat pocket tighten on the .45.

"We figure if the KGB tumbled to you they might make a try for your kids."

Mahoney said nothing, his mind whirling in a hundred different directions. He would not be able to tell Marge, and yet he knew it would be next to impossible to keep his emotions from her.

"It paid off," Carlisle said, definitely more in control of himself. "It is my understanding that John and Michael were both staked out and were on the verge of being grabbed. We got to them first, that's all."

"Zamyatin?" Mahoney asked through clenched teeth.

Carlisle shrugged. "We have no way of knowing that, but it would be logical. Zamyatin is evidently trying to convert you. He'd use your children as a lever."

"Where are they being held?"

"The Presidio in San Diego."

"I want to talk to them. Now."

Carlisle was shaking his head. "No way. We couldn't set up a secure channel. They'd know they had failed."

Mahoney's eyes narrowed. Was the man lying?

"We captured their agents before they could report back and forced them to send the affirmative signal. As far as anyone knows the Russians have your children. I want to keep it that way."

"I have no way of knowing if what you are telling me is true," Mahoney said. He took another step forward.

"For God's sake, Wallace, what do you take me for? I am on your side, you know."

Mahoney was shaking his head. "You're on Carlisle's side. How do I know you are telling me the truth?"

"You don't," Carlisle said. "But we have Zamyatin's children. You can go take a look at them for yourself if you want. They're in Congdon's apartment. So even if the Russians did have your children—which they don't—we have Zamyatin's. The lever is neutralized. They wouldn't hurt your children for fear of retaliation."

Mahoney could barely believe what he was hearing. The man *was* sick. But he also was holding all the trump cards. The Russians or Carlisle. What difference did it make? The lever was there, but Zamyatin was not wielding it, Carlisle was.

"What are we looking for?" Mahoney finally said. He felt physically ill with the thought of Marge. Dear sweet Marge. This would kill her if she knew.

Carlisle managed a thin smile, and he slowly withdrew his hand from his coat pocket. "Their organizational chart with all the names, specific duty assignments, budget codes, and actual office locations for starters."

"Zamyatin?"

"I'll leave that up to you. If he is still viable, if he hasn't compromised his own position by playing games with you, then I want him defected. I can't make that judgment sitting here. You'll have to figure it out."

"How about the operation? Sakharov? The president's trip?"

"The operation is still LOOK SEE, and you are still the kingpin, only now Zamyatin is the variable."

Mahoney just stared at the man.

"The president's trip is still on. It's too damned important to cancel. But I've got him to agree to a go-no-go decision point at ETA minus two hours. That would put Air Force One far enough outside Soviet air space for us to effectively defend him."

"And Sakharov?"

"You've seen the file," Carlisle said impatiently.

Mahoney had been given the file, but one all-important document had been missing. "I don't know who is running him."

"It doesn't matter."

Again Mahoney got the distinct impression that the man was lying. But why? Something was missing. The thought kept hammering at the back of his mind.

The music had stopped, and several couples from the dance floor were crowded around the bandstand talking and waiting for the next set.

Mahoney looked up out of his thoughts at Zamyatin who was staring at him. The man had a haunted look in his eyes, as if what he was doing was as distasteful to him as it was to Mahoney.

First of all find out what information Zamyatin was after so that he could be fed false data. And secondly, inform him that his children were being held and begin extracting real information from him.

It was sick.

"It's too damn bad we couldn't all go on vacation. Permanently," Zamyatin said, suddenly breaking the silence.

"What would you do?"

"I'd be a veterinarian. Outside of Moscow. Definitely outside of Moscow."

"Dogs and cats and all that?"

Zamyatin shook his head. "We don't do that sort of thing here. No, it'd be cows and sheep. Farm animals."

"How about presidents?" Mahoney said. The music had started again and he had to shout to be heard.

"He is still coming then? No change of plans?"

"We have a fail-safe for him," Mahoney said.

"At least there's that." Zamyatin looked away. When he turned back he seemed frightened. "The situation in the Middle East is heating up from what I understand."

"The Israelis will win again. It'll be another Six Day War or maybe even quicker." Zamyatin was fishing. Or was he?

"I don't know this time. No one might win. Or rather

we might all lose. Your Strategic Air Command is on alert. DEFCON TWO, I'm told."

Mahoney shook his head irritably. "What is it, Zamyatin? Why'd you go to my wife? Why'd you set up this meeting?"

"Our Missile Defense Service is on alert, too," Zamyatin said, ignoring Mahoney's questions for the moment. "Which is why there must be no incident on Soviet soil. You understand that."

"I understand a lot of things, Zamyatin. But not what you want."

The waiter finally came, and Zamyatin ordered a bottle of vodka and a bowl of pitted cherries. "*Pushkins*," he said, turning to Mahoney. "The fruit of your sweet tooth and the alcohol to warm your insides."

The band was playing mostly American rock-and-roll tunes from the fifties, and they listened for a while until the waiter came back with two stemmed glasses, a bottle of vodka, and a large bowl of pitted cherries.

"Like this," Zamyatin said, smiling. He poured half a glass of vodka, put a cherry in his mouth, bit half through it and still holding the cherry between his teeth, sucked down the vodka, swilling it around in his mouth before swallowing. "The cherry absorbs some of the vodka," he said, smacking his lips. "It tastes good. Try it."

Mahoney poured himself some of the vodka. "Are you still working alone on this?"

"As alone as any man in our position can work," Zamyatin said, staring at Mahoney's glass. "Try it with a cherry."

Mahoney sipped the vodka which was mild and quite

good. "I'll need more information if I'm to help out on this."

Zamyatin looked up. "Sometime early Monday morning a guard at Lubyanka Prison II just outside the city was murdered. We found his body early today in a shallow grave. Whoever killed him stole his uniform, his papers, and his weapon."

Mahoney poured more vodka for Zamyatin. "Have you come up with a connection?"

"Sakharov and the laser are still missing. We think he is still somewhere in Moscow, but beyond that there have been no leads except for one."

Mahoney stared at the man and wondered about his children. He had not looked in on them as Carlisle had suggested he should. He did not think he could face them. What did you say to a child who wanted to be with his father?

"There is a dissident group that operates mostly here in Moscow and to a lesser extent in Leningrad. It's an intellectual group. Mostly writers and artists and a few minor scientists who up until now have been considered a nuisance but quite harmless."

"They grabbed Sakharov and the laser?"

Zamyatin shrugged and went through the routine of the *pushkin* again. When he was finished he seemed almost angry. "The Democratic Movement, they call themselves. Human rights, whatever that is. That's what they are arguing about. Most of them are parasites. They prefer talking to working. Most of them aren't even any good at what they profess are their occupations."

"I've heard of the group," Mahoney said. "One of them is—"

Zamyatin cut him off. "The *one* exception," he said. "The man won the Nobel Prize for *literature*, if it can be called that. His claim to the prize was not that he could write, but that he was 'oppressed' and yet brave enough to write about what he considered intolerable conditions."

"Sounds like a Party line to me," Mahoney said sharply.

Zamyatin laughed lightly. "Yes it does. But when we compare this man to Tolstoy or Dostoevski, or even your Faulkner or Steinbeck, he comes out a very poor distant cousin." He shook his head. "No, it was merely the circumstances that won him the Nobel Prize. A political expediency, nothing more."

"You are saying that the Democratic Movement kidnaped Sakharov?"

"We think it is a possibility."

"And the Lubyanka guard?"

Zamyatin leaned forward. "President Forsythe will be arriving at Vnukovo Official Airport at 1100 hours Thursday morning. From there he will come by motorcade into the city. If a man in civilian clothes carrying the laser is accompanied by another man in a Soviet army uniform, carrying authentic papers and toting an AK7 automatic rifle, they may not be challenged."

What Zamyatin was saying was suddenly beginning to make a terrible kind of sense. It was plausible. And where there is a plausibility of action, guard against that contingency. It was in the handbook.

"Then it is a Soviet internal matter after all," Mahoney said.

Zamyatin looked startled, as if Mahoney had said

something totally unexpected. "I sincerely wish that were the case, my old friend. But it is not."

It was Mahoney's turn to be startled. What was the man trying to tell him?

"The Democratic Movement has been linked to the Central Intelligence Agency."

"You're nuts," Mahoney said.

"Nuts?" Zamyatin asked.

Despite himself Mahoney laughed out loud. "Nuts. Crazy. Insane. Off your rocker."

Zamyatin smiled. "Curious," he said softly, and then his expression darkened again. "I wish I was nuts, as you say. But it is true. Your Nobel Prize winner, Nikolai Gamov, has been seen on more than one occasion in contact with a known American intelligence officer. Until this moment we let the situation lie. We were curious about the relationship. But since Gamov was of no intelligence value—no hard intelligence value—we merely watched."

"When was the last time this American intelligence officer had contact with the Democratic Movement?"

Zamyatin fidgeted slightly. "I only just learned of the relationship this afternoon."

"How long ago, Zamyatin?"

"Six months."

Mahoney smiled sardonically. "And yet you are trying to convince me that the CIA has set the Democratic Movement up to assassinate President Forsythe?" He shook his head. "I won't buy it, Zamyatin. It doesn't wash. In the first place, six months ago the president didn't even know he'd be coming to Moscow now. No one did. And in the second place, an operation like that takes planning. Big planning. Detailed time tables. Gamov would have had to have lived at the embassy for a week or more to learn all that would be necessary—considering, even for a moment, that such planning could have gone on under my nose without me knowing about it.'' He shook his head again and started to rise. Zamyatin's children would have to be released. This operation was at a dead end.

''Aren't you curious about who Gamov's contact is?''

''The word you mean to say is *was*. And, frankly, no—I'm not interested in learning the name of some low-ranking embassy staffer who likes literature and who had the misfortune to run into Gamov at some party one night six months ago. Some poor hapless son of a bitch who is listed now on your files as a CIA officer.''

''Carlisle,'' Zamyatin said softly.

Mahoney just stared at him from where he stood over the table. The music no longer seemed loud, the room no longer smoky and stiflingly hot. Zamyatin was the only other person in the room. ''What did you say?''

''Carlisle,'' Zamyatin repeated no louder than before.

Mahoney sunk back down into his chair, took out a cigar and, never taking his eyes from Zamyatin's, managed nevertheless to open the package, withdraw the cigar, and light it.

''I was assigned to watch Carlisle from the moment he came here to Moscow,'' Zamyatin said evenly. ''I and one other man, whom I'm sure you know runs what you call the factory—Major Balachov—were assigned to watch Carlisle and make sure he got into no other mischief."

"This one got by you?" Mahoney heard himself asking.

Zamyatin nodded. "I received a Fifth Chief Directorate package on the situation only this afternoon. Complete with photographs."

Mahoney apparently still appeared doubtful to Zamyatin.

"It is no use, my old friend. We may lie to you and to others, but we do not lie to each other. Carlisle has had contact on more than one occasion with Nikolai Gamov, head of the Democratic Movement of dissidents."

"You are telling me that Carlisle is engineering the Democratic Movement in an attempt to assassinate the president of the United States?"

"It would appear so."

Despite his dislike of Carlisle he found himself unwilling to believe what Zamyatin was telling him. And yet much of what had gone on over the past few days fell into place now. Carlisle's insistence that the chief military attaché be present at the conference, for one. If Forsythe were to be assassinated there would have to be a quick and very solid link from the embassy to the Pentagon.

Then there was the business with Congdon. Had the man tumbled to Carlisle's connection with the Democratic Movement, not knowing that the dissident group may have kidnaped Sakharov and the laser? And did Carlisle know that if Congdon mentioned it out loud someone would put two and two together? If that was the case, what did Carlisle have on Congdon to assure his silence?

And the bug on his own office telephone, and the guards watching Marge and their apartment, and his children back in the States. Was Carlisle going to hold his own children's lives over his head?

Mahoney shook his head. Question everything. Especially that which seems most clear.

"It's a neat operation, Zamyatin," he said. "One that does you credit."

"What?"

"I'll admit you had me going for a minute there. You have tumbled to Carlisle, and now you want him out of Moscow. Permanently. Let a senior CIA officer charge Carlisle with an attempt to assassinate President Forsythe, and whether or not it can be proved, Carlisle is out. Neat."

Zamyatin was shaking his head. "No, no, it is not like that—I swear it."

"It didn't work. And it is going to backfire on you."

"Don't be a fool. You have everything to gain and nothing to lose."

"You're damned right . . . " Mahoney started, but Zamyatin waved him off.

"Let's say you are right in what you are saying. Then you have simply to do nothing about it. Don't blow the whistle on Carlisle. Say nothing to no one. You have already got plenty of hard intelligence about me and about the Komitet. Certainly enough to get rid of me."

Mahoney started to laugh, but bit it off. Zamyatin was disturbing him.

"But let's say for the moment that I am correct, Mahoney. Think, man . . . *think!* SAC is on alert. Our

Missile Defense Service is on alert. Shooting in the Mideast is imminent. What would happen if President Forsythe were assassinated?"

"It's frightening, but it's not going to happen that way," Mahoney said, not as sure of himself as he was making it sound. "What is going to happen is that I will go through the motions of checking out your story. I'll check on Carlisle. But meanwhile, you and I are going to discuss a number of other things. Among them your organizational chart, your personnel and budget lines, and . . ."

Mahoney stopped in mid-sentence. A look of infinite sadness had come over Zamyatin's features.

"No," he said, his voice barely audible over the loud music. "I need your help, but that does not make me a traitor."

"I can force it," Mahoney said. The thought of using Zamyatin's children this way was making him sick to his stomach.

Zamyatin shook his head. "The only point of weakness I have, Mahoney, is my children. I have them in protective custody."

Mahoney just stared at him, too shocked to say anything.

"It is you who are going to help me. I am saddened to have to inform you that your two sons, your daughter-in-law and your three children in the United States have been placed in custody by my people there. They will be held until Thursday."

XI

Early Wednesday Morning

WASHINGTON, D.C. (AP) . . . The White House announced today that President Forsythe would be traveling aboard a Concorde SST for his Moscow trip Thursday.

This will be the first official trip for the supersonic aircraft, which was purchased last year to be used as Air Force One.

The section of the United States Embassy in Moscow that was designated intelligence territory—as if no one else in the huge building had any intelligence—was called the White Room. The name came from a curious little electronic device that generated what the scientists called "white noise": random bits of electronic noise that could not be heard by the human ear, but that screwed up any electronic eavesdropping device such as phone taps and even some kinds of microwave scans.

The White Room at the Moscow embassy, quiet on

this night, was in actuality a half-dozen rooms at the back of the main building including the basement, first and second floors, plus the corridors and stairwells, as well as a few other isolated rooms and offices scattered throughout the building.

Outside of those areas were signs posted at irregular intervals on the walls warning that: "Listeners are Everywhere"; "Button Your Lip and Save Your Life"; and one poster which showed a hapless little man in a crumpled suit behind bars which proclaimed: "Even *Un*intentional Espionage is a Federal Offense."

Elsewhere in the embassy the staff was busy preparing for the president's arrival in less than thirty-four hours. The staff here was jocular although tired, and the bad jokes flew almost as fast as the paper work.

The correct grade of gasoline for the presidential motorcade, properly inflated tires, Bacardi rum in stock because it was the president's favorite drink, route security in cooperation with the Soviet Civil Police, accommodations for the presidential staff as well as the White House journalists, and a very sophisticated American-made defibrillation unit—everything had to be perfect. Although it was not public knowledge, the embassy had been informed by the chief White House physician that the president had a heart condition. Every detail was being planned. Every eventuality was being planned for.

Every eventuality, Mahoney thought as he entered the main front doors of the embassy and stopped at the marine guard's desk. Every eventuality save one. That someone, somewhere, was going to try to kill the president of the United States with a Soviet-made laser device.

"We're not signing in any longer?" Mahoney asked the young marine. The usual in/out log book was missing from the desk. Instead, a stack of blank three-by-five cards and a pen were neatly placed in front of the soldier.

"Yessir," the young soldier said. He slid a blank card and the pen toward Mahoney. "Your name and time in on the card, sir."

Mahoney signed his name and the time and pushed the card back to the marine. "When did this start?"

"This evening, sir. It was like this when I came on duty."

Mahoney nodded. "Let me see the cards for the last six hours."

The marine had placed the card in a small file box on the cabinet behind him and when he turned around he was shaking his head. "I'm sorry, sir, the in/out logs are closed."

"On whose orders?"

"Mr. Carlisle's, sir."

Mahoney stared at the young man for a long moment, then shrugged. "I see," he said and went down the corridor toward the elevator.

Upstairs, the White Room corridor was dark, and Mahoney shuffled down the hall to his office, unlocked the door and went inside. He did not turn on the light, but instead went behind his desk, sat down and stared out the window at the rain that was beginning to turn into wet snowflakes.

After awhile he poured himself a shot of whiskey from his bottle in a desk drawer, lit himself a cigar and again stared out the window as he smoked and drank, the whiskey not warming his insides this time, just laying sour in his stomach.

Once when Michael was eleven or twelve, Mahoney had taken him to his office, which at the time had been in the United Nations facility in New York City. His cover had been trade mission liaison between the American delegation and several of the delegations from Europe. His office was in a row of similar little cubicles, each occupied by a legitimate trade mission officer.

Michael had been impressed by the new building, by the foreigners in their strange garb, and by the immensity of it all, but in his father's office he had wrinkled up his nose.

"What's the matter, son?" Mahoney had asked, amused.

"I don't like it here, Dad," his son said.

"What's the matter with it?"

"It's too little."

"The offices are a lot bigger upstairs."

"I don't mean that, Dad," Michael said. "Everything is too little. I don't want to work here when I grow up."

"What do you want to do?"

"I want to work out in the woods. With the trees and the animals."

Mahoney had heaved a tremendous sigh of relief that day and every day afterward whenever Michael reiterated his desire to become a forest ranger or game warden.

He reflected now, however, that despite all the precautions, despite the fact that Michael had grown up to become a forest scientist, he had been dragged into the fray. All Mahoney's dreams for keeping his children insulated from his work had vanished. It had come as he had feared it might come all along.

Mahoney finished his whiskey, turned on his desk lamp, and put an Officer Contact form in his typewriter and began writing a report on his contact with Zamyatin, starting with Marge's phone call, and including the fact that his telephone had been bugged.

He worked for nearly two hours leaving nothing out, ignoring no speculation including the fact that it was a very real possibility that Carlisle himself was involved in a plot to assassinate the president.

The wind was blowing hard, streaking the snow against the window behind him, and howling around the building's corners, making him shiver.

Mahoney was very careful in his report not to step out of the bounds of his conversation with the Russian. Where the data seemed to support Zamyatin, Mahoney included them just that way. And where the facts seemed to point merely toward a Soviet plot to discredit Carlisle, Mahoney reported them without any special emphasis.

In this instance Mahoney was doing nothing more than acting as a conduit. A pipeline from Zamyatin to the intelligence pool. He would let the accusations, at least on paper, come from other quarters.

When he was finished it was nearly three in the morning, and he was dead tired. His eyes burned, his back was sore from sitting in one position, and he knew that when he got to his feet his legs would ache terribly.

He lit himself another cigar and poured himself a

second drink, then sat back in his chair to read over the half-dozen closely spaced typewritten pages he had completed.

These kinds of reports were supposed to be subjective. They were judged not only by their raw content, but on such things as the validity of the officer making the report. If the officer was a man such as Mahoney with long experience and a record of solid accomplishments, the report was taken quite seriously. Especially the sections of the report that contained such phrases as: "I believe that . . ."; "In my opinion . . ."; and "Considering past experience . . ."

But in this instance Mahoney had carefully avoided those terminologies. Instead he had called speculations just that, not gracing those thoughts with words like "opinion" or "believe."

He finally placed the report in a blank file folder and stuffed it beneath a stack of jackets on one corner of his desk. He stood up and stretched.

His legs throbbed, hurting him all the way up to his hips as he shut off his lamp and hobbled around his desk to the door.

Carlisle's office was two floors up and was checked like other White Room offices only at infrequent intervals during the night. The Citadel, as some of the staffers referred to Carlisle's domain, was the holy of holy places in the embassy, along with the ambassador's office. No one ever approached the door to either office without a direct invitation. And since embassy security as a whole was quite good, it was felt that infrequent checks by the night O.D. was sufficient.

Mahoney slipped out into the dimly lit corridor, closing and locking his door behind him, then silently made his way to the stairwell door, went through it and started the climb.

Deep inside of him where there should have been a wellspring of emotions, there was nothing but a dull, flat ache. He had blanked out his thoughts about his children, and of necessity his wife as well. It was a trick of the trade he had learned long ago.

"If you are on a mission, if you have a lot of straight thinking to do, your personal life must not intrude," he had told a junior staff conference once. "You have only so much mental and emotional energy available, and if you are to do a good job you mustn't squander it on thinking about your wife's new hairdo, or your mistress missing her last period. Those kinds of things will just slow you down."

He came to the landing one floor above his, and he had to stop a moment to catch his breath, to ease the pain in his legs.

Things at the White House would now be rising to a fever pitch as preparations for the president's trip went into full swing. Out at Andrews Air Force Base, the ground crew would be working hand in hand with the flight crew going over Air Force One with a fine-toothed comb. In times past, in other Air Force One aircraft, the president was supplied with a parachute. The only man aboard to be so equipped. But Mahoney idly wondered what was done to protect the president in an SST. Surely there was no possibility of parachuting from an airplane that flew 1,400 miles per hour nearly twelve miles above the earth. Perhaps the aircraft was equipped with an ejection seat.

Mahoney continued his climb and at Carlisle's floor he opened the stairwell door a crack and peered out.

The corridor here was only dimly lit, just like the downstairs halls, and it was deserted.

He withdrew a slender steel needle from a narrow leather case he kept in his pocket, slipped into the corridor and hurried to Carlisle's office door.

In less than thirty seconds he had picked the lock, entered the office, and had locked the door behind him.

Fifteen minutes later he had thoroughly searched Carlisle's office, his desk and file cabinets, and had slipped downstairs to the embassy library where he took his usual spot at the windowbox seat. Only now his wellspring of emotions was not blank, it was seething.

There had not been one single shred of paperwork on operation LOOK SEE in Carlisle's office. There was nothing on Zamyatin's children. No communiqués about his own children. Nothing in the daily logs about Mahoney and his contacts with Zamyatin. And nothing about the activities of the last weekend at Dzerzhinsky Square.

Mahoney had found, however, dozens of files showing, step by step, every movement the president would be making from the moment he got off Air Force One at Vnukovo Airport until he got back on.

And the most damning file of all contained only a single sheet of paper. It was a personal dossier on Nikolai Gamov, Nobel Prize winner, and head of the Democratic Movement of Soviet artists, writers, and scientists.

It was snowing so hard now that Mahoney could not see the gravel courtyard or brick wall below him, only the swirling gray snowflakes soft against a totally black background.

He stared out the window and the moving snow seemed to draw him forward. *A*, he told himself. Carlisle was indeed the nigger in the woodpile. He was engineering the Democratic Movement in an attempt on the president's life. Or *B*, all of this was a setup. Some kind of a twisted conspiracy. But for what purpose? For whose gain?

Slowly, the same name that had cropped up so many times in Mahoney's thinking over the past few days formed again in his mind.

Congdon. Perhaps he still held the key.

Mahoney got up, his legs much better than before, left the library, and worked his way through the maze of corridors to the housing wing of the embassy building.

At Congdon's apartment door he stopped a moment to listen before he knocked softly. There had been no sound from within, but a moment after he knocked he could hear someone coming, then the door swung open.

George Congdon, wearing nothing more than a pair of rumpled trousers and a dirty T-shirt, no shoes or socks on his feet, his hair mussed and his eyes red-rimmed and bloodshot, peered out at Mahoney standing in the corridor.

For a moment neither man spoke, but then Congdon cleared his throat. "You've come to see the kids?" he asked hopefully. His voice seemed raw.

"I came to see you, George," Mahoney said gently. "May I come in?"

Congdon just stood there holding on to the doorframe with one hand. He hadn't shaved in what looked like a day or more, and he looked as if he was on the verge of collapse.

"I could use a drink," Mahoney prompted, and

Congdon seemed to come slightly out of his daze. He moved aside and let Mahoney into the apartment.

A blanket and a crumpled pillow were spread out on the couch, and Congdon brushed past Mahoney and lay down, throwing an arm over his eyes.

"The kids are asleep in my bedroom. You know where the liquor is," Congdon said.

Mahoney went into the kitchen, which was immaculately clean, and poured himself a stiff shot of whiskey from the liquor cabinet next to the sink. He drank it down in one swallow, rinsed the glass and came back into the living room.

"Zamyatin's oldest daughter, Sandra, cleaned up the kitchen before she went to bed. She's quite a girl," Congdon said from the couch.

Mahoney sat down in an easy chair across from Congdon and studied his old friend's nearly inert form for a long time.

Congdon had always been a fastidious man. Neat not only about his dress and his personal appearance, but neat about his thinking.

"Everything has its place, and there is a place for everything," he used to say. "It is our job to see that the square pegs get put into the square holes, and the round pegs get stuck in the round holes, and not vice versa. Simple. No?"

"Carlisle is sitting on you, George. What has he got?"

Congdon didn't move, didn't speak, and for a moment didn't appear even to be breathing.

"It's too late for him now," Mahoney said. "Can't you see that? I know what is going on. He can't do anything to you."

Congdon slowly withdrew his arm from across his

eyes, turned his head and looked up at Mahoney. There were tears in his eyes, and Mahoney's heart skipped a beat.

"What is it, George? What has that madman got on you?"

"My wife," Congdon said, his voice low and raspy.

Mahoney leaned forward to better hear him. "What about her?"

"Jesus . . . Jesus . . . Jesus . . . " Congdon stammered, the tears streaming down his cheeks.

Mahoney tried to think. One year ago Janet Congdon had died of cancer. One day she had discovered several lumps in both of her breasts, had gone to the American doctor here in the embassy, and within ten days had been shipped back to the hospital in Washington, D.C., where she died.

Congdon had taken a thirty-day leave, but then had returned to Moscow where he had literally thrown himself into his work.

"Janet died of cancer," Mahoney prompted, making his voice as gentle as he possibly could.

Congdon was shaking his head. "She was murdered. They killed her."

It was like a knife cutting into Mahoney's heart. He couldn't find any words.

"Carlisle says he knows who engineered her death. He said he would tell me, if I cooperated. He says he will help me get the people, if I am a good boy." His words were bitter.

Mahoney let his breath out with a deep sigh. "He's using you, George. Janet died of cancer. She smoked. The doctors said it was lung cancer that spread. You saw the reports."

"Carlisle says they introduced a carcinogen into a

meal she ate at a Soviet restaurant. He says they do it all the time."

"No," Mahoney said. "Those chemicals can be detected. Carlisle is using you. Why? What do you know that he wants held back?"

Congdon just stared at him.

"He took Zamyatin's children, and he says he's got Michael, John, and the kids in custody back in the States. Can't you see what he's doing?"

Still Congdon held his silence.

"There's a good chance that the president will be assassinated on Thursday. Carlisle may be the man behind it."

"No," Congdon finally said.

"What?"

Congdon sat up. "I mean I don't know anything about that," he said wearily. He had stopped crying.

"What did Carlisle tell you to keep from me?"

"It doesn't make any sense, Wallace," Congdon said almost beseechingly. "It doesn't mean anything. It's so goddamned useless. So meaningless."

"What is?"

"All this time . . . all these days I thought you were working on the Mideast thing. The crises. Nuclear weapons. A Soviet plot to take over the oil wells. All this time." Now there as a note of wonder in his voice.

None of this was making any sense, but Mahoney said nothing because it appeared as if Congdon was going to continue.

"Dzerzhinsky Square was working at full tilt. Washington . . . New York . . . the embassy in Mexico City . . . everywhere it was the same. All the stops had been pulled out. Or so it seemed."

"What was it you discovered?"

"I went to Carlisle with it on Monday. It was so goddamned obvious." Congdon was shaking his head in wonder. "And then the roof caved in. Carlisle said I was not to mention this to you. I was not even to mention our conversation. Nothing. I was to play dumb. On Thursday he'd return the favor. He'd help me."

"And now?"

Congdon shook his head. "It doesn't matter. Carlisle was wrong when he figured you were working on the Mideast thing. He was afraid you'd do something to screw up the president's position on Thursday." He looked at Mahoney. "Deficit spending you asked me about. I said I didn't know anything about it."

Mahoney had a blank look on his face.

"Well, that's it, old friend. That's all of it. The Russians are *not* deficit spending. Nor have they pulled in anything but rubles. No hard Western currency, Wallace. Only rubles and not many of them."

Still Mahoney was not understanding, and it evidently showed on his face because Congdon sat forward on the couch.

"Don't you see, Wallace?" he said. "All this time we were worried about some big Russian push worldwide when it was nothing more than some little rinkydink operation right here in Moscow."

A glimmer of understanding began forming in Mahoney's mind.

"Everything else was a sham. There have been no operations outside of Moscow. No one gives a shit about the Mideast crises, except maybe the military. The Dzerzhinsky Square meeting was probably mostly nothing but a sham as well. It all had to be. There was no money for anything else. No hard Western money. You can't spend rubles in Washington or Lisbon or Mexico or even East Germany."

Mahoney got up from his chair, his mind spinning.

"Don't you see, Wallace, none of it really mattered. Even Carlisle will be able to see that now. It was all for nothing."

Without a word Mahoney turned and headed for the door.

"Don't you think she was poisoned, Wallace?" Congdon called after him.

At the door Mahoney hesitated a moment. "No, she wasn't poisoned, George," he said, and then he went out. He knew, finally, what was going on, what had been happening all along. Or at least he knew the highlights of the operation. Now all he needed were the details. And most importantly the reason why.

As he headed down the corridor toward the main embassy entrance, he reached inside his coat pocket and fingered his .45. He had found his gun in a desk drawer in Carlisle's office and had taken it. At first he had hesitated, because in some respects Carlisle was right. Being armed presented a new factor into the operation. A new and probably dangerous factor.

Only now Mahoney was glad he had the gun.

XII

Later Wednesday Morning

TEL AVIV, ISRAEL (AP) . . . Israeli Prime Minister Menachem Begin announced last night that he would be meeting with Egyptian leader Anwar Sadat later this morning here in Tel Aviv.

Begin refused to specify the nature of the meeting, but said it was a matter of "utmost urgency."

Zamyatin's apartment seemed hollow and empty without his children. It had seemed that way last night when he had finally come home from work and had flopped down on the couch, the lights out. And it seemed even more empty now at four in the morning as he lay awake still on the couch, sipping vodka.

Across the room on a low cabinet were photographs of the children that had been taken almost two years ago. He looked across at them and shook his head, smiling inwardly.

Sandra had become the mother hen of the family. She claimed that she remembered her mother, but she had been only three when Aleksei was born. It was more likely that she had formed a mental picture of her mother from the photographs she had seen and from the things Zamyatin had told her.

There was another side to his beautiful Sandra that in some ways disturbed Zamyatin, disturbed and at times frightened him. She was growing up under his nose. In the last year she had shot up in height, and lost her baby fat, her legs had lengthened and slimmed down, and she had developed breasts.

Sometimes when they were out shopping together Zamyatin would notice boys much older than his daughter looking at her in a way no boy should look at a baby.

He sighed deeply. The fact was, however, that his baby was no longer a baby. She was rapidly becoming a grown girl soon to become a woman.

It was partly because of the fact she had no mother and had to assume that role for them all, Zamyatin knew. But it was also partly because of her genes that she was maturing so rapidly. Her mother had matured early, had been a sensible girl all of her life. Back in Leningrad she had told him that as a girl her schoolmates had called her a forty-year-old teen-ager because she was so developed and was usually very serious.

In that respect Sandra was much like her mother. And at thirteen, she was already developing another of her mother's characteristics, one of simple beauty.

Lara, at twelve, on the other hand, was apparently not even close to making that transition toward womanhood. Her tiny, but developing breasts were a source of irritation and embarrassment to her; boys were good for only one thing: playing soccer. And the dresses she had to wear as a part of her school uniform were a hindrance to good fun.

Zamyatin had watched Sandra trying to teach her young sister the proper way to sit in a dress, but it was all to no avail. In a dress or not, when Lara wanted to sit down and cross her legs—ankle on knee—she did so and damn propriety and etiquette.

Where Sandra had a certain quality of aloofness about her—she always closed the door when she was dressing, was uncertain about being touched, even by her father—Lara was a bubbling little package of joyous energy who still loved her father's lap and who was never ashamed to hug and kiss goodnight whoever happened to be in the room.

And then there was Aleksei. Last year he had been accepted into the Young Pioneers and wore his red tie with the same pride a general wore his stars.

"Soon, Papa, very soon I will be in the *Komsomol,*" he said to his father almost daily. "Very soon now—you watch and see."

Number one in his class scholastically, number one in his class in sports, and number one in his father's heart. Where Sandra was reserved and Lara was an unabashed bundle of energy, Aleksei was a joyous boy of unbounded enthusiasm for nearly everything around him.

But he was a tender boy as well. He never forgot his sisters' birthdays, nor did he ever go to sleep at night without first very seriously kissing everyone.

"Good night, Papa, see you in the morning," he

would say in his tiny little voice. "Sleep well, sisters," he would hug and kiss them.

Sandra doted on him like any mother would a son, and Lara, even though she was his senior, looked up to Aleksei almost as if he were an older brother. A God. He was a Young Pioneer, after all. He wore the red scarf. Soon he would be in the *Komsomol*.

Zamyatin sat up and leaned forward, his face buried in his hands, his elbows on his knees. They would not let him see his children for some inexplicable reason. It made no sense.

The apartment building was quiet. Zamyatin could hear his own breathing, and near the front door the eight-day clock he had bought in Helsinki ten years ago suddenly chimed four times, and he looked up.

Several times during the afternoon and early evening he had reached for the telephone intending to call General Ganin. To plead with the man about his children. All he wanted was five minutes with them. Three minutes. Sixty seconds.

But each time he had pulled his hand back. There simply was no mechanism within the entire Komitet for such an action. Directorate administrators could and sometimes did cross directorate lines during specific operations. Ganin had done the very thing at noon yesterday. Department heads did not. So he had thrown himself into his work, repressing for those hours the fear he felt for his children.

There had been literally hundreds of individual movements in and out of the American embassy during the afternoon and early evening hours. Most of the individual surveillances, however, had uncovered no other pattern from that of an ordinary shift change. Some personnel had come from their apartments to work, while others who lived off embassy grounds had gone home.

A few had stopped at restaurants, others had shopped, two of them at GUM downtown, and one low-ranking embassy staffer had secretly—or so he thought—met a young Russian girl and they had gone back to his apartment and made love.

The American could prove sooner or later to be useful to them in a minor fashion. His wife had returned to the States for a short vacation, and the photographs Balachov's people had taken of the liaison would be useful for blackmail should the staffer ever find himself in a position where he had access to sensitive information.

Other than that there had been nothing. At least nothing concerning the scientist Sakharov and the missing laser device.

Zamyatin had left the Center around 9:00 P.M., and took a staff car to the First Department's headquarters, slowly cruising past the U.S. Embassy on his way.

The rain had not yet turned to snow, but it was freezing to ice on everything it struck so that Zamyatin had to roll down his window to get a clear view of the huge yellow brick building.

The American military guard at the front gate, in his guardbox, had watched the car go by and had probably taken down the license number. It would tell them nothing other than the fact the car was an official government vehicle.

Five blocks away, Zamyatin pulled up and parked in

front of a building that looked like a deserted warehouse. The facade fooled no one, of course, but in diplomatic relations appearances often were more important and carried more weight than actual fact.

He entered the building by a side door, the only entrance that was ever open, showed his identification to the guards just inside, and went upstairs to the third floor where Major Balachov maintained his office.

A young, good-looking second lieutenant jumped to attention in the outer office as Zamyatin came through the door.

"Please go directly in, sir," the lieutenant snapped. "Major Balachov is awaiting you."

Zamyatin smiled, amused, went past the lieutenant and entered Balachov's office.

The First Department Chief was standing behind his desk just lighting a cigarette when Zamyatin came in, and he shook out the match, threw it in an overflowing ashtray, and beamed.

"Comrade Colonel, come in, come in and sit down."

Zamyatin crossed the large room and sat down in a chair in front of the desk. For a moment Balachov remained standing, looking down at Zamyatin, but then he, too, sat down and offered him a cigarette.

"They are American. I just bought them fresh at the exchange store."

Zamyatin shook his head. "You are coming up in the world, Boris Balachov."

Balachov returned the pack to his breast pocket. "I have no wife, as you well know, comrade, to spend my money on. There is no one. I do not even have the luxury of children as you do."

The man seemed expansive to Zamyatin, and for some reason it made him slightly uncomfortable.

"To what do I owe the unexpected pleasure of your visit this evening?" Balachov asked.

His eyes were hooded, Zamyatin decided. And although in many respects the man was deficient as a Komitet officer, he still was dangerous. Beware of sinking ships lest you get taken down in the suction.

"Sakharov and the laser," Zamyatin said softly. "What progress?"

Balachov held out his hands. "You asked for no reports, comrade."

Zamyatin said nothing, and he was satisfied to see that Balachov fidgeted somewhat uncomfortably.

"There is no progress so far, comrade," Balachov said.

Zamyatin looked at him. "Let me see your log." The American Air Force had borrowed time-motion accounting procedures from General Motors in the sixties, and the Soviets had in turn borrowed the system for their own use.

Officers of Balachov's rank and below were required by Komitet regulations to account for every moment of their time on computer punch cards. Each day the cards were sent to data processing from which time-motion and efficiency studies were distributed to all division and directorate heads.

Balachov handed over his thick plastic folder that contained his daily cards without comment. Zamyatin flipped open the folder and began going through the cards.

When he was finished he looked up, disappointed. There had been no card outlining any trip to

Kutuzovsky Prospekt. Balachov had not been the one who had picked up his children. One card was, however, curious.

"Vnukovo Airport. What were you doing there?"

Balachov blinked. "An embassy staffer went there to check on preparations for the president's arrival Thursday. I followed him."

"And?" Zamyatin asked sharply.

Balachov shrugged. "Nothing else, comrade. The man checked with the airport security division, and then returned to the embassy."

Blind alleys. It seemed to Zamyatin that he had spent half his life chasing down blind alleys.

If the CIA had grabbed his children they would have used them as a lever against him. As it turned out, his own people had his children. His own people were using them as a lever to make him do their bidding.

Only he was finding he was caring less and less about Sakharov and the laser, about the American president and about peace anywhere in the world. He wanted his children back, and he had come here this evening hoping blindly that somehow Balachov could help him, or would at the very least know something.

But it had been foolish.

Zamyatin stood up abruptly and handed the card folder back to Balachov with a weak smile. "Continue with what you are doing. I want Sakharov and the laser."

"Yes, comrade," Balachov said, getting to his feet.

Zamyatin looked at the man for several seconds longer then turned on his heel and left the way he had come.

The first snowflakes were just beginning to fall when

he climbed back into the staff car, started the engine and drove slowly away.

At Smolenskaya Plaza he turned right toward the river, his thoughts as black and as bleak as the night he was driving through. A few great blocks of ice still drifted with the flow of the river, their gray masses only slightly lighter than the black of the water.

Spring was always the strangest season in Moscow. Filled with hope and promise for a respite from the terrible, long winter, spring often was the great disappointer. The rains that always fell in the spring, more often than not turned to snow like this evening. Despite this, however, the heating systems in most public buildings were shut down by mid-April, so for many, spring was a time of misery.

He crossed the Berezhkovskaya Nab bridge, made a U-turn on the deserted street and went back over the river toward his apartment.

Before his wife had died they had had friends, people they could drop in on at any time of the day or night. Sandra had insisted on it.

"I will not live my life in isolation," she had insisted one evening shortly after they had gotten married. It had been one of their very rare arguments.

"You know my position," he had said.

"State Security Service or not, we *will* have friends."

"No one will trust us. We will be looked upon as spies."

"Only if we act like spies."

And she had had her way. Over the next few years they had developed many strong and, Zamyatin had supposed, lasting friends. But after Sandra had died all their friends had drifted away. Zamyatin was an officer in the Komitet. Sandra, by the sheer force of her personality, had overcome that social handicap. Zamyatin alone could not.

There was no place he could go on this evening other than back to his office, back to Balachov's office, or to his empty apartment. None of those options seemed comforting. Nor did the thought of going to some noisy, crowded restaurant interest him. And Zamyatin needed comfort.

As he drove he let his mind wander back and forth over the activities of the past few days, ever since the weekend call-up of officers to the Center.

Nothing had been the same since then. Not his job, not his relationship with the people who worked for him, and now not even his children.

As he passed the American Embassy again he cranked his window down several inches. The marine guard was not in sight and now even fewer windows than before showed light.

They sleep like we do, he thought, and yet like us they never sleep.

There was some traffic on Tchaikovsky Street despite the weather and despite the relatively late hour for Muscovites, and Zamyatin only idly noticed that a black car a block ahead of him had slowed down and had pulled over to the curb.

Neither speeding up nor slowing down, Zamyatin drove past where the car was parked across the street from him, its lights still on and its engine idling.

He glanced that way and for several seconds his heart seemed to stop, and he nearly pulled the steering wheel off its column.

There were two men in the car. And in the brief moment that he had been able to see through the windshield he had identified both of them.

Two blocks farther down the street Zamyatin pulled up and once again parked in front of the Department One headquarters, and with shaking hands fumbled for the car door handle.

He had to be sure, he told himself, his heart racing. He had to make absolutely certain.

Just inside the doorway the guards once again checked his identification papers, and he took the stairs up as fast as he could run, and barged into Balachov's outer office.

The same second lieutenant as before was seated behind his desk and he jumped up, obviously flustered when Zamyatin came through the door.

"Comrade Colonel . . . " the lieutenant stammered.

"Major Balachov," Zamyatin snapped. "Get him out here, now!"

"I am sorry, sir, Major Balachov is not here."

"Where is he?"

"I don't know, sir."

Zamyatin quickly moved past the lieutenant and before the young man could object, stormed into Balachov's office and flipped on the lights.

The lieutenant came after him. "Comrade Colonel, please . . . "

"Return to your post, Lieutenant," Zamyatin said, not bothering to turn around as he surveyed the office.

"But, sir . . . "

Zamyatin turned and glared at the young man. "Lieutenant," he barked.

"Yessir," the young man said, and he turned and

went back to the outer office. Zamyatin closed the door.

In ten minutes he had made a thorough search of Balachov's desk and of two of the three file cabinets in the room. The third cabinet was locked with a heavy combination lock and steel bar, but Zamyatin did not need to look through it. He had found what he had come looking for.

Returning to the outer office, Zamyatin stopped in front of the young lieutenant's desk. "On your feet, soldier," he shouted.

The lieutenant jumped up into a pose of rigid attention, his eyes straight forward.

"When Major Balachov reports back here I want you to give him a message from me," Zamyatin snapped. "Do you understand?"

"Yessir."

"Tell Major Balachov that I will expect a report—in full—on my desk first thing in the morning on his meeting this evening with Nikolai Gamov. Do you have the name?"

"Yes, comrade. Nikolai Gamov."

"Very well, Lieutenant. Carry on."

Zamyatin turned and stormed out of the office, down the stairs, past the two guards at the door and back to his car, which he had left running.

Holding himself in check just a little longer he carefully put the car in gear and headed toward his apartment, the reunion with his children now seeming very far away and perhaps even impossible.

Zamyatin had just looked at his wristwatch that showed it was exactly 4:45 A.M. when someone knocked softly at his door. He smiled sadly as he looked up from where he still sat on the couch.

"Come in," he said in English. "The door is unlocked.

He could hear the door open, and then close, and almost immediately he could smell the odor of a cigar.

Mahoney came around the corner into the living room, and he stopped short. Even in the very dim light Zamyatin could see that the American was soaked.

"Take off your coat and come in and sit down," Zamyatin said.

Without a word Mahoney took off his raincoat and hung it and his hat in the vestibule, then returned to the living room where Zamyatin indicated a chair for him to sit down.

"Vodka?" Zamyatin asked, but Mahoney shook his head. He seemed grim.

"They are doing a number on us, Yurianovich," Mahoney said softly.

Zamyatin needed no translation of that idiom. "Who has my children?"

"We do," Mahoney said.

Zamyatin could feel the ache in his heart as if someone had grabbed his insides and were squeezing with a powerful grip. "And now?" he heard himself asking.

"Now we talk," Mahoney said.

7:00 A.M. Wednesday

It was still dark when Major Boris Balachov, dressed in civilian clothes, emerged from the First Department headquarters five blocks away from the American embassy.

The snow, which had fallen heavily all through the night, lay in dirty little piles against the curbs and around the corners of buildings.

He turned away from where his car was parked around the side of the building, thrust his hands in his pockets and walked purposefully down the street away from the embassy.

He was deep in thought.

With slightly more than twenty-four hours to go, Zamyatin had begun putting it together. Balachov did not worry about a confrontation with Zamyatin as much as he was deeply concerned about a confrontation with his own boss.

"Why wasn't Zamyatin followed? Why wasn't the man watched?"

Those were the questions Balachov feared most of all, because he could not give the truthful answer: vanity, pride, and ambition.

Simply put, there was not one man in Balachov's department who was good enough to watch Zamyatin without being detected. If Balachov could not supply the expertise, then someone else would. And whoever that someone else was, he would end up taking over Political Services. Balachov could not allow that to happen, so he had gone out on a limb.

The basic premise Balachov had operated under could not be faulted. Only his limited vision of it could be argued.

Zamyatin was a loyal Soviet citizen, a loyal officer of the KGB and therefore could not deliberately become a traitor, and therefore did not *need* to be kept under surveillance.

That view was correct as far as it went. Zamyatin's loyalty was unquestioned and unquestionable. The man had proved almost from birth where his loyalties lay, and had worked hard all of his life to maintain the highest standards of any officer within the Komitet.

Balachov's point of view was limited by his lack of understanding of two relationships.

The first was the relationship between a father and his children. Balachov had never been married, had never sired children, and in fact seldom thought about sex. On the rare occasions he did have sexual thoughts they usually were concerned with men or finding creative ways to masturbate. For most of Balachov's life his sexual drives had been sublimated to the State. To the Communist Party. And finally to the Komitet.

As a result, many of Balachov's views about people around him were naive or, in the case of Zamyatin's relationship with his children, totally ignorant.

Balachov, because he had never had the experience, could not conceive of one human being caring more about someone else's life and safety than his own. He could understand a subjugation to the State, or even to a high principle, but not to another person. Especially not to a child, or in this case, three of them.

He knew that the Americans had picked up Zamyatin's children, and General Ganin had made it quite clear that another mistake like that would mean the end of Balachov in more than one way.

General Ganin had repaired the mistake, convincing Zamyatin that his children were being safely held in the Center. How long that fabrication would hold was anyone's guess. But they only had until Thursday. A little more than twenty-four hours.

The second relationship that Balachov had no understanding of was the nature of loyalty, or to be more exact, the difference between loyalty and blind obedience to rule.

Balachov was blindly obedient to the State, whereas Zamyatin was loyal. Where Balachov did as he was told—exactly as he was told with little or no finesse, with little or no initiative and with little or no imagination—Zamyatin knew at all times what he was doing and why he was doing it.

Zamyatin believed in Communism. Believed in the grandeur of the Union of Soviet Socialist Republics. In the world-unifying cause he fought for.

Balachov believed only in martial order. A captain was more important than a lieutenant. A major higher than a captain. And a general was near the top.

Which was why Balachov was worried at this moment that General Ganin would ask him questions that he had no answers for. Vanity, pride, and ambition were all qualities outside the realm of what he thought was correct behavior for an officer in the Komitet.

Yet all of those things indicated at least a tiny spark of humanity within the man.

And then there was Nikolai Gamov. Somehow Zamyatin had found out that he had met the man this morning. It was a stupid mistake, but one that could be side-stepped for at least twenty-four hours.

The entire setup was sloppy and was now coming apart at the seams. But Balachov felt like a man in a leaky rowboat far out to sea; he would have to do everything and anything he could to plug the holes, lest the boat sink and he drown.

It took him fully forty-five minutes to circle around the Tolstoy Museum and finally make his way into the Old Town section of Moscow where, from a back alley courtyard, he entered a ramshackle ancient wooden building, and descended down a flight of rickety stairs into a dark, dank basement.

At the bottom of the stairs he stood perfectly still in the near absolute darkness, holding his breath and listening. The only sounds he could hear, however, was the wind outside and the rain beating against the door.

Then a single light bulb hanging down from the ceiling in the middle of the large room came on and for a moment he was blinded. He held his right hand over his eyes.

"Boris Azarov," a deep, man's voice boomed from the shadows beyond thc light. There were others in the room; Balachov could hear them shuffling around.

"Nikolai Gamov?" he said, lowering his hand.

"More accurately I should say *Major* Boris Azarov, chief of the special security detail, Vnukovo Official Airport."

Someone came down the stairs, and Balachov turned as a young man with long hair, a pockmarked complexion and deep black eyes stopped short. He eyed Balachov, and then looked beyond him toward the shadows at the back of the room.

"It's all clear, Nikki. He was not followed."

"Search him."

Balachov raised both of his hands as the young man moved forward and quickly searched him. When he was finished he stepped back.

"He has no weapons."

"Welcome to Samizdat House," the deep voice said, and several other lights hanging from the ceiling were switched on.

Balachov turned as Nikolai Gamov, a huge bear of a

man, came forward and held out his hand. Behind him were half a dozen other men.

"We are sorry for the indignity we had to put you through," Gamov said, taking Balachov's hand and pumping it. "But we cannot be too careful."

He half turned and indicated the others. "May I present the activist faction of the Democratic Movement," he said with a tinge of irony in his voice. "Gentlemen, this is Major Boris Azarov. I've already given you his title. And now you will be able to meet and talk with the man who has made our little project possible."

"This is the man you met last night, Nikki?" asked a middle-aged man wearing a heavy army overcoat with the insignia removed. He did not offer his hand, and did not come closer to Balachov than a few feet, almost as if he was afraid Balachov was a wild animal who might attack at any moment.

"One and the same, Vladimir," Gamov said, and he turned again to Balachov. "I'd like you to meet our conscience. Vladimir Protopopich Simenof, *artiste excellent.*"

Balachov extended his hand, but Simenof ignored it, directing his comments to Gamov, who towered above his slight figure.

"Pray tell, at long last are we finally to learn what all these nocturnal wanderings and heinous acts we've been doing lately mean?"

Gamov laughed. "Poor Vladimir is not only an artist on canvas, he fancies himself an artist with words as well." He laughed again. "Yes, Vladimir, this morning you will learn everything, and before this meeting is completed you will shake Major Azarov's hand."

Simenof grunted and turned away as the other men, some of them very young, but most middle-aged or older, seated themselves around a long table.

Gamov took Balachov's arm and led him over to the head of the table where they both sat down.

"This place at one time housed the underground press that was operated by the Free Artists and Writers Union," Gamov explained as a samovar and glasses were set up at one end of the table.

"Which is why you call this place Samizdat House?" Balachov asked. He took out a cigarette, lit it and inhaled deeply.

"Yes," Gamov said. "Self publication—the only way in which the former occupants of this room could express themselves freely."

A younger man at the far end of the table had just poured himself a glass of tea, and he looked their way. "Our government has become unresponsive to its people's needs. It will change or crumble."

Balachov peered down at him. "You sound like Andrei Amalrik."

The young man swore and several of the others around the table chuckled.

"Our young friend at the end of the table is Pavl Ivanovich Gorsky. He is our resident politican. And yes, he does sound rather like that ineffectual troublemaker."

Again there were more laughs around the table, and the man next to Balachov handed him a glass of tea.

"But the time of speaking and of merely writing has passed for us, my friends," Gamov said, addressing himself to the group. "The time for action has come."

Several of the men around the table rapped their knuckles against the tabletop in approval.

Gamov nodded toward Balachov. "Major Azarov came to me two months ago at a party. From that beginning I knew that he was not an establishment man. That his philosophy was very much related to ours, only with one important difference." Gamov paused for effect. "The difference is that until this moment we have been men of talk, whereas Major Azarov has been a man of action."

"Are you proud then, Nikki, of what you accomplished at Lubyanka II?" The question came from Simenof.

Gamov was shaking his head. "No, I am not. It was the most despicable thing I have ever done in my life. My soul grieves for what I have done."

"We have gone along this far on your word and good honor alone. It is time now for you to tell us what you have done. To what course of action you have committed us." Simenof had looked directly at Balachov when he said the last.

"Major Azarov, with help from friends, has managed to kidnap Professor Doctor Leonid Sakharov from his office at Moscow State University."

There were several gasps around the table. The enormity of what Gamov was saying to them was almost too much to grasp. Balachov smiled inwardly. They had heard nothing yet.

"I have Doctor Sakharov in a safe place," Balachov said, speaking for the first time. "And the less you know about my methods and contacts, and the less I know of yours, the more protected all of us will be."

There were no comments from the others, and Gamov continued.

"In addition to Doctor Sakharov, Major Azarov has also managed to steal a device which emits a beam of laser light. A weapon."

"Doctor Sakharov developed this device to be used as a hand-carried military weapon," Balachov again spoke up. "My special security forces were involved with the initial field testing, which is how I knew of its existence."

"It can kill a man?" one of the men at the table asked.

"Yes," Balachov said. "And there is no effective defense against it. At least not in the standard security procedures we use. Armor plate, bulletproof glass, nothing offers any sure protection. The device has been able to penetrate up to seven inches of armor plate in less than four seconds, making it very uncomfortable for anyone so protected."

"Is this what we are to become?" Simenof shouted, half rising out of his chair. "Are we to become common murderers? Has the taste of blood at Lubyanka tainted your soul, Nikolai?"

Gamov was holding up his hands for silence. "On the contrary, my dear Vladimir. The device that Major Azarov will supply to us will be used for peace. I repeat that word. For *peace!*"

"Then why the army uniform, the papers, and the weapon?" Gorsky asked.

"The plan is simple," Balachov said. "But I must first warn you that it is at the same time dramatic and very desperate."

"Can it be any more dramatic or desperate than what we have already done?" Simenof asked in disgust.

"Yes," Balachov said, and his simple answer silenced the man.

"Please continue," Gamov said. "Tell them everything we have agreed upon. Leave nothing out."

Balachov nodded, took a deep drag on his cigarette and exhaled the smoke slowly. "At eleven o'clock tomorrow morning the president of the Unites States will arrive at Vnukovo Official Airport. It is our aim to kidnap the man."

For a seeming eternity there was absolute silence in the room, and Balachov could hear the wind outside moaning around the building. And then pandemonium broke loose with everyone shouting at once.

Balachov sat back in his chair, stubbed out his cigarette in an ashtry in front of him and lit himself another.

For several minutes the debate raged until finally Simenof's voice began to win out over the others.

"Is this the insane course of action you have been plotting for us, Nikolai?" Simenof shouted. "Are we to become nothing more than international terrorists?"

Gamov was calm. "On the contrary, Vladimir, we are going to do exactly what we originally set out to do. Guarantee our human rights in our own country under rule of law, and guarantee peace—*worldwide peace.*"

Balachov sat forward. "At this very moment the American military is on alert. Poised and ready to mount the attack. Our own Missile Defense Service is also poised and ready for the command. We are on a collision course toward nuclear holocaust."

"And this insanity you propose will help?" Simenof asked incredulously. He was no longer shouting.

"Yes it will, my impassioned Russian comrade," Balachov said.

Once again there was silence in the room for several moments until Gamov spoke up.

"The president will be taken back aboard his aircraft, which will be refueled and ordered into the sky. Several of us will be on board. The pilot will be ordered to fly in a holding pattern directly above Moscow from where radio communications will be set up with our own government as well as the American government. Our demands will be simple." Gamov looked around the table. Even Simenof was hanging on his every word.

"First we want the immediate organization of a congress for human rights in the Soviet Union. This congress will be made up of members of our government as well as representatives from every walk of life.

"Secondly, we will demand an immediate meeting of the heads of state from all nations that currently have a nuclear capability. That meeting will be held in Moscow for the purpose of permanent nuclear disarmament."

"You are a foolish man, Nikki," Simenof said. "What guarantee do you have that once you release the American president all of us will not simply be arrested and executed?"

"Our demands will be broadcast on such frequencies that almost every man, woman, and child in the world will be able to hear us." Gamov said. He nodded toward Balachov. "Major Azarov tells me that onboard the president's aircraft is enough communications equipment to insure that happens."

Simenof was shaking his head; the others around the table were staring at Gamov and Balachov in wonder.

"And how will this noble act be accomplished?" Simenof asked.

Balachov sat forward. "At ten-fifty A.M. tomorrow I will personally escort Sakharov and the laser device up into the control tower at Vnukovo. At that same moment Nikolai and as many of you who want to be present will be in the crowd waiting to see the president's arrival. At the edge of the crowd working security control, will be one of you dressed in the Lubyanka guard's uniform, carrying his weapon and carrying his identification papers—with the name changed."

"You can arrange all of this?" Simenof asked.

Balachov nodded. "It has already been done," he said. "As the president steps off the aircraft, the laser will be aimed at him and an announcement will be made over the airport's public address system informing everyone present what will happen if we do not receive immediate and absolute cooperation."

"And then?" Simenof said softly.

"And then your people at the edge of the crowd will be escorted by your man in uniform to the president, where you will take him back aboard his aircraft and order the pilot to circle the city."

"Insanity," Simenof said wonderingly.

"To peace!" Gamov suddenly shouted, jumping up.

A moment later everyone else around the table had jumped to their feet and were joining the cry. "To peace! To peace!"

Even Simenof finally joined them as Balachov sat back once again in his chair, lit himself another cigarette, and to himself said: "'To the naiveté of the pure."

XIII

Wednesday

A176BULLETIN

WASHINGTON, D.C. (AP) . . . In a joint communiqué this morning Egyptian President Anwar Sadat and Israeli Prime Minister Menachem Begin informed the White House that nuclear weapons are being stockpiled in Syria.

The communiqué, released to the press in Washington by members of Sadat's and Begin's staffs, said intelligence sources had uncovered the weapons, which are of a tactical nuclear class.

"Tactical nuclear weapons have and are being stockpiled outside the Syrian capital city of Damascus," the message said in part.

It seemed as if he had never slept. His mouth was foul from the vodka he had drank all morning with Zamyatin. And his mind seethed with everything they had talked about.

There were two final hurdles for him to face this morning. The first was Marge. Dear sweet Marge.

He would not be able to hide from her the fact that Michael, John, and the children had been dragged into this mess. Nor would he be able to hide from her his worry about it.

Marge, for all her apparent dowdiness, was a bright and highly perceptive woman. Combined with the fact that they had been married for nearly forty years, it made her almost clairvoyant when it came to what was on her husband's mind.

He had walked from the embassy to Zamyatin's apartment what seemed like a million years ago, but shortly after eight o'clock he had taken a bus from Kutuzovsky Prospekt to within half a block of his apartment building.

Moscow was a city of the day, and now it had come alive. The sidewalks were filled with pedestrians hurrying to work, the subways were crammed, and there was even a moderately heavy amount of automobile and truck traffic along the streets and broad thoroughfares.

The second hurdle he would have to face this morning was the situation at the embassy between Carlisle and Congdon and this operation. There were too many incongruities. Too many loose ends that had to be tied up.

As he walked up from the bus stop he was deep in thought and did not notice the black Ford Cortina embassy car waiting outside his apartment building.

Finch, the night O.D., was behind the wheel and he rolled down the window. "Mr. Mahoney," he called out.

Mahoney stopped and looked up. Finch had a worried expression on his face.

"Mr. Carlisle sent me here for you. Said you're needed."

Mahoney approached the car. "How long have you been here?"

"About half an hour, sir."

Mahoney turned. The Soviet guard by the front door was watching them.

"I knocked on your door, but there was no answer," Finch was saying. "We were getting worried. We didn't know where you were."

"I was out . . . " Mahoney started to say turning back, but then his blood ran cold. "What did you say?"

Finch looked up at him confused. "Sir . . . ?"

Mahoney reached through the open window and grabbed the man by the coat collar and pulled him forward so that his head banged on the doorframe. "What did you say about no one being home?"

"Please . . . Mr. Mahoney . . . you're hurting me."

Mahoney let the man go, turned and ran up the stairs into his apartment building, then took the stairs two at a time, his heart pounding and his breath ragged.

He would not let himself think it. He forced his mind blank. But his insides felt as if someone had kicked him.

On the third floor he rushed to the rear of the building, taking out his keys as he ran. The door was unlocked.

He entered his apartment and stopped short in the middle of the living room. It was deathly still. He could hear someone coming up the stairs at a run, probably Finch, as he strained to hear a sound, anything from the kitchen or the bedroom.

"Marge?" he called out as he moved slowly into the bedroom.

The bed was neatly made, and Mahoney could not tell if it had been slept in last night or not. The bathroom was empty and the kitchen was cleaned, the dishes stacked in the drain.

Finch came into the apartment as Mahoney went back out into the living room and threw open the closet door. Marge's coat and her umbrella were still there.

He stood for a moment holding onto the doorframe with one hand and the closet door with the other staring at Marge's coat and umbrella. She would not leave without them. Not on a day like this. She would not have left, that is, voluntarily.

Mahoney turned slowly to look at Finch who was staring at him. "Where is she?" he asked, his voice low and menacing.

Finch backed up a step. "Your wife, sir?"

"Where is she, Finch?" Mahoney said, closing the closet door and advancing a step.

"I don't know, Mr. Mahoney. There was no one here when I arrived," he said as he backed out the front door and into the corridor.

Mahoney followed him relentlessly, almost like an animal stalking its prey. "Carlisle said nothing to you?"

Finch was shaking his head. "Nothing, Mr. Mahoney. He just told me to come and pick you up, and bring you back to the embassy immediately. He said it was urgent. For your own safety."

"Zamyatin," Mahoney said half under his breath. He slammed the apartment door behind him, grabbed the obviously frightened O.D. by the arm and hustled him down the stairs.

The Soviet guard stepped out of his box as Mahoney and Finch emerged from the door. Without breaking his stride, Mahoney just glanced at the guard and said, "Don't," in Russian and continued down the stairs and across the sidewalk to the car.

He released Finch. "You drive."

Finch just stood there confused. "Back to the embassy, sir?" he asked.

Mahoney shook his head. "Get in, goddammit," he shouted, and he opened the door and climbed in the passenger side.

A moment later Finch came around the car and slipped in behind the wheel. He started the engine, put the car in gear, and then turned to Mahoney.

"Mr. Carlisle was upset. He gave me specific orders . . ."

"Screw Carlisle," Mahoney said savagely. He pulled out his .45, yanked the slide back and pointed the gun toward Finch, keeping it below the level of the window so that the Russian guard who was watching them could not see. "Kutuzovsky Prospekt. Number eighteen. Now!"

Finch's eyes had grown wide. "Yessir," he said, and he pulled away from the curb.

The entire fucking thing had been a setup. The thought burned deeply in Mahoney's mind. He put his gun away. But why? They wanted something from him. But what?

It was not merely hard intelligence. Or at least it did

not seem that way to Mahoney. At least not on the basis of what he and Zamyatin had talked about last night.

But it was some kind of Russian operation. Mahoney was almost certain of it. It was an operation that had been deliciously elegant, at least to this point. It was almost like some sort of vast chess game, a game at which the Russians were masters.

It had begun legitimately enough in the KGB, Mahoney thought, and he held on to that premise almost like a drowning man holds onto a life preserver. Or was it a straw?

"The kidnaping happened around midnight Saturday," Zamyatin had said looking up from where he sat on the couch.

Mahoney had taken a small glass of the vodka and he sipped at it thoughtfully. "Why are you telling me this?"

Zamyatin looked at him through red-rimmed eyes. A picture of George Congdon looking similarly distressed popped into Mahoney's mind, and he wondered at the similarity between the two men.

"Something is going to happen tomorrow morning," Zamyatin said. "Can't you see that? We've got to stop it. You and I."

"Why us? Why have we been dragged into this?"

Zamyatin shook his head in despair. "Why is anyone dragged into anything? We're in the business, that's why. We were handy."

"It doesn't wash, Yurianovich," Mahoney said. "We have your children."

"Almost better you than us . . . " Zamyatin said

under his breath. Mahoney did not quite catch the words.

"What did you say?

Again Zamyatin shook his head. "Nothing," he said and stared at Mahoney, then took a deep swallow from his glass. "You have my children?"

"No. But they are in the embassy. I am sure of it."

"And your children? Michael and John and his wife and your three grandchildren?"

Mahoney's gut tightened. "My own people picked them up just as your agents were about to grab them. We forced your men to send the affirmative signal."

"Who told you that?"

"Carlisle."

Zamyatin smiled. "And you believed him? You have spoken with your children?"

Again Mahoney's gut tightened. "I spoke to them on the telephone," he lied. "Carlisle was telling me the truth."

Zamyatin looked away. "I proposed the order to have them picked up. We needed a lever against you."

Mahoney said nothing, thinking of his own order against Zamyatin's children. An order that had successfully been carried out.

"I didn't like it. I didn't want to do it, you must understand that. I withdrew the order, but it was too late. You were to be converted. They wanted you as a double. You are in a good position. You could have proved very useful."

"What was I to you?" Mahoney asked, feeling a sense of pity for the man.

"If your president is assassinated tomorrow there

will very likely be a war. No matter whose plot it was. Your government could not sit still."

"And your government would have to make a preemptive strike."

Zamyatin shrugged. "It would be a moot point. Once the shots were fired there would be no end to it." He looked into Mahoney's eyes with a strange intensity. "That cannot be allowed to happen. We must stop it. You and I."

Mahoney's right eyebrow arched. "Spell it out."

Zamyatin smiled, but the gesture was not a happy one. "Communications, Mahoney. That is what you and I need before it is too late for even us to do anything."

Mahoney inclined his head slightly. "The Center was lit up like a Christmas tree all day Sunday. Why?"

"Sakharov and the laser device were kidnaped. General Barynin himself called the Komitet's officer corps together for a meeting."

"Unusual."

"Unprecedented. The budget was unlimited. All standard operations were suspended for the duration, and each duty chief, each section head, each division commander, and each directorate administrator was instructed to operate as if someone in his area of expertise, some organization internal or external to the Soviet Union, had kidnaped the scientist and his deadly machine."

"Did Barynin tell you why Sakharov had been kidnaped?"

"No. He only told us that two men identifying themselves as Fifth Chief Directorate officers came for the professor and took him away. We were given composite drawings of the two men based on the university guards' descriptions."

"And?"

Zamyatin shrugged. "They are Russian, but beyond that I do not know."

"Anyone else in the Center recognize them?"

"We do not have interdepartmental communications at my level."

"No," Mahoney said, sighing. "Neither do we." He was thinking of Congdon's and Carlisle's relationship. "So you went on a full Center alert to find Sakharov and the laser."

"Yes," Zamyatin said. "But with one curious provision. That the operation, which has been labeled CLEAN SWEEP, be completed no later than 1100 hours Thursday."

Mahoney's breath caught in his throat. "That is the president's ETA at Vnukovo."

Zamyatin ignored the conclusion. "My department concerns itself with every foreign embassy in this town except for the Chinese. The completion time and date General Barynin imposed on us made me think of the American embassy."

"I don't follow you."

Zamyatin laughed sardonically. "Kennedy's assassination was a CIA plot."

"Don't be an ass," Mahoney snapped. "Some of the best investigators in the world have been over that theory a hundred times. It doesn't hold up. Oswald killed Kennedy. If anything, the man had connections with *your* people."

"Let us not argue the point. It is meaningless at this late date. Suffice it to say my feelings about the matter—my beliefs—caused me to take a look at operations in your embassy."

"Our surveillance told us that the Center was on full alert, so we geared up an operation, labeled LOOK SEE to see what you people were up to. We were using the preparations for our president's arrival as a cover."

"The presidential preparations were a cover, all right," Zamyatin agreed. "But for what?"

Mahoney said nothing, his thoughts once again going back to Congdon and to Carlisle. What *was* going on under his nose in the embassy? Stewart Anderson was not in on it, Mahoney was certain of it, although this mess had come up when the ambassador himself was conveniently out of the country.

Zamyatin had gotten up from the couch, and had gone to the window and was peering out at the falling snow. "Whoever is pulling the strings is doing so on two levels," he said, not turning around. "Either that or someone is taking advantage of an existing situation."

He turned around finally and came slowly back to the couch. Before he sat down he poured himself and Mahoney more vodka from the bottle which was now nearly empty.

"To life," he said, holding up his glass.

Mahoney toasted with him, and they both drank. Then Zamyatin sat down.

"We went on full Center alert, and your people found out about it. You in turn went on embassy alert and my people found out about that."

"The opening moves," Mahoney said, putting his glass down.

"Yes, my old friend, but you must understand those

were the opening moves for only one of the games. There are two operations going on at the same time. I'm convinced of it."

"Go on," Mahoney said.

"Whoever was calling the shots for this operation was looking for a contact. We're busy, you're busy—what better time for tendrils to snake out? We wanted to know what your people were up to and you wanted to know what was going on with us."

"You're saying some kind of a contact had to be made?"

"Exactly. Sooner or later there had to be a point of contact between our two services. It just happened to be between us."

"You mean *you*," Mahoney said. "It was you who contacted me, remember?"

"Yes, but it had to happen sooner or later. If not between you and me, then between your cook from Tennessee and one of my people."

"Zeta-one, I believe he was called," Mahoney said. The class six review of personnel had uncovered the man's regular contacts with the Soviets. Last night he had been shipped back to the States to stand trial.

"Congratulations," Zamyatin said.

"He couldn't have been much help."

"No, he wasn't," Zamyatin admitted. "But he was better than nothing until you and I came along."

"We did," Mahoney said after a moment's hesitation. "And the game moved into high gear."

"I had to be sure of your cooperation," Zamyatin said, obviously with much distaste. "And you had to be sure of mine. I ordered the kidnaping of your children and you ordered the kidnaping of mine."

"Two minds working along the same path. I didn't like it any better than you did, Yurianovich," Mahoney said. "I, too, withdrew my recommended order."

"Carlisle?"

Mahoney nodded. "He wouldn't leave it alone."

"Neither would my people."

"It would appear, however, that the weapons we were to use against each other have been neutralized."

Zamyatin looked startled.

"My people picked up your children as planned, and in addition they picked up my kids and placed them in protective custody. But you don't believe that."

"No," Zamyatin said. "I have it on the highest authority that my children are in protective custody in the Center, and that yours are being held someplace in Montana."

"You have spoken with your children?"

Zamyatin nodded. "It is a holiday for them—no school. And I promised to take them on a regular holiday as soon as this is over with."

Zamyatin was lying, of course, but Mahoney derived no pleasure from that knowledge, because it was very possible that Carlisle had lied to him about his children being in protective custody in San Diego.

"So," Mahoney said. "As it turns out we have no levers to use against each other. The operation is neutralized."

"So it would appear."

"Then why are we talking with each other?"

"Because there still is the problem of Sakharov and the laser and your president."

Mahoney looked up out of his reflections at Finch

who was glancing at him from time to time as he drove. The rain was falling so hard that the windshield wipers were nearly useless, and Finch had slowed the car to a crawl.

"Mr. Carlisle is going to raise hell when we get back," Finch said.

"You're a good man," Mahoney said. "Don't get yourself involved in this. You'll get mauled."

The man flinched. "Yes, sir. I hope you know what you're doing."

"I don't," Mahoney mumbled, and he went back to his thoughts.

"I found no connection between Carlisle and Nikolai Gamov." Mahoney said, telling another lie.

"Nevertheless it is documented," Zamyatin said. "But there is more now, much more. Some of it puzzling."

Mahoney had not smoked since he had arrived, but he pulled out a cigar now and began unwrapping it. "Are you still on the idea that the president is going to be assassinated."

"That's the second part of the operation," Zamyatin said with feeling. "It will happen, I am sure of it now."

Mahoney stopped what he was doing, the lit match held in mid-air several inches from the end of his cigar. The clock in the vestibule chimed five times, and Mahoney shook out the match. "What have you learned?"

Zamyatin jumped up and began pacing the room. "I'll tell you everything. But you're going to have to help now. There is no way around it. Both of us are in it."

"Go on," Mahoney said, stuffing the unlit cigar back in his breast pocket.

Zamyatin continued his pacing. "First of all there is no disputing the fact that Nikolai Gamov, the Nobel Prize winning writer, is nominally a CIA agent. More specifically we believe that Gamov has and is supplying Carlisle with information about prisons throughout the Soviet Union. Additionally, Gamov is the leader of at least one faction of the Democratic Movement."

"Therefore, Carlisle may be pulling some of the Democratic Movement's strings."

"Exactly."

Mahoney no longer felt the idea was ridiculous. Carlisle was a highly capable man. If indeed he was in partial control of the Soviet dissident group, he would use them to his own best advantage, whatever that might be.

"A Volvo station wagon was found yesterday eight miles from Lubyanka II prison. Inside was found a very small blood stain—the same blood type as the murdered guard—and one clip of automatic rifle ammunition."

Mahoney just watched Zamyatin pace.

"The station wagon has been identified. It belongs to a close personal friend of Nikolai Gamov's. A fellow member of the Democratic Movement. He is missing at the moment."

Mahoney spoke up. "Carlisle is connected with Gamov. Gamov is connected with the murder of a prison guard. Therefore, Carlisle needed the prison guard's uniform, papers, and weapon for some reason."

Zamyatin had stopped and he was looking across the room at Mahoney. "Don't toy with this, Wallace," he said earnestly. "Please."

"I am not, Yurianovich," Mahoney said. "I promise."

"Something else came up . . . last night," Zamyatin said. Now he seemed agitated although he had stopped his pacing and was still staring at Mahoney. "One of my own people—Major Boris Balachov—chief of the department that is charged with watching your Embassy—I saw him with Nikolai Gamov last night."

"We're here, Mr. Mahoney," Finch was saying. "This is eighteen Kutuzovsky Prospekt."

Mahoney looked at the man hunched over the wheel peering through the windshield at the apartment building across the street.

Carlisle, Gamov, and Balachov. The American, the dissident, and the Russian.

Did *Carlisle* maneuver Gamov and the Democratic Movement into planning the assassination of President Forsythe tomorrow morning?

Did *Major Balachov* maneuver Gamov and the Democratic Movement into planning the assassination of President Forsythe tomorrow morning?

Or did *Gamov* himself for some reason or reasons unknown plan the assassination of President Forsythe tomorrow morning?

Mahoney wanted to be convinced that if Carlisle was behind the plan it was not intended to lead to the president's death, that it was some kind of an operation designed to upset the Russians—cause a flap and therefore cause someone, somewhere some embarrassment.

Mahoney shook his head.

That was too thin. Too weak. There was something else. Something missing.

He focused on Finch and then looked out the window. Zamyatin's apartment building was across the street.

"Wait here," he said and reached for the door handle, but Finch pulled his arm back.

"I don't know what you've got in mind, Mr. Mahoney, but I hope you have thought it out."

Mahoney looked at him, but the image of Marge in his mind's eye was overwhelming. "Just be here; I'll need some quick transportation."

Finch looked alarmed. "Sir," he said. "What . . . I mean you aren't . . . ?"

"Just be here," Mahoney said. "And keep the car running." He got out of the car, crossed the street in the heavy rain and entered Zamyatin's apartment building.

Zamyatin had apparently known that his children were at the American embassy, and he had also known that Mahoney's children were safe. The only point of weakness left was Marge. And for that, the sonofabitch would die.

Heedless of the odd looks he had gotten from a number of people in the lobby of the building, Mahoney took the stairs up to Zamyatin's fifth floor apartment where he stopped at the door to listen. He could hear someone moving around inside.

Evidently Zamyatin had not yet gone to the Center. When they had parted less than an hour before, they had agreed to return to their respective offices and dig for more answers. If there indeed was a plot against President Forsythe's life, it would have to be stopped.

Mahoney pulled his .45 from beneath his coat and tried the door. It was unlocked. He cocked the hammer of the gun, took a deep breath, threw open the door and leaped inside.

The apartment was in a mess. Furniture was overturned and cut apart, stuffing strewn everywhere. Drawers were out of cabinets, picture frames broken apart, and even the walls and ceilings had been broken into; gaping holes in the plaster exposed the studs and joists.

A wet overcoat and hat were flung carelessly atop the overturned couch.

Mahoney advanced a step, his mind racing to a dozen different possibilities, his heart hammering nearly out of his chest, and, curiously, Marge's soft, womanly smell of soap and perfume and shampoo sharp in his mind.

A large man, obviously Russian, appeared at the doorway from one of the back rooms.

For an instant he stood frozen, but then he grunted, dropped to one knee and fumbled beneath his coat.

Mahoney extended his right arm, almost in slow motion, and pulled the trigger of the .45. The gun bucked in his hand, the roar so loud it felt as if the entire room would collapse on his head, and the man in the doorway seemed to leap backward.

And then everything speeded up. Mahoney raced across the room, flattening himself against the wall next to the doorway. He cautiously peered around the doorframe into a bedroom that was in the same state of total disarray as the living room. No one was there except for the man at his feet whose legs were jerking spasmodically. Half the man's forehead was gone, the white matter of his brain mixed with bits of bone and frothy blood.

Mahoney bent down and quickly went through the man's pockets until he found his wallet. He straightened up and opened it. The man's photograph on a KGB identification card stared out at him.

Mahoney pocketed the wallet, went back to the front door and opened it a crack. The corridor was deserted, but for how long it would remain that way was anyone's guess, although Mahoney was fairly certain it would not be for long.

He slipped out of the apartment, carefully closing the door behind him, and with the .45 in his coat pocket, his finger on the trigger, he forced himself to walk at a normal pace to the stairwell, and then down the stairs to the ground floor.

The lobby was deserted when he came through the stairwell door, but as he went out the front door he could hear sirens in the distance.

Finch was still across the street in the embassy car, the motor running, and within a few seconds Mahoney was piling into the front seat beside the man.

"I want you to drive to the embassy now," Mahoney said. "But normally. Not too slow, not too fast. I don't want to attract any attention."

Finch put the car in gear and pulled away from the curb. He rolled up the window. "What happened up there? It sounded almost like a gunshot."

"It was," Mahoney said absently. He was thinking about Marge . . . dear sweet Marge . . . so he did not see the color drain from Finch's face.

XIV

Wednesday

A351FLASH

DAMASCUS, SYRIA (AP) . . . ISRAELI JETS ATTACKED THE SYRIAN CAPITAL CITY SHORTLY BEFORE DAWN.

A352BULLETIN

DAMASCUS, SYRIA (AP) . . . Israeli jets attacked the Syrian capital city shortly before dawn this morning killing, one official estimated, at least 100 civilians.

Meanwhile, Israeli troops and armored divisions poured north of the Sea of Galilee toward the city.

Observers here believe the specific military target is the Duma Military Supply Depot just north of the city.

The Israeli and Egyptian governments had

claimed tactical nuclear weapons were being stockpiled at Duma.

Mahoney barged into Carlisle's office. Stewart Anderson was seated across the desk talking with him and they both looked up, startled.

Mahoney pulled his .45 from his shoulder holster, cocked the hammer and pointed the gun directly at Carlisle. "Where is she?" he said, his voice low.

The color drained from Carlisle's face and Anderson's mouth was opening and closing, but no sounds were coming out.

"Where is she, goddammit!" Mahoney shouted. He could feel what little control he had leaving him.

Carlisle reached for the telephone, but Mahoney was across the room in three steps and with his free hand knocked the phone off the desk. He pressed the barrel of the .45 directly against Carlisle's forehead.

"If you move, I'll kill you," Mahoney said.

Carlisle's face was beginning to turn red.

"I want to know where my wife is."

"She's here. In the embassy," Anderson said.

Mahoney glanced down at the man hunched in his chair, and then looked back at Carlisle. "Is that true?"

"Yes," Carlisle said, the word choking out of him. "We had to get her out of the apartment. They were closing in."

Mahoney began to shake as the relief washed through him. He stepped back, uncocked the gun and put it back in its holster. "Where is she?" he said.

"In VIP housing. Unit two," Anderson said. He had regained his control. Carlisle, however, was still plainly shook.

Mahoney turned to go.

"Wait," Carlisle shouted.

At the door, his hand on the knob, Mahoney paused.

"It's about your children," Carlisle said.

Something stabbed at Mahoney's gut, and his breath caught in his throat. He slowly turned back to face the man. Anderson looked sympathetic, but Carlisle looked worried.

"John and his wife and your three grandchildren are at the Presidio. We're sending you and Marge back to the States tomorrow morning. You will be able to see them."

The children. Mahoney could clearly remember what he and Marge were doing each time they got the call that John's wife had had a baby. And each time after the telephone call Marge had phoned Michael with the news and invariably she got around to her favorite subject. When was Michael going to settle down, marry, and have children.

"Michael," Mahoney mumbled. "Where is Michael?"

Carlisle got up and came slowly around from behind his desk.

"I said where is Michael?" Mahoney snapped. The harshness of his voice stopped Carlisle short.

"I'm sorry . . . " Carlisle began to say.

The ache was in Mahoney's gut again. He wanted to lash out and hit something. Anything. Carlisle.

Carlisle had selected a piece of yellow paper from his desk and he held it out toward Mahoney. It looked like a copy of a teletype message.

Mahoney moved away from the door and took the paper from Carlisle and quickly scanned the story. It was an Associated Press dispatch, dateline Missoula, Montana. Three men who had apparently burglarized the Forest Products Laboratory near Missoula had burned to death when the car they were in crashed.

One of the men was believed to have been an employee of the FPL. The other two men were unidentified.

Mahoney looked up. "Michael?" he asked.

Carlisle nodded his head. "We missed them by half an hour."

"Michael?" Mahoney said again. His legs felt like rubber, and his head was spinning.

"Marge has not been told yet," Carlisle was saying. "Perhaps you should go to her."

Mahoney looked at Carlisle for a long time before he spoke. He was aware of Anderson out of the corner of his eye. The man was still seated by Carlisle's desk, but he was staring toward the window.

"How about the operation?" Mahoney asked. "The president tomorrow."

Carlisle shook his head. "The operation is over with. It is finished."

"Zamyatin? Gamov?" Mahoney asked. "Do you know about Balachov?"

"Yes I do. But the operation is finished. You and Marge are going home."

Mahoney took a step closer to the man and Carlisle backed up.

"It's not what you think, Wallace," Carlisle said in alarm.

It had been a setup. From day one it had been nothing more than a Carlisle scheme. And whatever else happened now, he was getting out. Quitting the company, just like Marge had suggested. He had had enough. More than enough.

He turned without another word and left Carlisle's office. It was nearly ten in the morning. The last time he had slept had been Monday night, and now everything that had happened in those hours was catching up with him. His legs throbbed, his gut ached, and his head felt as if it were detached from the rest of his body and floating somewhere near the ceiling.

The corridors and offices were filled and busy, and as he worked his way over to the housing section of the embassy complex several people called greetings to him. But he heard none of it.

How could he tell Marge that her favorite son was dead? He had not been shot down in Vietnam. He had not given his life saving a drowning boy. He had not even gotten himself lost in the woods and died of exposure in the line of duty for some Forest Products Laboratory project.

How could he tell Marge that Michael had died because his father was in the wrong kind of a business for a man with a family?

How?

The VIP guest quarters of embassy housing looked like any Holiday Inn the world over. Here was carpeting, wood paneled walls, recessed lighting and piped-in music. A marine guard stood duty at the entry door, a precaution taken only when the president, vice president or secretary of state was due to arrive.

Unit one, which was reserved solely for the president if and when he ever visited the Soviet Union, would now be sealed off until the Man arrived. Marge had been given the second best unit.

Mahoney showed the marine guard his identification, signed the visitor's log, and shuffled down the wide corridor past the presidential suite to the second unit.

He hesitated a moment at the door, took a deep breath and went inside.

Marge was seated on a long divan in the large, well appointed sitting room, sipping coffee from a silver service with Mrs. Leland Smith, the ambassador's wife.

Both women looked up, Marge's face lighting up with a bright smile that almost immediately darkened to a frown.

The ambassador's wife put her cup down and got up. "Mr. Mahoney," she smiled, her voice smooth and confident. "Your wife and I have had the loveliest of chats." She came forward and held out her hand.

Mahoney shook it delicately as Mrs. Smith looked into his eyes. There was a certain shrewdness about the woman that in itself commanded respect.

"Mrs. Smith," he said politely.

"I understand that you and Margery will be leaving us tomorrow," the woman said conversationally. "I for one will be sorry to see your delightful wife go. I had no idea how charming a woman she is."

"Yes," Mahoney said, and he felt slightly foolish that he could think of nothing else to say.

The ambassador's wife glanced back at Marge. "Well, my dear, I will leave you two alone. But remember we are scheduled for tea with some of the other ladies at four."

Marge had not moved from her spot on the couch,

nor had she even put down her coffee cup. She was staring at her husband.

"See you then," Mrs. Smith said, and she went out the door, closing it softly behind her.

Mahoney remained where he was standing and after a moment, Marge reached forward and set her coffee cup down, and then managed a slight smile.

"I was so excited when the ambassador's wife herself came calling for me this morning that I completely fell to pieces."

Mahoney said nothing.

"I forgot my raincoat and my umbrella, and I even forgot to leave you a note, poor dear," she said. "But when she came to my door personally and said a car was waiting, I just lost my head. We came right here and had coffee. She is such a wonderful lady. She said that we were leaving tomorrow. And that certainly came as a surprise."

Mahoney came all the way into the room, sat down on the couch next to his wife and took her hands in his.

"We must leave," he said. "I am in danger of being arrested by the Russians for spying."

"There has been some trouble?"

Mahoney nodded. "Yes, Marge, there has been some trouble."

"You poor dear," she said. "You must have been out of your mind with worry when you came home and found out I was gone. I didn't leave a note or anything. I'm sorry, Wallace, I'll never . . ."

"Margery," Mahoney said, interrupting her.

She looked at him, her eyes gentle and understanding, almost like a salve on a wound. She had been there when Michael was a baby, as any mother would be. She had been there when Michael was five and he fell off his tricycle and broke his arm. She had been there when he fell out of his tree house and broke his nose. He was only twelve. And she had been there when, as a senior in high school, he broke his leg skiing. Only this time she could not be there. Never again could she be there. It was too late.

Mahoney started to cry, the sobs wracking his entire body. Marge cradled him in her arms and made soothing sounds as she rocked him back and forth like a mother would a child.

It had been so useless, so fucking useless, one part of his brain cried out in despair. But another part of him, the rational, more professional self, remained detached. It was his training and experience.

"Intelligence coups are the stuff of spy novels, and spy novels alone," he himself had told a young staffer once.

"Shoot 'em ups, cloaks and daggers, fake passports, safehouses, planes to Lisbon, wild Nazi plots for a new Third Reich . . . all those are elements of a James Bond movie, and hardly ever the real world.

"A good intelligence officer is nothing more or nothing less than an astute observer of human nature. Have dinner with a foreign diplomat and his wife and observe their reactions to what you say for a clue to how they feel and what they are doing.

"Read a foreign newspaper or watch a foreign news broadcast, pay attention to local elections, and haunt the news venders to see just what books and magazines the government you are studying allows its populace to read."

John had been the good boy. The boy they never had to worry about. Straight A student all the way through school. The one to volunteer to cut the grass. Up early on Saturdays. The one to go to church with his mother without being asked.

Michael, on the other hand, was their rascal. Until his last year in high school he only ever had two grades. The D's were for the serious subjects and the occasional C's were for the snap courses.

He had been the one to first sass back. He was the one who was never able to make it home from a date on time. He was the one who was forever borrowing against his allowance although he never wanted to do a thing around the house.

But Michael was the one whose cup ran over with love and enthusiasm.

Steady John. Rock of Gibraltar John. Free and easy Michael. Michael, the boy with the laughing eyes.

Mahoney was drifting. He knew he was drifting and he wanted to stop it but he could not.

He was only faintly conscious of Marge moving away from him and laying him back on the couch. What seemed like years later she was standing over him, pulling a blanket up under his chin, and then taking off his shoes.

Then nothing.

Mahoney sat straight up with a start, the blanket falling away from him. The room was dark, the only light coming from under the corridor door.

The telephone rang again, and he realized that must have been what had awakened him.

He pulled the blanket off his legs, got up and headed

for the door as the phone rang again. In a moment he had found the light switch and he flipped it on.

The telephone was across the room on a low table. He stumbled over to it as it rang again, and picked it up. "Yes?"

"Do you feel better now that you've slept?" It was Carlisle.

"Where is my wife?"

"At Congdon's apartment with Zamyatin's children."

Mahoney looked at his watch. It was nearly ten o'clock. He had slept for twelve hours. "I don't want her involved."

"Like I told you this morning, Wallace, this operation is over with. You and Marge are leaving in the morning. Everything you own has been packed and shipped from your apartment out to Vnukovo. We've got diplomatic passports for both of you. There will be no trouble tomorrow."

"How did you do that?" Mahoney heard himself asking, although he didn't care. He was seeing Michael again in his mind's eye.

"The ambassador returned this afternoon. He has been appraised of the situation, and he arranged it."

Mahoney said nothing.

"I'm in my office. I want you to come over here now."

"No," Mahoney said flatly.

"I need your report," Carlisle said. "Finch told me there was a gunshot."

Mahoney sighed deeply. "I'll be right there."

"Good," Carlisle said and hung up.

Mahoney put the phone down, went into the bathroom and splashed some water on his face. He looked like hell. His eyes were bloodshot and baggy, he needed a shave, and he felt as if he hadn't taken a bath in years.

What he wanted most of all now was a hot bath, a stiff drink or two, a little something to eat and another twelve hours of sleep with Marge by his side.

But those pleasures would have to wait. Above all else Mahoney had always been, was now, and would probably forever be, a man of duty.

He dried his face and hands, went back into the sitting room and pulled on his shoes and his jacket, went out the door and shuffled down to the guard post at the end of the corridor.

The young marine on duty had watched Mahoney coming and at the last moment he jumped up. "May I see your identification, sir?" he asked in a Southern drawl.

Mahoney stopped directly in front of the young man who towered over him, and smiled.

The marine seemed startled. "Your identification, please," he repeated, this time with a certain amount of sternness in his voice as if someone who looked as bad as Mahoney had absolutely no business being here.

Mahoney reached inside his coat for his wallet and the marine reached for the gun strapped at his hip. When he saw Mahoney had only pulled out a wallet he relaxed slightly.

Mahoney flipped the wallet open and handed it to the young man who took it and looked down at the ID that identified Mahoney as a trade mission specialist.

"Has the president arrived yet?" Mahoney asked taking the wallet back.

"No, sir," the marine replied with the same sternness.

"Then relax," Mahoney said with obvious amusement, and he turned and headed down the corridor toward White Room territory, leaving the marine wondering just who the hell he was.

Carlisle was in his office when Mahoney knocked once and entered. He indicated a chair for Mahoney to sit down as he poured a drink from a decanter into a large glass.

"Bourbon. No ice. Is that right?" Carlisle asked, handing the drink across the desk.

Mahoney accepted the glass and took a deep drink, the liquor warming his insides and straightening out the knot in his stomach. "Did you bring my cigars as well?"

Carlisle smiled. "You were out, actually, so I got you some more. Probably the last Cubans you'll get for a while." He opened his desk drawer, took out a cigar box and handed it across the desk.

Mahoney took out a cigar and after he had it lit he sat back in his chair and took another deep drink.

"The gunshot," Carlisle said. "Was it Zamyatin?"

"No," Mahoney said, and he took the KGB agent's wallet out of his pocket and handed it to Carlisle. "He had Zamyatin's apartment pretty well torn up."

Carlisle had flipped the wallet open and was looking at it. "You thought Zamyatin had Marge picked up?"

Mahoney nodded. "The president is in no real danger tomorrow, is he?"

"No," Carlisle said.

"And Nikolai Gamov?"

"I was running him. But he was nothing more than a very low-level intelligence source. It was a favor, as a matter of fact, to the State Department. They wanted something on prisons. Gamov supplied it."

"And Sakharov?"

"He was mine also. It was a multi-station project. I ran him here, and the chief of station in Zurich ran a friend of his there. There was a lot of good material while it lasted."

"How about the laser Zamyatin was worried about?"

"No such device exists. Or rather I should say the lasers that had been developed that have any military potential would take a battleship to carry. Too much electronics."

"Zamyatin?" Mahoney asked, holding himself in check. He felt as if he were on the verge of exploding—literally exploding—into a million tiny pieces.

Carlisle shrugged.

"One last question," Mahoney said, setting his glass down on the edge of the desk.

Carlisle's eyebrows rose.

"Why?"

"Why what? Why weren't you informed from the beginning? Or why are you being shipped out? Why what?"

"Why did my son die?"

Carlisle looked uncomfortable. "It was an accident, Wallace. Nothing more than an unfortunate accident."

Mahoney still held himself in check although it was difficult. "You owe me an explanation."

Carlisle looked even more uncomfortable. "No," he said. "You are put out of the operation. There is no longer a need to know."

"I'll go to the newspapers."

"You'll go to jail," Carlisle said. Sweat was forming on his forehead.

"I'm an old man. It doesn't matter. My son is dead."

"Leave it alone," Carlisle pleaded. "Leave here tomorrow and forget about it."

Mahoney was shaking his head. "No chance. You want my report on Zamyatin, I want your explanation. It will be a trade."

"I can't."

"I'll name names. Yours included."

"I'm shipping out within the month myself."

"I'll find you if necessary."

Carlisle looked like a cornered animal. "Why are you doing this, Wallace? What can you possibly gain?"

Mahoney sat forward. "My son is dead. I want to know if it was worth it. I want to know if I am going to be able to face myself in the mornings."

Behind Carlisle the window was nothing more than a dark square, and Mahoney could see his reflection in the glass. It was as if he were looking over Carlisle's shoulder at himself. He looked like a desperate man.

"What do you want to know?" Carlisle said finally.

Mahoney shifted his eyes to him. "Everything. Right from the beginning."

"And once you have that information?"

"Marge and I will go home. I am retiring."

Carlisle nodded. "I see," he said. "There are no records of this operation."

"Not even my RTA on Zamyatin's children? Or my contact reports?"

"Those," Carlisle conceded, "but nothing more. They are in one jacket, classified top secret. They won't be placed in our archives here. We're shipping the jacket back to Langley tomorrow in the pouch."

"Why?"

"That one I can't answer. The brass ordered it, that's all I know. When you get back you'll be debriefed."

"How did it begin?" Mahoney said. He sat back again with his cigar.

"About a year ago, just before I was assigned here, State asked me to look up a man by the name of Nikolai Gamov. He had won the Nobel Prize for his book on civil law and prisons within the Soviet Union and it was felt that he could be what they called 'a friend of the West.' "

"You came here and looked him up. Was he receptive?"

"Very," Carlisle said. "His philosophy is that all Russians should be friends of the West. Everyone should be friends with everyone else."

"Cozy."

"Rather," Carlisle said dryly. "At any rate, it was a low-level operation. Strictly extracurricular. I'd send a brief back to State every so often and everyone seemed happy. Until one month ago.

"I saw Gamov at a party and he told me that a Major Boris Azarov was attempting to infiltrate the Democratic Movement. He said he was afraid the KGB was closing in on them because of his contacts with me. He wanted to cool our relationship for a while."

"Azarov?" Mahoney asked. The name was not familiar to him.

"I put Switt on it. If the KGB was interested, then I figured we'd better take a closer look. As it turned out Azarov was really Major Boris Balachov, head of Zamyatin's Department One. Balachov had also gone under the name Leonard Skyles, supposedly an American businessman. He's used that ploy before to fool his fellow Russians, but of course the cover would never hold up with another American."

"So you informed Gamov that the KGB was indeed interested. In fact, since Balachov was head of Department One—the department that watches us—and since he was trying to infiltrate the Democratic Movement, then he must have known about your contacts with Gamov."

"I didn't tell Gamov a thing."

"You left him in the dark? Exposed like that?"

Carlisle nodded. "Gamov is a writer, not an actor. I wanted to see just what Balachov was up to."

"Which was?"

Carlisle smiled. "It was a fantastic plot, actually. Balachov convinced Gamov and the others that he could kidnap Sakharov and a portable laser device. His plan was to use the laser to kidnap President Forsythe when he arrived here in Moscow."

"Jesus," Mahoney said. "But why? What was the ransom going to be?"

"World peace. Human rights in the Soviet Union. The usual crap."

"And Gamov went along with this?"

"Only because I asked him to."

"Asked him, or forced him," Mahoney said sardonically. "I can see it now. You would have had photographs, perhaps tape recordings of your contacts with the man. Send those in a package over to Dzerzhinsky Square and Gamov would be on the first train to Siberia."

"Something like that," Carlisle said evenly.

"Gamov let Balachov into the fold and gave him a gold star for his plan."

Carlisle nodded. "As far as we can tell, someone from the T Directorate did the actual kidnaping of Sakharov and his briefcase. Meanwhile Balachov reported back to Gamov that he had the scientist and the laser in hiding. The morning the president arrived he could arrange to be in the control tower with the laser and Sakharov to operate it. From there the laser beam would have been aimed at the president. An announcement over the airport's public address system would have announced the fact, the president would have been hustled back aboard Air Force One, and the pilot would have been forced to take off and circle above Moscow. Meet our demands or else."

"How about the Lubyanka II guard? Who killed him, and how did he fit in?"

"The Komitet's thinking becomes a little thin at this point, but it goes back to the reason Balachov was ordered to infiltrate the Democratic Movement in the first place," Carlisle said. He paused a moment to marshal his thoughts, and Mahoney puffed on his cigar.

"The Democratic Movement had been a thorn in the Kremlin's side for a long time. First came Andrei Amalrik's book, *Will The Soviet Union Survive Until*

1984? Then came Solzhenitsyn's *The Gulag Archipelago,* which won him the Nobel Prize. And finally came Gamov's *Punishment Without Crime.* When it, too, won the Nobel Prize, the Party was shook up all the way down to the lowliest commandant in the boondocks."

"President Forsythe's comments about human rights in the Soviet Union could not have helped the situation either."

"Exactly," Carlisle said. "The Democratic Movement was becoming an embarrassment. But the kind of a thorn in the Kremlin's side that could not merely be plucked out. It would bleed all over the place. The harder the Kremlin would push on the Democratic Movement the more martyrs they would make. The entire Western world would have been in an uproar."

"The plan was to infiltrate the movement, set them up for an act of terrorism that would look bad in the eyes of the world, and then expose them. No hue and cry would be sounded if Gamov and his followers were executed. Kidnaping the president of the United States. A clear act of terrorism."

"That's correct as far as it goes," Carlisle said. "But there was much more."

"Weren't you taking a terrible risk that Gamov himself was playing the double? And that the kidnaping would actually take place?"

"I didn't think so at first," Carlisle said, and he looked somewhat uncomfortable again.

"Gamov did go for it, didn't he?"

Carlisle nodded his head very slightly. "We didn't tumble to it until the Lubyanka II guard was killed.

They needed a uniform, papers, and a weapon so that Gamov and his people could get close enough to the president at the airport to pull it off."

"And still you didn't call the president off?"

Carlisle said nothing.

"There's even more isn't there?"

Again Carlisle nodded. "General Barynin himself was in on this. Under orders, I presume, from the Kremlin."

Suddenly everything fell into place. Zamyatin's story, what Congdon had told him, what Carlisle had just said. All of it fell into place.

Mahoney got to his feet.

"Don't you want to hear the rest?"

Mahoney shook his head. "No need. I know what happened. But what about Congdon's wife, you bastard?"

Carlisle looked away.

"You used Gamov, you used me, but worst of all you used Congdon."

Still Carlisle held his silence.

Mahoney placed his hands on the desk and leaned forward, taking some of the pressure off his legs.

"General Barynin never does things one at a time. He is famous for his multiple operations. The Democratic Movement would be taken care of. Their plan with Balachov was working beautifully. So well, in fact, that Gamov—a man supposedly of peace—was moved to actually murder a Soviet guard. The Democratic Movement was in their pocket.

"They knew of your connection with Gamov, or at least guessed it, so Barynin ordered the entire shooting match over at Dzerzhinsky Square cranked up on alert to find Sakharov and the mythical laser. He was lying to his own people.

"Barynin and his planners knew damn well that Zamyatin could be maneuvered into contacting someone over here. And he did."

Something else suddenly and sickeningly came clear in Mahoney's mind.

"You knew that, didn't you, Carlisle?" he said, amazed. "You outthought Barynin almost from the start, didn't you?"

Carlisle would not look up.

Mahoney straightened up. "I was set up," he said softly. "From the beginning I was the patsy. You must have had a great laugh when I submitted the RTA on Zamyatin's kids. I was doing exactly what you wanted me to do. It was big. A worldwide KGB operation. So big I'd fall for it. Which is why you stepped on Congdon. If Congdon had told me that the Soviets were not deficit spending, and had no hard Western currency available I would have realized the operation was nothing more than a local push." Mahoney was tired all over again. "I was set up."

"Not really. Not at first. Not until Zamyatin contacted you. From that moment on I could not tell you the entire story. You would not have been as effective a contact."

"If I would have by chance been converted I would have had too much inside knowledge to give them."

"Right," Carlisle said.

"And Zamyatin—he was nothing more than a dupe like me. They were using him just like you used me."

"Hold it right there, mister," Carlisle said, looking

up. "What the hell do you think this was all about? Some Boy Scout picnic? I was doing my job. Nothing more. This didn't start out as my idea. It was a conspiracy all right. But not mine. The Kremlin came up with it. I just decided to play in the same ball game."

"A Kremlin conspiracy," Mahoney said softly. "I go home in one piece, more or less. But let's take a look at the casualties. First of all my son is dead. And for what reason I still don't know. For that alone I could kill you."

Carlisle started to protest, but the look in Mahoney's eyes stopped him. He suddenly knew that Mahoney was not lying.

"Gamov and the entire Democratic Movement is wiped out. Or will be shortly. So *they* won that inning. But Zamyatin is finished, so *we* won that round." Mahoney's eyes bored deeply into Carlisle's. "What about Zamyatin's children? They had no mother, and now there is no way we can give them back to their father."

"We'll drop them off in front of their apartment."

"What?" Mahoney shouted. "Their father is a traitor. What kind of a life will they have?"

Carlisle shrugged. "It can't be helped. Zamyatin is going to be a dead man very soon. We won what we started out to win. He was a highly effective officer. We've ruined him. As far as his children go, I am truly sorry, but there is nothing I can do about it. I'm sure the Soviet government will put them in a State home. They won't starve."

Mahoney suddenly turned away and stalked out the door no longer able to stand the sight of Carlisle. No one had come out unscathed in this operation except for

Carlisle himself, and his Soviet counterpart, Major Boris Balachov. Both of them would have promotions. They had earned it.

But there was one final question that Mahoney needed an answer to. Something that had plagued him for a very long time.

And before he and Marge got on that plane tomorrow morning, he was going to get the answer, and if possible set a few things straight.

XV

Early Thursday Morning

WASHINGTON, D.C. (AP) . . . President Forsythe left this morning aboard the Air Force One SST from Andrews Air Force Base for his scheduled meeting in Moscow with Soviet leaders.

Meanwhile, fighting stopped in Syria with Israeli troops surrounding the city of Damascus.

The president, before he left, said this would be the last war in the Middle East. His talks with Soviet leaders would assure that.

The marine guard at the front gate of the U.S. Embassy had not been told Mahoney could not leave embassy grounds so he thought nothing of it when the man, bundled in a raincoat, his hat pulled low, signed out and headed down the street on foot.

It was raining, as it had been all week, and Mahoney had to admit to himself a vast relief that he and Marge would be getting out of the Soviet Union for good. In only a few more hours their plane would be leaving for New York.

Zamyatin's children were the problem, he told himself. If Zamyatin was to be eliminated, what would become of his children?

The streets were dark and completely deserted as they usually were this late at night. Mahoney felt old, tired, used up. And no matter how hard he tried, he could not keep his thoughts from drifting back to his son Michael. His baby boy who could not stand to be confined to an office. Who had finally made something of himself. At Syracuse University he had become a straight A student almost overnight and an outstanding scholar all the way through his doctoral thesis and postdoctoral work in plant pathology.

God, what a waste. What a terrible waste.

The face of the KGB agent that Mahoney had killed in Zamyatin's apartment merged in his brain with the faces of Michael, of Marge, and of Zamyatin's three children.

They were still awake, playing the children's card game Go Fish with Marge, when Mahoney had left Carlisle's office and went down to Congdon's apartment.

Congdon was in his bedroom, and when Mahoney came in he came to the door. There were cardboard boxes strewn around the room and several half-packed suitcases lay open on the davenport and easy chair.

"I'm leaving in the morning on the same plane with you and Marge," Congdon said.

"I'm sorry George . . . " Mahoney started to say, but Congdon cut him off.

"The hell with it," Congdon said. "If it hadn't been

Carlisle it would have been someone else, somewhere else. It was time for me to bail out anyway."

The children had looked up and were staring wide-eyed at Mahoney, obvious fear in their expressions.

"Why don't you come with us, George," Marge said brightly. "We're having a family get-together in Montana. The mountains would be a nice place for a vacation. Michael could show you around."

Congdon did not look at Marge, and Mahoney knew that he had heard about Michael.

"I'm sorry Wallace. I'm truly sorry."

Marge's eyes had darted from her husband to Congdon and back to her husband again. She put down her cards and got slowly to her feet. "What is it, Wallace? You said there had been trouble. What kind of trouble?"

Congdon went back into the bedroom, and Mahoney went to his wife and took her in his arms.

"It's Michael," he said, and Marge stiffened. "There was a highway accident outside Missoula."

She pulled away from him and looked up into his eyes. "Michael is dead," she said with no trace of emotion, only tiredness, in her voice.

Mahoney barely nodded his head.

It took several seconds for her to react, and when she did it was as if she were melting. "Oh . . . Wallace . . . our son . . . our baby . . . " she mumbled, and she collapsed into her husband's arms.

Mahoney was crying, and Zamyatin's children were staring frankly at him, their mouths open and the fear that had been on their faces turning to an expression of bewilderment. They did not know what to do or where to go.

Despite his grief Mahoney's heart went out to the

children, and he managed a slight smile for them. "You will be safe here," he said softly to them over Marge's shoulder.

The oldest girl flinched. "We would like to go to our father," she said. Her English was heavily accented, but understandable.

Marge again pulled away from her husband. "It's all right now," she said, looking up into his eyes. And then she turned to look at the children. "What about the children's father?"

The boy said something to the oldest girl that Mahoney could not quite catch, but the other girl looked as if she was about to cry.

"Is this the American embassy?" the oldest girl asked.

"Yes, it is," Mahoney said.

"Why are we being held here?"

"My papa," the boy cried in Russian. "I want my papa."

The oldest girl moved around the table and took the boy in her arms. The other girl instinctively moved next to them.

"We don't care if you torture us. We will tell you nothing," the girl said.

"Oh, my God," Marge cried, stifling a gasp. "Wallace?" she said, glancing at her husband. Then she went around the table and put her arms around all three of the children.

"No one is going to hurt you," she said gently. "I promise."

The children were looking up at her, their expressions gradually softening. Marge was a woman who, no matter what the situation, people instinctively trusted and liked.

What she was doing was dangerous, Mahoney thought. She was transferring her grief about Michael to protectiveness toward these children. But it was a situation that could have no satisfactory solution for her. And he was worried for his wife.

"Marge . . . " he started to say.

"Don't worry about us, Wallace," she said. "I'm going to put them to bed. It's late."

"Are you going to stay here with them?"

"Yes," she said.

Mahoney stared at her for a moment longer, then sighed. "I'll be back in a few hours," he said.

A look of abject terror briefly crossed her face. She took a half step forward. "Wallace . . . don't do anything foolish . . . " she said.

"Don't worry, old woman," he said, smiling. He came around to her and kissed her on the cheek. "There is something that has to be attended to. I'll be back in a couple of hours."

"Must you?" she asked.

Mahoney nodded.

"Then be careful, old man," she said, and Mahoney turned and went out of the apartment.

His thinking had been very straighforward and even a bit company-oriented this morning, he told himself tiredly as he rounded the corner onto Kutuzovsky Prospekt and stopped in the shadows.

Zamyatin's building was across the street and half way down the block. There were a few lights shining from windows here and there in the building, but not in Zamyatin's apartment.

There was a good chance that the man was not at home. Possibly he was at his office, or he might have already been arrested.

Zamyatin was of no further use to the KGB. Carlisle was correct about that. But the man certainly would be of vast importance to the CIA if he could be gotten out of the country. And he was of even greater importance to his children.

There were no cars parked in front of Zamyatin's building and Mahoney could not detect any surveillance team.

So far as any of them knew, the KGB operation CLEAN SWEEP was still on the active list and would remain so until later this morning when the president arrived. Which meant that there was a possibility that Zamyatin was still around in one piece. At least for the time being.

The timing would be tight, but Mahoney figured if he could get to Zamyatin, convince him of what was happening, and what had been happening, they could return to the embassy, and later this morning he and his children could somehow be smuggled out to Vnukovo and gotten aboard the diplomatic plane for New York.

After that, Zamyatin would be debriefed, he and his children given new identities, and they could slip into anonymity in the United States.

That was the plan, as thin as it was, Mahoney told himself where he stood. But General Barynin's operations were never run on a single level. Maybe this too was a setup. Maybe at this point Zamyatin was being used as bait.

He moved out of the shadows and slowly walked toward Zamyatin's building. There was someone watching. Mahoney was almost certain of it. He could feel it in the air.

Across the street he entered the deserted lobby and

started up the stairs. The biggest problem, he told himself, might not be getting back to the embassy. It could very well be convincing Zamyatin to come with him.

He stopped at the first floor landing to listen, but there were absolutely no sounds except for his own breathing. No one was following him. Yet.

They would be watching the Finnish border and probably would not be paying too much attention to Vnukovo which would be crowded with people coming to see the American president. They could do it. But only if Zamyatin cooperated.

On the second floor landing Mahoney paused again to listen. And again there were no indications that he was being pursued.

At the very least, Zamyatin would be fired from his job and would be banished from Moscow. Internal exile, they called it. A very effective weapon against a man like Zamyatin with three children.

Mahoney resumed his climb to the fifth floor landing where he stopped long enough to take the .45 out of his shoulder holster and with his finger on the trigger stuffed it into his coat pocket. With his other hand he opened the corridor door and silently hurried to Zamyatin's door.

There were no sounds from within, and like before, the door was unlocked. Just inside the vestibule Mahoney closed the door behind him and carefully moved a few steps forward, stumbling and almost falling over something large on the floor.

Mahoney bent down and reached out in the darkness, and his fingers brushed the cold, firm flesh of a dead man's face. He recoiled, almost falling backward.

And then he heard the sound, low and animal-like coming from somewhere within the apartment. He strained to hear more clearly and suddenly he realized what it was. Someone was crying. Sobbing. But very softly.

"Yurianovich?" Mahoney called.

The crying stopped, and the apartment was deathly still.

"Yurianovich," Mahoney called again. "It is Mahoney. Wallace Mahoney."

"You have my children," Zamyatin's ragged voice came from the living room. Something crashed in the dark, Zamyatin swore, and a moment later a light came on.

Major Boris Balachov lay on his side on the floor directly in front of Mahoney. His eyes were open and his skin was a pasty white. He had been dead for several hours. The handle of a butcher knife protruded from the middle of a large dark stain in his back.

Suddenly Zamyatin was standing there, obviously drunk, his hair disheveled, his eyes bloodshot, and his clothes a mess.

"This heathen came looking for me. Said I was a traitor. Said he hoped I would never see my children again," Zamyatin slobbered. He peered down at Mahoney still on his hands and knees. "But I believed him when he told me that you have my children. You do have my children?"

Mahoney got slowly to his feet, the effort taking almost more strength than he had. "I have your children. They are safe. They are with my wife."

Zamyatin lurched forward, stumbling over

Balachov's body and falling heavily into Mahoney's arms.

"They're all I have, Mahoney. Don't you see?"

Mahoney helped Zamyatin back to his feet, stepped over the body, and led him back into the living room. Zamyatin had evidently turned the couch upright, but had done nothing else to straighten up the apartment. The body of the KGB agent Mahoney had shot earlier was gone, and he wondered if they knew or suspected who had killed the man.

He sat Zamyatin down on the couch and quickly rummaged around the apartment finally finding Zamyatin's coat and hat in a pile in the kitchen.

When he returned to the living room Zamyatin was drinking out of a half full bottle of vodka. An empty bottle was laying near the couch.

Mahoney took the bottle away from Zamyatin and threw it down, then pulled the man to his feet and helped him struggle into his coat and hat.

"I'm taking you to your children. And then all of us are getting out of the country."

"No," Zamyatin shouted, pulling away from Mahoney. He was still drunk but he seemed suddenly more in control of himself. "I'm not a traitor, Mahoney. Despite what Balachov thought, and despite what you are trying to do."

"The operation was a setup from the beginning," Mahoney said. They did not have much time left. "Both of us were set up. And now it's over with."

Zamyatin was shaking his head. "Balachov and the Democratic Movement are going to kidnap the president. *Kidnap* him, not assassinate him."

"No," Mahoney said. "That was a setup, too. Your people wanted only to discredit the Democratic Movement. Meanwhile, you and I were supposed to convert each other. Our children were the trump cards."

"But the president," Zamyatin mumbled.

"There was no real plot, Yurianovich, you've got to see that. Balachov was running the Democratic Movement for your people, and Carlisle was running the movement for us. We got caught in the middle."

"You grabbed my children anyway," Zamyatin said bitterly. "You are no better than the rest of them."

"My youngest son was killed when your people tried to grab him," Mahoney said softly.

Zamyatin just looked at him.

"My son is dead. Your children are safe and sound."

Zamyatin reached out and touched Mahoney's arm. "I'm sorry, Wallace. I am sorry. None of this should have happened."

"Just like World War II," Mahoney heard himself saying. He was angry. Where Marge had transferred her grief into concern for Zamyatin's three children, Mahoney was turning his grief into hostility against Zamyatin.

"What?" Zamyatin asked confused.

"World War II. Remember? The Obersalzburg? The German soldiers you tortured for information? Remember?"

Zamyatin said nothing.

"I can understand you the way you are now, Yurianovich. I can understand you and your children. And, God help me, I can even understand why you proposed kidnaping my children to use them as a lever against me. I did the very same thing. But I cannot understand how you could have changed since the war. Unless you haven't."

"The Nazis tortured and killed my mother, my father, my sisters and my younger brother. They thought they were Jews. There were people who survived. I learned about it. I knew it before I was assigned to the Obersalzburg. A lot of us knew."

"I understand," Mahoney said simply. And after more than thirty years, he really did understand finally.

"Do you?" Zamyatin asked, his voice intense, bordering on maniacal. "You live in a country that has never been invaded. How can you understand? How?"

Mahoney took Zamyatin's arm and guided him to the front door, stepping carefully over Balachov's body. "I understand, Yurianovich. And now you must understand that I am taking you to my embassy. To your children."

Zamyatin stiffened in his grasp. "I am no traitor."

"Do you want to stay here and die?" Mahoney snapped. "What about your children?"

"My children . . ." Zamyatin repeated dumbly, and then he trailed off.

Mahoney opened the outer door a crack and peered out into the corridor. It was deserted. A moment later he was guiding Zamyatin toward the stairwell door.

Just a little longer. Even a few minutes to let them get downstairs and clear the building. Then fifteen more minutes and they would be through the gates of the embassy. From that moment they would not be alone. They would have help.

They started down the stairs, one at a time, Mahoney careful not to let Zamyatin stumble and fall.

"Are there any surveillance people on this place?" Mahoney asked as they passed the second floor landing, and headed down the last flights of stairs to the ground floor.

Zamyatin shook his head. "I don't know."

At the bottom was a metal door with a small square window set about eye level. Mahoney propped Zamyatin against the wall and peered out the window. Nothing had changed. The lobby was still deserted.

"What did you feel like when you signed the order to have my children picked up?" Zamyatin asked.

Mahoney turned to him and buttoned up his raincoat and pulled his hat low.

"What did it feel like?"

"Shut up," Mahoney said.

"I mean it," Zamyatin said, pushing himself away from the wall and grabbing Mahoney's lapels. "Did it make you feel powerful? Like a god?"

"For Christ's sake, how did *you* feel?" Mahoney snapped. "How do you feel now? Are we gods?"

"I feel terrible," Zamyatin said miserably. "I kept thinking about my own children."

Mahoney opened the door with one hand and with the other guided Zamyatin out of the stairwell, across the lobby and out the front door where he headed them across the street.

Even if there was a surveillance team on them they could not be certain what he and Zamyatin were up to. For all anyone knew he and Zamyatin were heading someplace to exchange information.

If there would be trouble, it would probably come near the embassy when it would become obvious what was happening.

They made it across the street and headed toward the corner. It would be the case, that is, Mahoney thought, if the KGB had not already tumbled to Zamyatin as Balachov apparently had.

It was cold and the rain beat against them in sheets driven by a rising early morning wind. And for the first time in a long time Mahoney suddenly wondered if he had not bit off more than he could chew.

He had left the embassy with no thought other than to get to Zamyatin and bring him back. He had not stopped to think about the consequences or possible consequences of that act. Nor had he stopped to tell anyone where he was going, or ask for help.

At this moment he was one man alone in a city of nearly ten million people. A hostile city in which he could be arrested and executed as a spy.

About fifty yards from the corner it happened.

A Zil limousine pulled up and parked across the street from them and four men got out.

"Mr. Mahoney. Comrade Zamyatin. Wait a moment, please," one of the men called out.

Mahoney grabbed his .45 out of his coat pocket, turned and snapped off two shots, the bullets ricocheting off the concrete building beyond the car.

The four men scrambled for cover and Mahoney bolted toward the corner with Zamyatin in tow.

"Stop!" one of the Russians shouted.

It was a long way back to the embassy and Mahoney knew there was very little possibility that they would make it. But he did not let himself think about it. The corner. They only had to make it to the corner.

A shot was fired, and then another and Zamyatin went down. Mahoney spun around, crouched down and snapped off a shot at a solitary figure running toward them. The man stumbled and fell forward.

Mahoney jumped up and literally dragged Zamyatin the last few feet around the corner of the building as several more shots were fired at them from behind the parked limousine.

Blood was pumping from Zamyatin's neck in huge spurts completely covering his shoulders and one side of his face. His eyes were open but glazed.

Mahoney dropped down to his knees, the pavement cold and wet through his trousers, his face just inches from Zamyatin's.

"Your children love you, Yurianovich. You must know that."

Zamyatin's eyes blinked rapidly, and he tried to move but gave up almost immediately.

"We will take care of them. Unless you want us to return them to your government."

With a superhuman effort Zamyatin managed to shake his head no. The movement was very slight, but Mahoney understood.

"We will take care of them. My wife is a very good woman."

Zamyatin was not moving now, and the blood was no longer pumping out of him.

Mahoney stared at his old friend's face for a long moment, and then scrambled to the corner of the building in time to see two of the Russians running his way.

He fired two more shots. One of the Russians went down, and the other turned and headed in a zigzag pattern back to the car.

Mahoney got to his feet and began running as fast as he could toward the labyrinth of dark, winding, narrow streets in Old Town. From that point there was a chance—only a chance—that he could make it back to the embassy before they caught up with him.

11 A.M. Thursday

It was raining furiously, but the clouds were very high, and from the southeast the sun was just peeking from a small blue break. It was the first sun anyone in Moscow had seen for at least ten days.

Ambassador and Mrs. Leland Smith, Margery Mahoney, and Zamyatin's three children all in the back seats of a long, black Cadillac limousine, were passed through the security gate at Vnukovo Official Airport outside Moscow by a bewildered and uncertain captain of the guards.

His pass manifest showed none of the passengers in the car except for Margery Mahoney. But captains of the guards, of any guards, simply did not question the ambassador from the United States, so he waved the car through.

"I don't know how I can thank you for all you have done," Marge said to Mrs. Smith, and the woman smiled, reached out, and patted Marge's hand.

"I think you will find that it will all work out, Mrs. Mahoney," the ambassador said. His voice was deep, very rich and warm. He and his wife made a wonderful couple.

Marge glanced at the children seated next to her, and her heart ached so deeply that she wanted to cry.

The embassy chief of medicine had sedated the children with mild injections of Valium so that they would offer no resistance.

Congdon had helped her approach Carlisle with the request that the children be taken out of the Soviet Union, but the CIA chief of station had denied the request.

"They are not our responsibility," Carlisle had said, and she had not argued with him.

Wallace had not returned as he promised he would, and yet she had to think of the children's welfare. They could not be left behind. So she had gone to the ambassador's wife, and explained everything. Suddenly doors had begun to open and Carlisle became a highly cooperative soul.

Marge turned and looked out the car window toward the sun. Behind them were the administrative buildings but ahead and to either side in the distance were birch forests, looking green and white and fresh in the sun despite the heavy shower.

The sun she had missed during their time here in Moscow. Church she missed. Black pepper at times. American newspapers less than three days old. American television, especially *One Day At A Time* and *All My Children*.

A 727, gleaming silver in the sun and rain, stood ready on a utility parking apron away from the administrative building where the president's Air Force One would be parking and discharging its passengers.

Back at the ceremony area were gathered a large crowd of people, a great number of Soviet military troops and most of the dignitaries who would be greeting the U.S. president in just a few minutes.

At the 727 however, there was only a small contingent of American marines, an equally small contingent of Soviet military honor guards and two low-ranking Soviet officials from the Ministry of Protocol, both obviously flustered.

Several American technicians in white coveralls, stationed at the embassy, had finished the final preflight check of the 727, had loaded the remainder of the baggage including the diplomatic pouch that was not allowed to be touched by Soviet baggage handlers, and were waiting now to load personal luggage aboard the plane.

The limousine pulled up and parked near the boarding stairs; a marine guard opened the door and the ambassador climbed out of the car and shook hands with both the Soviet officials as his wife and Marge helped the three children out.

"Highly unusual, Mr. Smith," one of the officials was saying.

"On the contrary," Ambassador Smith boomed heartily. "I am not leaving on this flight. As a matter of fact, we should all get back for my president's arrival."

Both Soviet officials glanced at the children. They both were clearly uncomfortable.

"Then we do not understand, sir," one of them said.

The ambassador smiled. "There is nothing to understand. My wife and I merely wished to accompany an old friend of ours and her children to the airplane. They are returning home."

"But this was not scheduled, sir. We were not informed."

"Informed?" Ambassador Smith said, his right eyebrow arching aristocratically.

"What I mean to say, Ambassador, is that this lady was on the passenger manifest, but the three children . . ."

"Are you questioning my word, sir?" Ambassador Smith said angrily. "Must I have a word with Mr. Brezhnev personally about this?"

The color had drained from both men's faces. "By all means no, sir. I merely meant that we felt badly that we could not provide the proper ceremony for a close personal friend of the ambassador himself."

Ambassador Smith was beaming. "No need, my good man. Absolutely no need. Let us save the ceremony for the president who should be arriving momentarily."

"By all means," the one Soviet diplomat said.

Marge was staring at the four white-suited technicians who were carrying several pieces of luggage up the boarding stairs and into the aircraft. One of the men . . .

The ambassador had come over to her and he hugged her and kissed her cheek. "Everything will work out, my dear," he said softly in her ear so that no one else could hear him.

Marge looked up into his sparkling eyes, and she could barely believe what she was seeing. "Thank you, Leland, you're a dear," she said loudly enough so that the Russians could hear her.

The ambassador laughed, and then Marge hugged his wife. "Thank you . . . oh God, thank you," Marge said into her ear.

"Absolutely," Mrs. Smith said, parting. "I would be delighted, my dear. Please write."

And then Marge was herding the children to the

boarding stairs and they were climbing up toward the open door. The children went in first and at the top Marge paused, turned and waved at the ambassador and his wife. She would never forget them.

The children were already seated and strapped in when Marge stepped into the airplane. A stewardess led her toward one of the rear seats as another stewardess closed and locked the main door.

Almost immediately the engines began coming to life and many of the 127 passengers who were taking this flight back to New York watched as the dowdy-looking little woman in a mouse brown raincoat suddenly lit up, her face suddenly radiating joy and happiness like piles of diamonds glittering under a summer sun. And then she was in her husband's arms as the plane began to move toward the runway.

"You didn't come back. I didn't know. Carlisle said you would be delayed. That I had to go without you. I thought that you were . . . that you . . . that you were never coming."

The stewardess, a young woman in a pretty blue uniform, was gently pulling them apart. "I am afraid you both will have to be seated and put on your seat-belts. We are about to take off."

They separated, sat down, and the stewardess helped them with their belts.

"How?" Marge said when the young woman was gone.

"I was in the trunk of the car," Mahoney said laughing. He looked infinitely tired. There were heavy bags under his eyes, and he looked old and lined. "They dressed me in white coveralls, stuffed me in the trunk at the embassy and while Smith was giving those

Russians hell I just slipped up the steps into the plane."

"Why wasn't I told?"

"It was my idea, dear Margery. I didn't want that burden on you. You're just not a liar."

Marge smiled. "I did all right with Leland in front of those Russians?"

"Leland?" Mahoney said, laughing.

"Yes," Marge said, and she turned and looked across the aisle where the children were strapped in their seats. Already they were asleep.

For the next year their little lives would be difficult if not nearly impossible. But Ambassador Smith had promised to pull the right strings back home to provide the children with new identities and the proper education. Summers they could spend in northern Minnesota with Wallace and her. That is, if they wanted to.

The way the little boy, Aleksei, had sat on her lap earlier this morning left her no doubt about their outcome. All they needed was love. Just like any child.

Marge turned to her husband and smiled. "I love you, old man," she said.

"I love you, old woman," he replied.